CORAL BAY

A MICHAEL BENNETT NOVEL

BY:

SHAWN MICHAEL DEAN

Published by Electric Lemmons, LLC
Key West, FL 33040

Cover art and design by David Barens

This edition was formatted for print and digital by EBook Launch

Content Editing by The Editorial Department.

Print ISBN: 979-8-218-69120-2
Digital ISBN: 979-8-218-69121-9

First printing edition 2025

This book is dedicated to my late mother, Betty

For always loving and supporting me in whatever of the

many paths I have taken on life's journey.

I'm only able to live because of you.

Acknowledgments

A VERY SPECIAL THANK YOU to the only person to have ready my manuscript as many times as I have, my great friend and writing mentor, John H. Cunningham. Thank you for your invaluable advice and direction as I fumbled through this first book and for the continued motivation to complete it.

Thank you as well to all my beta readers: John Cunningham, Bill and Linda Klipp, Ed Kertis, and Susan Silverman. Your feedback and encouragement were instrumental.

A Note on People and Places:

Island Blues and The Quiet Mon on St. John are now gone, but for those of us who spent time in those magical places, their legacy will live on forever in our memories and our hearts. Thank you for all the great times.

The character, Captain Charles, A.K.A "Big Kahuna", was modeled after my good friend Charles Hoffman who left us back in 2016. Kahuna didn't fly planes or serve in the Navy, but he loved the islands and when I was writing his lines, I could hear his voice. I know he'd get a big kick out of being in the books and coming along for the ride. Cheers, brother.

"In the end, we will conserve only what we love, we will love only what we understand, and we will understand only what we are taught."

— Baba Dioum

PROLOGUE

DAVID BLANKENSHIP TRIED TO OPEN HIS EYES. One was already swollen shut and his head throbbed. He could hear the dying hiss from a propane tank as it emptied. The gas made it hard to breathe and the taste of blood filled his mouth.

Trying to focus he looked around the cabin of his little sailboat. It had been torn apart by the two men. They never said what they wanted, and despite not resisting, they had beaten Dave nearly to death. He tried to sit up, but the slightest movement sent shockwaves of pain through his body, and he collapsed back onto the deck, grasping his broken ribs.

An open hatch on the ceiling offered some fresh air. He laid still on his back, staring into the night, and searching for sounds of the men. But all he could hear was the ship's bell lightly ringing as the boat rocked on her mooring.

Feeling that the men had left, he started to relax. Finding the strength to push through the pain and sit up, he took a deep breath and closed his eyes, then rolled onto one elbow and reached for the table for support.

But he froze when he heard a voice outside.

"Come on, we got what we came for, let's get the hell out of here before someone sees us," one of the men said.

Fear shot through his body as he felt the boat rock when someone came aboard. Dave, wincing in pain, quickly slid into the shadows under the table, pushing as far back as he could, then quietly lifted the seat of the galley bench and retrieved his Mossberg Mariner 12 gauge.

The first round was birdshot, meant to clear a deck or give a warning, the rest were slugs. He was a peaceful man by nature, but that night he had no intentions on a warning shot so he quietly ejected the first round and chambered the second, then inched further under the galley table and leveled the shotgun at the companionway.

His hands trembled as he removed the safety and lightly rested his finger on the trigger.

Filled with fear, he knew this had to be a last resort. His small boat was now a propane filled powder keg floating on Red Hook Bay. One spark from the gun and it was over for anyone onboard.

The other man came into the salon, shouting back, "I'm almost done. We need to do this right, so it looks like an accident."

Dave, hidden in the darkness took aim at the shadow. But focused on his task, the man never looked towards him. He quickly placed the dead tank back into the cabinet under the stove, opened the valve on the fresh one, turned the main burners to max, then quickly exited. Dave feared what was next.

His knee was badly injured and he had several broken ribs, but he had to get out. He was suffocating from the gas and knew at any moment the boat could explode. Clenching his teeth as he moved, he tried to be quiet. Then as he neared the companionway, he heard the sound of a small outboard starting and felt the boat rock as someone stepped off. The small engine's RMP's came up and slowly moved away.

Dave, relieved, let out a sigh and with what energy he had left, he pulled himself up the stairs and flopped into the cockpit, gasping for fresh air.

He could still hear the motor and pulled himself onto the bench, leveling the rifle into the night towards the sound. Only able to focus with one eye, the lights of St. Thomas in the distance were a blur, the men in the boat a silhouette.

He relaxed his aim and with a deep breath rested his head on the gunwale. His heart still raced, but he felt a calm knowing the men were leaving and he was alive.

Then, the motor came to an idle. Dave looked up but was unable to see. He wiped the sweat from his eyes and tried to focus, his hands still gripping the shotgun, his finger pressed harder on the trigger as he scanned the night.

Then a light, a small flame like a candle, pierced the darkness and the sound of the motor's RPMs again came up, but now grew closer. One of the men held it as the flame grew. Dave pressed the butt stock deep into his shoulder, took aim towards the light, and pulled the trigger.

The silence of the misfire and the click as the hammer feel quietly on the round was chilling.

Shocked, Dave looked down at the rifle and pulled hard on the fore stock, the dead round flew into the night. He heard the motor again come to an idle as he slammed the fore stock forward and chambered the next round.

Looking up he again focused on the flame, but his heart sank as the flaming bottle flew through the darkness towards him, over his head and into the cabin.

Dave drew in a deep breath, took aim and squeezed the trigger. The man spun to his right and fell hard as he yelled out in pain. The small boat quickly turned and sped away.

Dave dropped the shotgun and lunged for the rail. His hands just grasped the top lifeline as the gas filled boat erupted in flames. Air hissed as it rushed from the cabin and the fire ejected him into the night, smashing his head hard against the dinghy davits.

His blood ran cold as he splashed into the warm Caribbean waters.

He struggled for a moment as he tried to purge the saltwater that had filled his lungs. His chest burned, and his head throbbed. He fought to keep his head above water, but his injuries made it hard. The seconds passed like hours but soon he heard a siren in the distance and saw blue lights coming towards him.

Dave let out a labored call for help and took a deep breath, trying desperately to hold on, his eyes fixed on the approaching boat. He could now see the lights reflecting on the water as they drew closer, but he felt his consciousness slipping away. In a short burst of panic, he began grasping for anything, flailing in the darkness and screaming for help with what little breath he could gather. But it was of no use.

Tears filled his eyes, and he reached towards the moon and took a final breath before slipping beneath the surface. With his hand still extended and eyes cast upward, he watched the blue lights flashing overhead. The search light darting around. But unable to move, numb, he slowly faded into blackness and sank into the dark waters of the bay.

CHAPTER 1

"SIR…SIR," SHE SAID. I twitched with a hard breath and opened my eyes. She took a step back and placed a hand over her mouth, which did little to conceal her grin.

"I'm so sorry, Mr. Bennett, but we've landed."

"Thank you," I replied with a yawn as I stretched my arms over my head.

"Take your time, sir. I'll have your bags waiting for you," she said, then walked towards the front of the plane.

Still foggy with sleep I looked around to make sure I had everything. On the table in front of me was an untouched and now watery Bloody Mary. The flight from Key West to St. Thomas was short, especially on a private jet, but I was deep asleep shortly after takeoff, the sounds from the previous night still echoing in my ears.

I stood and headed towards the door where the attendant that woke me was standing with my bags next to her.

"So much for making the most out of the company jet," I said.

"Maybe on the ride home, sir. It was very nice to meet you, Mr. Bennett," she said and lightly shook my hand.

I lingered for a moment in her eyes and smiled back. "Looking forward to it," I replied, then stepped outside.

The warm Caribbean air was thick with humidity from a recent rain and my glasses immediately fogged. I pulled them off and looked around. The storm clouds were moving away, leaving a clear blue sky. A warm breeze blew down the tarmac. As I wiped the fog from my sunglasses, I watched two seagulls overhead, fighting over a small fish one carried in its beak. They tumbled through the air, their playful calls breaking the noise of the airport. I took a deep breath and smiled.

A black sedan pulled up, stopping near the jetway. The driver, an older but energetic West Indian man, leaped from the car. He was dressed neatly in a suit and smiled as he greeted me.

"Good afternoon, Mr. Bennett. My name is Amos," he said quickly in a thick Caribbean accent.

"Nice to meet you, Amos. But just call me Mike."

"OK, OK, Mr. Mike. As you wish. Before we get going though, Mr. Vincent sends his apologies for not being here to greet you. I'll take you to the ferry terminal at Red Hook. Ms. Kim will be picking you up on the other side."

"Who's Kim?" I asked.

He took my bags and moved to the back of the car, talking over his shoulder as he walked. "Ahh, she is such a lovely woman. Beautiful inside and out. You won't be able to miss her. She'll be the very pretty girl in a blue Jeep. She's a very good friend of Mr. Vincent," he said, closing the trunk.

Quickly he moved to the side of the car and opened my door. Then with a redolent smile he continued. "And sometimes I think, maybe a little more." He laughed as I climbed in, closing the door.

Amos was talking to the attendant on the plane, so I pulled a newspaper from the seatback. Dave's picture was on the front-page with the headline FATAL BOAT FIRE RULED INCONCLUSIVE. My heart dropped and my stomach felt heavy. Staring at the picture I didn't notice Amos, now in the front seat.

"Are you OK, Mr. Bennett?" he asked, speaking more slowly with a soft expression.

"Yeah, I'm – I'm fine."

He looked to the paper now sitting in my lap. "Did you know Doc Blankenship?"

"Yea," I said with a heavy sigh. "Dave and I were close friends once."

He glanced out the window, seeming to search carefully for his words. "Did you already know?"

"I knew. His picture just shocked me, I guess. I haven't seen him in a while."

"Sorry my friend," he said as he turned around and started to drive towards the gate.

"Mon, it's a damned shame," he said, talking over his shoulder as he drove. "Doc Blankenship was a great guy. A tragic accident and a loss for these islands, no doubt."

I folded the paper and placed it back in the seatback. "So, have you worked for Larry long?" I asked.

"Humph. I don't work for Mr. Vincent. I work only for me. This is my car. Amos's Car Service. Best on the island. You need anything, just call me," he said and handed me his card.

We moved slowly through the congested roads. There were a few cruise ships in port and Charlotte Amalie was alive with activity.

"I can't stand those things," I said. "Giant pollution factories."

"I agree, mon. But, these days, they're a necessary evil. Lots of money in those boats being here. Some folks' livelihoods rely on them."

"I guess so," I replied.

"Hey, Mon, I agree with you. It's a sad reality. But, it's the reality, ya know. Besides, how's it different from the marina Mr. Vincent is working on? And I guess, you too?"

I stared out of the window towards the ship. A large building was being constructed on the far side of the bay near the port. "Good question, my friend," I said with a heavy sigh.

We rode in silence for a few minutes. Lee Scratch played on the radio. Breaking free of the heavier traffic we started to move faster. I stared out of the window as we wound through the island roads, watching as the people and places passed by like stills in a flip book.

"I've been coming here for a long time my friend," I said. In some ways this really is a piece of the world time forgot. But change being the only constant in life, I guess it's inevitable."

"True words, my friend. The islands, like the world, are always changing," Amos replied. "Lots of folks know that there is big money to be made here. Unfortunately, the folks who stand to profit from it the most aren't from here, and most don't even live here. To them, It's all about the money. It brings needed jobs, sure. But it's also changing a lot of things. Some of the magic gets lost. Ya know?"

"All in the name of progress," I said.

In the rearview mirror his eyes found mine.

"Progress huh? – Change isn't always that, mon."

"I couldn't agree more," I said.

***

We arrived at the ferry terminal in Red Hook. I pulled the paper from the seatback and tucked it under my arm. Amos had retrieved my bags, and I handed him forty dollars in a handshake. He squeezed my hand firmly and smiled.

"It's always nice to meet good folks. If you ever need a lift, or anything at all, give me a call," he said.

"I'll do that. Stay well my friend."

I picked up my bags and headed for the terminal, making it just in time to grab a beer and my tickets to St. John, then board the ferry. I always loved the ride over and preferred to sit up top in the open air. The breeze coming over the water seems to strip away the warm blanket of the Caribbean heat.

Over the port rail, the British Virgin Islands were barely noticeable through the haze of the Saharan dust, blown across the Atlantic by the trade winds. I thought for a moment about the last time I was in the islands and how much my life had changed since then.

Before I was there to celebrate finishing up a big job I did with Larry. Now I'm there to work, as a favor to a friend, but also at a time I could use the extra money.

I finished the rest of my beer then took the hat from my bag and pulled it low over my eyes. My head back, I stared into the blue sky and took a deep breath. It was good to be back, I thought, then closed my eyes. The sun was warm on my face and still being a little tired, I quickly drifted off.

CHAPTER 2

THE FERRY PULLED INTO PORT and I sat quietly and watched as both locals and tourists quickly funneled towards the stairwell. Once the top deck was clear I walked to the rail and looked across the bay then to the passengers as they spilled out onto the ferry docks. A young couple stopped and studied a tourist guide map. The river of bodies parted around them, several people letting their irritation be known as they passed. Happily unaware though, they found their destination, pointed down Prince St., then excitedly moved off.

"Sir, it's time to disembark. Please head down now," a voice said from behind me.

"OK. I was just waiting for the masses to clear," I said and picked up my bags.

"Smart man," he said with a half grin, as he started to scan the deck for trash. "Have a good day, sir."

There was nobody waiting for me on the dock, so I walked to the park across Kongens to wait in the shade, looking for the blue Jeep and a pretty face. After several minutes I tried calling Larry, but it went to voicemail. Finally, a text came through from a 912 number.

Hey, this is Kim, Larry's friend

I am sure you are off the ferry by now

I was delayed by a donkey roadblock but am not far out

I'll meet you at the Beach Bar in Cruz

Get me a dark rum and Coke on deck, but tell the bartender

it's for me, so no V.I. pours. He'll know what that means

I walked in the water along Cruz Bay, looking out over the horizon. The sun was starting its initial descent on the latter part of the day, and the wind coming off the ocean was cool and refreshing. Looking back towards St. Thomas and Red Hook, I thought of Dave. We'd lost touch the last couple years, but he had called just days before his death. Sadly, I missed the call and he didn't leave a message.

A lump formed in my throat, so I drew in a deep breath of Caribbean air, tilted my head back, and swallowed hard. Wiping the tears from my face, I walked into the bar.

I found two stools facing the water and ordered two dark and Cokes. I needed something strong, so mine was a V.I. pour. A heavy serving of dark rum with just a splash of Coke.

With Dave still on my mind I pulled the newspaper from my bag. The article went on to talk about how he was a respected and noted professor at the University of the Virgin Islands and led several environmental advocacy groups, including The Coral Bay Alliance, a group of citizens who are opposed to the marina project I was there to work on.

I was staring out over the water, lost in thought about how Dave and I left things between us, and wondering why he called. My mood was getting heavy so trying to shake it off I put the paper away, took a long pull from my drink and tried to focus on anything else.

Watching the people on the beach I noticed two very attractive women walking together. They stopped, standing in the water as they talked and laughed. One of them caught my stare, smiled and talking to her friend, nodded in my direction. They both waved pointedly, letting me know I had been caught. I returned the smile and nodded, offering a subtle wave back.

A man in his twenties was a couple stools down, he leaned over and slapped my arm, laughing. "They caught ya looking, bro."

I chuckled at myself. "Yea, they did. Oh well."

"She didn't seem to mind though," he said.

"Yeah, at least they smiled."

"Well and the fact that one of them is walking this way." He nodded to the beach as he turned back to his friends.

I looked up just as she walked in. Her tanned skin was contrasted by the white sailing shorts she wore and the beach sand that stuck to her legs. Her blue shirt flapped freely in the ocean breeze, revealing her pink bikini top. Her long black hair was pulled back in a ponytail and her piercing blue eyes seemed to smile as she approached and found mine.

"Mike?" she said.

"Good guess," I replied, standing to greet her and offering her my hand.

She ignored my handshake and hugged me. "Well, you are the only one sitting alone and Larry described you as a little older than me, tall, and a good-looking guy with a nice tan. Though he did note, not as good-looking as him."

"Ahh, Larry. Always the humble one," I said.

She laughed. "Sure, that's what he is."

"Here ya go, Kimmy," the bartender said and handed her the glass.

"Thanks, Tony," she said.

Standing back as if to study me, she smiled and conspicuously looked me over as she drank from her glass. "But – I think I disagree with his assessment."

"Oh yeah, in what way?"

"You're definitely better looking."

I smiled. "Well, thank you."

Kim took her seat at the bar. "So, Mike. First time on the island?" she asked.

"No, I've been coming down here for years. Usually sailing out of Nanny Cay, on Tortola. But I've spent a lot of time on St. John as well. Mostly in Coral Bay."

"Oh, I love sailing. I grew up doing it. Oddly though, since I moved here, I don't do it as much."

"Well, I'm actually staying on a friend's sailboat in Coral Bay and will definitely be doing some sailing."

"Which boat?" she asked.

"She's a Lagoon 440 called *Second Wind*."

"OK. I know the boat. Never seen her move though."

"Yeah, Chris bought her and got super busy. He's seldom on island. Maybe we'll take her out one day while I'm here."

She grinned. "Mr. Bennett, we just met and already you're asking me to sail off with you."

"No, just to asking a fellow sailor to help me check her out. I promised Chris that I'd get her off the mooring and go over everything to make sure she's ready to sell."

"Well, time will tell."

"Always does," I replied.

A silence carried for a moment. She looked me in the eyes and grinned, then shook her head and took a drink from her glass.

"What?" I asked.

"So," she said, clearing her throat and ignoring my question, "how long have you been working for Larry?"

"Well first, I never worked for Larry as an employee. But we go way back. I used to own an environmental consulting and permitting business in Miami and Larry and I worked on some projects together."

She laughed. "OK, noted. You worked *with* Larry."

"So then," she said, leaning in closer and resting her head on her hands, feigning a deep interest. "I know what he does. What's your role, Mr. Bennett?"

I smiled and leaned forward on my elbow. Then with the most serious expression and voice I could conjure, I replied. "Well, it's quite serious you see. And very complicated. I'm not sure you'd understand."

"Oh, do tell, Mr. Scientist. I'll try to follow along," she smirked sarcastically.

I laughed and sat up, grabbing my glass and abandoning the act. "It can be complicated, but it's pretty straight forward really. Larry liked to build around sensitive areas because the view is always better. But the permitting process is harder in those places. So, that's where I came in. I made sure the projects didn't damage the environment, or at least had minimum impacts, and I handled the permitting applications with the state and the corps."

"Corps?" she said with a puzzled look.

"Yeah. The Army Corps of Engineers. Basically, the federal permitting agency for building in those areas. All super boring, I'm sure."

She sat up and smiled. "That's fantastic. So that's why you're here? The Coral Bay Marina project?"

"I took a drink from my glass. "That's the one."

"Oh good. I know Larry's been having a lot of issues with getting it going. Especially with the permits. They actually just fired some other people that were working on that."

"Yea, he mentioned that when he called me."

"Well, I'm sure you're good, but it'll be an uphill battle though. A lot of people here don't like the idea and are fighting against it."

"Not surprising. Any new building projects around sensitive areas will have its detractors – What do you think?" I asked.

She sighed. "Well, I see Larry's vision, but I like Coral Bay as it is. It's quiet and simple. There's a great culture there. I'd hate to see that lost."

"Easy for you to say, Kim," the bartender said as he made a drink. "You know how many jobs that place would bring and the money that could be made."

"Tony, you live on St. Thomas and never go past Mongoose Junction, so what do you know?" Kim replied.

"I know it's expensive to live here and those rich folks would tip big," he said.

"Take it from me, Tony, they don't. And if you need more work, go back to New York," she said with a stern look.

"I guess you'd know about how rich folk act, princess," he said firmly, leaning on the bar in front of her. He stared at her intently and narrowed his eyes, glanced to the beach then back to her and smiled. "But nah, I think I'll stay here."

"Smart man," she said, playfully tossing a piece of ice at him as he walked away.

"What about you, Mike?" Kim asked.

"I definitely see your point and agree with you. But I don't have any control over that. like I said, my job is to help them get the permit approved, if we can, and with minimal damage to the environment."

"So, there's no guarantee? I thought maybe you had some magic touch or something."

"No magic. If it works, it works – Sometimes it doesn't."

"Well, I know Larry is super stressed over getting this moving. We had a trip planned and he canceled it because he was too worried about it all to leave."

"That's too bad. Hopefully I can help him there. So, you and Larry are an item?" I asked.

She sat back and raised her eyebrows. "That's very forward of you, Michael. We only just met." She leered at me and sat quietly.

"Kim – I'm – I didn't mean to – um…" I couldn't find my words.

The bartender started laughing and slapped his hand on the bar. I jumped and looked over. He was turning red. Looking back to Kim she was trying her best to hold her laugh in.

"Mike, wow, you're an easy one. I really had you there."

"Funny," I said and downed the rest of my drink.

"Another one?" the bartender asked.

"Just a beer."

He slid the bottle down the bar. "On me, man," he said still laughing.

"To answer your question, Mike, no. Well, not right now. We've dated off and on, but it never stuck. We had fun. We still do. It just wasn't a good fit."

"Well Larry is quite the charmer," I said.

She grinned. "You have no idea."

CHAPTER 3

WE DROVE ALONG NORTH SHORE ROAD. Sea grapes and mangrove trees lined the right side, the crystal blue waters of the Caribbean were to our left. The sun was fading, and the sky was alive with color. In the distance through the haze, were the British Virgin Islands. Sailing and motorboats dotted the waters.

"God, I love it here," I said, breaking the silence.

"Yeah, it's a magical place. Certainly captivated me," Kim replied.

"How long have you lived here?" I asked.

"Almost five amazing years."

"So many times, I've considered it. Just a couple years ago in fact," I said.

"Where are you living now?"

"Key West."

"I've never been. It's on the bucket list though."

"It's a lot like here in some ways. Mainly, because of all the great people."

"That's my favorite part of the Virgin Islands really. The people and the culture here are so beautiful."

"Yeah… the people really are the magic in a place," I said.

I was quietly staring straight ahead as we wound through the small island roads. A few moments passed and we made the turn onto Centerline at King Hill.

"Are you OK, Mike? You kind of drifted off there," Kim said.

"Yeah, I'm fine. It's just – well, like I said, in Miami I didn't have to worry about affecting the culture of a place. And until I got here, I never really considered it."

"Well, I guess it can't stay this way forever. The only constant is change, they say."

"As long as the price doesn't outweigh the value," I said.

We pulled up to the dinghy docks at Coral Bay and climbed out. She paused and looked out over the waters of the Bay and smiled. "Well, Mr. Bennet here you are."

"Thanks for the ride. Now I just need to find my buddy's truck. Chris said it's here somewhere and the keys to the dinghy are in the glovebox."

"Well, if you want, I'm meeting some friends at Skinny Legs for dinner and drinks," she said as she hugged me. "I'd love for you to join us."

Her smile was both shy and alluring. She lingered, waiting for a response.

"Sounds good to me. I just want to drop my stuff on the boat and I'll meet you there."

"Great," she said, hugged me again then headed off. She walked excitedly, as if to a party of old friends.

I turned around and started to scan the parking lot for the truck. Looking back towards Kim, I shouted after her. "Hey, Kim."

She turned around and walked backwards. "It was really great meeting you," I said.

In her best Barrie Chase voice she replied, "Mutual, I'm sure."

***

Chris's truck was easy to find. It was an older beat-up green Toyota lifted on thirty-three-inch wheels and a light rack across the top. On the dash was his old faded red hat that simply read, *Relax*. The truck was unlocked, and the dinghy keys were right where he said they would be. I grabbed them and headed to the dock.

To my dismay though, after searching and going to every boat, I realized the dinghy wasn't there. I tried calling Chris, but he was in the UK, so his phone was likely off since it was the middle of the night there. It was dark so I couldn't see his boat on her mooring, so I locked the truck doors and headed to Skinny Legs.

Walking in I saw Kim and her group of friends at the far end of the bar. She noticed me and motioned me over. As I arrived, they were wrapping up what I guessed was one of a few rounds of tequila shots. I was greeted as if I were an old friend. I didn't know them, but it made me smile.

As Kim introduced me to everyone, the bartender approached and placed a shot of tequila and a beer in front of me. Kim simply looked at me and smiled as she kissed the back of my hand and shook cinnamon over the spot. She then picked up an orange wedge and stopped. "Your move," she said. Her grin now devious, she placed the orange slice rind first between her teeth and raised an eyebrow. Waiting.

Feeling like the entire bar was watching, I followed suit. I licked the cinnamon from my hand and tossed back the shot. She gasped as I placed my arms around her and dipped her backwards, retrieving the orange wedge from her lips, holding her there for a moment before slowly standing her back up. The bar cheered. I smiled at her and chased the tequila down with a long pull from the beer.

Kim looked at me, bewildered, still standing close, her hand on my chest.

"My. I wasn't expecting that," she said.

"Well, such a bold move requires one in return." I grinned at her as I took another pull of beer, satisfied in her reaction.

She bit her bottom lip, her stare lingered, a euphoric look in her eyes. "Indeed."

The bartender set two more shots in front of me as one of Kim's friends, an Irish man named Gabriel, put his arm over my shoulder.

"I don't want a kiss from ya there, lad, but that was one helluva move," he said slapping me on the back. "I don't think I've ever seen Kimmy so stunned."

I smiled and toasted his glass, downed the shot, then quickly finished my beer as well. "Welcome to St. John," he said and patted my back, laughing as he walked away.

I made the rounds, getting to know Kim's lively group of friends. A band was setting up and the night was getting into full swing as locals and tourists began to fill every space. The tequila was making itself known and I was happy when my fish sandwich arrived. I looked down the bar, Kim was watching me and smiling. She motioned to the stool next to her. Trying to maintain an air of confidence I walked over and sat down.

"Quite the group of friends you have here," I said.

She didn't reply. She just looked at me with a shy smile.

"I'm really glad you came."

CHAPTER 4

GABRIEL AND TAMARA BOTH WERE TOO busy getting the dinghy ready to notice me on the stern of their boat, stripping down to my skivvies and shoving my clothes into a small bag I found on their deck. "Catch," I shouted to them, tossing the bag just as I jumped from the afterdeck.

I splashed into the cool waters of Coral Bay, letting my momentum carry me as deep as it could, then I slowly drifted back to the surface with just the buoyancy from my lungs. The water was refreshing. For me, a swim, especially in the saltwater, has always seemed to have an ability to at least partially rinse away a hangover.

"Feel better?" Gabriel asked as my head broke the surface.

I poured myself over the side and onto the deck of the small inflatable boat. "Too soon to tell," I said. "I think some food may be just what I need to shake this hangover though."

Tamara handed me a cup. "Here, drink this, it'll calm your stomach."

I took a sip. It was ginger beer with the beautiful distinctive taste of Angostura Bitters. I took a few long pulls from the cup and then placed my head back against the rail and let out a sigh.

"I don't really recall what happened last night, but I blame this all on Kim," I said holding the cup to my forehead.

She grinned and replied. "Well, we had to give you a proper welcome to our island."

"I have been here many times before," I said.

Without missing a beat, she tossed me a small box of Ginger Snaps and said, "well welcome back then."

"Yeah, thanks," I replied.

"Where's Kim?" I asked.

"She stayed at a friend's house up the hill. You guys were really hitting it off, but since you just met, she decided it'd be best if you crashed with us. You told us about your dinghy situation but given how late it was and how drunk we all were, we just brought you back here to our boat.

"Right, the damned dinghy. I still have to find it."

"That's where we're heading now. *Second Wind* isn't far," she said.

She pulled once on the motor's chord and the tiny engine came to life. She gave it some gas, and we were off.

We made a hard turn and passed around the bow of an old sloop. From the companionway I heard an old Jimmy Buffett tune. "My head hurts, my feet stink…it's that kind of morning, really was that kind of night." I laughed at the irony, which only made my head hurt more, and thought how appropriate that song was in that moment.

"At this rate, if I don't die by Thursday, I'll be amazed," I said to myself.

We approached *Second Wind,* and I could see the dinghy on davits behind the boat. We came around her stern and could see that it was locked.

"Damn it. My keys are in the truck," I said.

"We can run you out later," Gabriel replied. "We have to get to work though."

"Fine with me. I need food before anything anyway."

As we approached the dinghy dock, I was looking down, gathering the painter line and my bag.

"You could at least put some clothes on," a woman's voice said.

I looked up, ready with a witty comeback. But when my eyes met hers, my mind went blank and all that came out was an unintelligible garble of sound.

"Well hello to you too, stranger," Kim said with a grin. "You look like you could use some food. So could I. What do you say we grab some lunch?"

I cleared my throat and climbed onto the dock. "Sounds good to me," I said.

"Well, let's start with you putting some clothes on first. It's not that I don't enjoy the show but…" She gave me a once over and walked a few steps before turning around.

I sighed, dumped my clothes onto the dock and quickly got dressed. I couldn't find my phone and was frantically searching for it when Gabriel appeared from behind me and slapped me on the back. If you're looking for your phone, it's about thirty feet down on the bottom of the bay. You lost it last night climbing on the boat."

"Perfect." I muttered to myself.

I tossed the rest of my stuff into my bag and walked towards the truck. I was digging for a clean shirt when Kim's phone rang, it was Larry.

"Hey Larry"

"Yeah, he's here."

"No, he lost his phone in the water."

"Heading to get some lunch somewhere."

"We're in Coral Bay, not sure where yet."

"OK, sounds good to me. Meet you there."

"Bye."

"Larry says to meet him at High Tide in Cruz. He's heading there now," Kim said.

"I need some food sooner than that." I replied.

She was already in the passenger seat and started digging though her bag. "I have some fresh mango and coconut water. That should hold us over."

"Guess it'll have to do," I said. "Larry beckons."

Never mind Thursday, I thought to myself. *If I don't die by lunch, I'll be happy.*

***

We were on our way down Center Line Road, heading towards Cruz Bay. Kim had one bare foot out the window, her dark hair blew freely in the wind. She was looking out over the island as we drove atop the steep cliffs, playfully moving her hand through the wind like a glider drifting on the breeze. I smiled as I watched her.

My attention though was abruptly brought back to the road as I drifted onto the shoulder, loose gravel loudly struck the wheel wells. I took a deep breath and glanced over to her from the corner of my eye.

"Keep her between the buoys there, Captain," she said with a smile, never moving her gaze from the window.

"Um – yeah. Will do," I replied, trying to hide my face, and embarrassment.

"So, how'd you end up down here?" I asked her.

She chuckled. "Not a subtle misdirection, but I'll go along." She looked down at a ring on her right hand and sighed as she rubbed the red stone set in the otherwise humble band. "Honestly, escaping my family."

"Not a unique story to the islands, I guess," I said.

"Nope. Lots of people here escaping something. It's a perfect spot for it."

"Family that bad?" I asked.

"No, not at all. They're all good people. I just, I had enough of being a Blackwell in Agusta Georgia. See, my family is one of the prominent families in the area and I was expected to act a certain way and be a part of certain social group. Basically, fit into the world I was born into. Don't get me wrong, I love my family and know I am lucky to be born so privileged, but – it just never fit me to be the socialite. So, five years ago after I graduated from college, I traveled some and ended up here. I just, never left."

"That explains the bartender's princess comment," I said.

"Yeah, Tony was raised polar opposite to me. He's great, he just loves to pick on me."

"Sounds amazing. So, you have a trust fund then or they send you an allowance?"

She was quiet for a second then made a disapproving look. "No!" She let the punctuated word hang in the air for a few moments. "Well, my father does give me a small allowance…for now anyway."

She paused for a long moment, staring blankly out of the window. Then, as if answering a question, one that was never asked, she continued.

"Look! At least he isn't paying for grad school, or a new car like he does for my siblings. It's not forever, just until I decide what I want to do with my life. Then I'll return to the world and pay my own way, or I won't go back, and I will figure it out. Either way, I'm twenty-eight and it's my life."

"I'm sorry," I said. "I didn't mean that to be insulting. Of all people, I am not one to judge. I know what it's like to come from a prominent and domineering family. Hell, your escape was better than mine. After undergrad I joined the Army to get away."

"Really?"

"Yup, spent four years jumping out of perfectly good aircraft. Figured it was as far from what Pops wanted me to do as I could get. Eventually though, I still ended up at NYU and got my MBA as was expected of me. That's where Dad went to school. Legacy BS. You understand."

"Oh, I know that all too well," she said.

"Look, sorry I went off like that. It's a touchy subject and I just had a long argument with my 'dear mother' recently, so it's fresh. That was uncalled for." She smiled at me and patted my leg. "Forgive me?"

"Already forgotten," I replied.

She squeezed my leg gently. "Good."

Chapter 5

I FOUND A PARKING SPOT NEAR MONGOOSE JUNCTION. We walked to High Tide and grabbed a table with a good view of the water. It was a slow day, so the server was at our table quickly. I needed something to calm my stomach, so I ordered a Dark Rum and ginger beer with two dashes of bitters, an order of conch fritters, and a grilled Mahi sandwich.

"You know what, that sounds perfect," Kim said. "Make it two."

The day was warm and there wasn't a cloud in the sky. A gentle breeze cooled my skin. Leaning back in my chair I watched a pelican crash into Cruz Bay, then emerge victoriously with his catch, soaring overhead then out of sight.

I could feel Kim watching me, so I glanced over and smiled. She grinned, then leaned back in her chair, rubbing my leg with her foot.

"So, Mike, tell me more of your story? What did you do after NYU?"

"Well, I eventually got roped into the family business, so I worked for my dad for a while."

"It wasn't something you wanted to do?" she asked.

"Not at first, but it had its perks. I made a lot of money, had a nice condo, boat, great car… everything you could want as a young man living in Miami Beach."

"That sounds lovely. What was your job?"

"More or less to serve as my father's protégé. He owns a real estate development company. He loves to say that he changed the Florida skyline. I was being groomed to take over, even though I wasn't sure it's what I wanted to do. But he knew how to keep me in the fold. And it worked for a while."

"Daddy bought your loyalty, huh?"

"When you grow up a certain way, you get used to that way of life. When I went in the Army, he made me do it on my own. I think it was his plan, to let me fend for myself so I'd come running back to daddy and his money. You get it."

She laughed. "Oh yes, all too well. Our affection was constantly paid for. I had an opposite reaction though. It pushed me away."

I chuckled. "Well, maybe you were more virtuous than I was."

She shook her head laughing. "Well, I don't know about that. I'm far from a saint extolling the virtues of poverty. I do still get my allowance after all."

"Can't fault you there," I said.

"So, what changed? Why did you leave?" She asked.

I sighed. "Living in South Florida you hear all the time about the wetlands disappearing, what the sugar barons have done to the everglades, overdevelopment … and on and on. So much so that it becomes commonplace, just part of the life there. But being in that business it started to eat at me. Seeing how some of it really gets done … so many things swept under the rug or paid off through various bullshit legal channels, using unethical biologists … I couldn't ignore it anymore. I felt like I was selling my soul."

"So, you quit?"

"Yup. And he cut me off. Most of my stuff, my car, the condo, almost everything was owned by the company. So, he took it all. He said he didn't raise some 'damn hippie environmentalist'. Bastard even took me out of his will."

"Damn hun, that's rough. What'd you do?"

"I hit pause. Sold everything I had left and found a boat for sale in Miami Marina. I lived there a while and ran charters."

"So, when did you work with Larry? When you were at your dads' company?"

"No. That was with my own company. I started a small firm aimed at helping construction be less impactful on the environment."

"Wanted to really go against daddy, huh?"

"Not just him. Look, I understand that growth is inevitable. I can't stop development. But I had my MBA and learned a lot about construction and the business of it working for dad. So, I knew it could be done better. I went back to school and got a degree in environmental science while I built my firm. Even went against dear old dad on a big project he was bidding on. I helped a different developer get the job, which really pissed him off.

"Wow, sounds like you were pretty successful."

"Yea, it was. The firm grew rapidly and before I knew it became a hero among the movement to make construction greener. I actually met Larry after my company got a big writeup in an architectural journal. We completed a couple of huge projects, and the sky was the limit."

"Until it wasn't, eh sport," a voice said from behind me. "Recounting the Waterford Project? The one that almost sank us both."

I knew Larry's voice. I hadn't seen him in years, but he hadn't changed. He was tall with the build of a runner and all the confidence and swagger of a movie star. He was in his mid-fifties but appeared ten years younger. He wore a short sleeve white button-down linen shirt and tan mid length shorts with expensive looking leather sandals. His only adornment was his green Rolex Submariner.

"Larry Vincent, been a long time. You look great," I said, standing to greet him.

"You too. Key West has been good to you," he said.

"Well, a hell of a lot less stress these days."

Kim sat staring at us both blankly then interrupted. "You can't just leave that hanging out there like that. What almost sank you both. What the hell happened?"

Larry looked to me. "Not a what, so much as a whom," he said, nudging my arm.

"Yeah, thanks buddy," I said, shooting him a hard glance before turning back to Kim.

"Look, I don't' want to recount the fall of Michael Bennett here, but I made a mistake, blindly trusted someone I shouldn't have, and it cost me everything. But it was my business, so the onus is on me."

"That's it? How did that almost sink you too, Larry?" Kim asked.

"I know Mike doesn't want to discuss this, and neither do I honestly. Bringing it up was a poorly thought-out friendly jab at Mikey here. Let's leave it there."

"I will say though, after the dust settled, Larry was one of the few people in that business who was there for me. As much as he could be anyway," I said.

"Wow. Sounds like a juicy story. But I understand. One day though, I have to hear the rest," Kim said.

We sat down and Larry put his hand on my arm. "Mike, I know I didn't mention it on the phone, but I'm really sorry to hear about Dave. He was a good man. The best person you had on your team in Miami."

I sighed. "Yeah, he was. You know he called me just a few days before his accident. I missed the call though.

"Did he leave a message?" Larry asked.

"No, he didn't. And by the time I saw the missed call … he was gone."

Everyone was silent, Larry and I both staring off and recalling the past, Kim likely unsure what to say. I stared out at the water watching an older man loading a guest into the little dinghy he'd pulled onto the beach. His skin was well weathered, and his clothes tattered. His smile and laughter though were that of a man who had found his place in life. He spoke to his guests as he pushed the boat off the beach, and they all erupted in laughter as they turned and headed to the small sloop waiting on her mooring out in the bay.

The waitress approached with our food, breaking the silence. She brought Larry a Jack & Coke and a shrimp salad. "Here ya go, Larry, the usual for ya."

"Thanks, Missy," he said then looked back to me as he mixed the shrimp with the greens on his plate.

"Well, Mike, turns out our work will be a little delayed. There was a fire a couple days ago at the trailer on site, and an office worker was injured. So, the fire marshal has to do an investigation. He said it shouldn't take long though. Maybe in the next couple days."

"What happened?" I asked.

"The marshal said it's likely just bad electrical. Not sure yet though."

"OK, so what do we do till then?" I asked.

"There's still lots of work we can do. You still get your daily consulting fee. But for now, I need you to do something for me. Since it's outside of your normal job, I'll pay you $500 cash. Once you get back, maybe we'll be able to get to work."

"What do you need done?" I asked.

"I have work on Tortola for a couple days. But I need Charles Winters picked up on St. Croix and brought over to St. Thomas. He's the COO of Bowling Green Holdings, the group behind the marina project."

"He has that massive yacht, why can't he come here?" Kim asked. "I'm enjoying hanging out with Mike."

"Because he's a pain in the ass and likes to be catered to. That's why. Once that boat hits St. Croix, it doesn't leave until he does. But hey, you can go with him if you want, Kim."

Turning back to me he continued. "Mike, you'll take the company boat, head over, and stay at my place. I just got it a couple months ago and have only stayed there once. It has a great hot tub on the balcony overlooking the water, and a private beach. Call it a personal favor. Hell, I'll owe you one," he said as he sat back in his chair, taking a long swallow from his drink, waiting for my reply.

"I guess I don't have anything else going on. Why not," I said.

"Good," he said loudly, then tilted his glass up and swallowed the last bit from the highball. "Look, our base of operations is St. Thomas, I have you setup in a room at the resort there. But you have a spot in Coral Bay for now, right?"

"Yeah, for now. Taking care of a buddy's boat."

He reached into his pocket and pulled out a cell phone. "OK, that works. Look, I have to run but meet me at the Coral Bay dinghy dock at 8am." He handed me a phone. "I'm the only one with the number to this, so if it rings, it's me. I'll have all of the details and your money tomorrow morning."

"Well, this should be fun," I said to Kim.

She sighed and spoke quietly. "I don't think I'll go, Mike," Kim replied. "The trip sounds fun, but we just met." She straightened her posture and lifted her chin, feigning pretentiousness with a grin. "I am a lady, after all."

She winked at me then continued.

"I do want to get my Jeep though, so I'll ride back to Coral Bay with you. Maybe we can go for a quick swim at Lamesure. But after that I may just head home and rest. I still have a little recovering to do from last night."

Larry quickly shoveled a few more bites of his salad into his mouth then pulled a hundred dollar bill out and sat it on the table in front of me. "This is for lunch," he said and stuck his hand out. I stood and we shook hands. "Really good to see you again, sport," he said, tapping me on the chest.

As he hugged Kim his phone rang. "Hola, Miguel. Un momento por favor." He placed the phone against his chest and in a lowered voice, said he'd see me at the docks at 8. He kissed Kim's' cheek, then quickly turned and left.

I looked at Kim. "A lady, huh?"

She replied simply with shrug and a grin.

CHAPTER 6

LAMESURE BEACH WAS EMPTY. KIM AND I SAT IN THE SAND, letting the warm sun bathe us as the waves gently lapped at our feet. She was leaning back on her arms, her eyes closed, smiling to the sun.

Opening one eye she noticed me watching her, smiled and leaned against me. "Let's go for a swim," she said quietly.

She grabbed her snorkel gear then headed to the water. I sat for a moment and watched her. Her beauty was so natural. Her allure, effortless. I watched as she gently slid beneath the surface and started towards the middle of the bay. "Are you coming?" she asked, turning back briefly towards the beach. I quickly followed after her.

The day was picturesque. The seagulls outnumbered the clouds in the sky and the sun's rays penetrated the crystal-clear water, illuminating the life below. The scenery was magical both above and beneath the surface. I trailed behind paying as much attention to her as I was the tangs, clownfish, and snapper that peeked in and out of the rocks as we swam by. Far off I could hear the clicking of dolphins. I peered into the blue in hopes of seeing one, but none appeared.

We swam a while, playing flirtatiously in the cool waters and I pointed out different species of fish and plant life, trying to impress her.

As we swam back to the beach, I grabbed one of her fins, pulling her gently backwards. She spun around and, pushing off the bottom, tackled me. I caught her and we both sank into water. We came up, both laughing hard, our faces inches from one another. As we caught our breath our eyes met. Our laughter quickly faded as the tension built between us.

I slipped one arm around her waist and pulled her in closer. She put her forehead to mine and tugged at my waistband. My heart was pounding. Slightly biting her bottom lip, she ran her hands up my chest, then behind my head, pulling me to her and kissing me deeply. The world faded to obscurity, and we were alone, lost in the moment, drawing each other closer.

I pulled gently at the string that held her top on. She stopped and slowly broke from our kiss, holding our faces close together. We were both breathing heavily, our eyes locked in a silent exchange of thoughts. I was shaking with anticipation. The energy between us was ethereal.

She smiled and kissed my lips gently then took a step back as she re-tied her top, our eyes still locked. Her face softened and I could feel the tension of the moment release. I took a deep breath and slowly let out a heavy sigh.

"Yeah," she said. "Me too."

"Still a lady?"

She nodded slowly.

"For today."

***

"Hey, y'all," a man's voice said. I opened my eyes and sat up. He was a large man with a clean-shaven head and a full beard. Any intimidation I may have felt due to his size was softened by his warm smile. Anchored behind him in the deep waters of the bay was a Yellowfin center console with a dozen or more fishing poles on the T-top and Mahalo Charters emblazoned on the side.

"You're gunna cook you lay there too much longer," he said.

"Yea, you're probably right, thanks, man," I groaned as I stretched out.

"Wow, I needed that little nap," Kim said.

She looked up at him. "Oh, hello."

"Sorry to wake you folks, but I see a lot of tourists out here. More than one has succumbed to the rum and woke up looking like a lobster. Though I guess y'all look pretty tanned."

He approached us, extending his hand. "My name's Captain Charlie. Most people call me Big Kahuna."

"Nice to meet you, Captain," I said, standing and shaking his hand.

I stretched again and he pointed to the tattoo on my chest.

"Those jump wings?"

"Yeah. I was in the Army, 82nd Airborne. Long time ago."

"Ah, a fellow veteran!" He pointed to a tattooed set of wings on his shoulder.

"I was Navy. Dating myself a little here, but I flew the A6 Intruder. Big Kahuna was my call sign."

"Well, damned glad to meet you, Captain," I said, shaking his hand again.

"You too, brother. Where y'all from?" he asked.

"I live here, over near Chocolate Hole. Mike is in from Key West," Kim replied.

"No shit. Damn, I lived in the Keys and ran charters there for a long time all up and down those waters. Still know a lot of folks there."

"Glad you came along, Kahuna," Kim said.

"Yea, it's a favorite spot for me to cool off after a charter. I have a spot up on Sugar Apple and keep the boat on a mooring in Coral Bay."

"I'm staying in Coral Bay too. I'm on *Second Wind*," I replied.

"The blow boat near Island Blues?" Kahuna said.

I laughed. "Yeah, that's the one. – But, since we're all heading back to Coral Bay, do you think I could charter you for a few minutes when we get there? That's my buddy's boat and he left the damned dinghy on the davits."

"No worries at all man. Tell ya what, I'll pick you up at the dinghy docks. My fee is a couple cold beers. How's that sound?"

"Works for me," I said.

Kim and I decided for a final swim and made our way out to Kahuna's boat with him. He climbed onboard and donned a bright aloha shirt then brought the anchor in on the windless. We moved away from the boat and watched as she came onto plane and slid across the bay towards open water. Kahuna offered a final wave in the form of a shaka hand gesture as he made his turn.

I swam backwards, Kim followed me, smiling. I slowed and she swam into my arms. I pulled her in for another kiss, tugging again playfully at the ties on her top. She turned away and held up a finger in a scolding manner.

"Now you be good. A lady requires a gentleman."

She winked then swam towards the beach. I watched for a second then turned back to the open water, taking in the moment and reflecting on the day, now fading into night. In the distance a pod of dolphin finally emerged, rolling in the waters. One breached, flying through the air and landing sideways as it splashed back into the sea. I smiled and floated on my back, kicking gently towards shore, my eyes still on the horizon, now orange and red with the setting sun.

Chapter 7

KAHUNA WAS WAITING ON THE DOCK WHEN WE ARRIVED. I waved as I pulled my bag from the bed of the Jeep.

Kim gave me a kiss on the cheek. "See you in a couple days," she said.

"If you change your mind, you know where I'll be. 8am." I said, playfully pulling on the beltloop of her jean shorts.

She hugged me then standing close, spoke quietly. "I had a great day with you, Mike. I really want to go. Which, is why I shouldn't."

She kissed me once more then climbed into her Jeep. "Have fun and be safe. I put my number in your phone and sent myself a text. Call me when you get back."

I watched as she drove away, blowing a final kiss before turning onto Centerline Road. As I grabbed my bag, I shook my head to snap myself out of the dream she left me in, then walked towards Kahuna, still in a daze.

He had a huge grin on his face and started laughing as I approached. "Man, that girl sure has you under her spell."

"I've only known her two days! But yeah, I can't deny that man."

He slapped me on the back as we walked. "It's good to see, brother. I haven't felt that in a long time."

"Where's your boat?" I asked looking for the Yellowfin.

He scoffed. "That thing is way too big for the dinghy dock. My tender is down here though."

We loaded into his dinghy and were to *Second Wind* in moments. Entering the salon, I did a quick check and found a fully stocked bar and plenty of beer in the fridge, but no food.

I grabbed two Kalik's and walked onto the aft deck. "Want to have a beer out here?" I asked. "I'll need to get some food soon, but we can have one or two here first."

"Got us covered, brother," Kahuna said. "I have lots of leftover fried chicken and a couple sandwiches from my charter today. Island Blues and Skinny's both look to be jumpin', so a quiet beer on the deck sounds perfect to me."

"Great," I said. "Me too."

"So how long were you in the Army for, Mike?" he asked as he sat down.

"Only about four years," I replied. "My life took a slightly different trajectory than planned, What about you? How long was your Navy stint?"

"I did my twenty. Flew with the Black Falcons off the America then moved to flying heavies after the Navy retired the A6. That's actually how I got to the Keys. I flew into NAS Key West a long time ago and the beauty of those islands really captivated me. I managed to get Key West as my final duty station as base XO. After I got out, I stayed and started my charter business."

"Yeah, that seems to be a common theme down there. Several former base COs did the same. It's like a little commander's club. – Why'd you leave though?"

He sighed. "A story for another time, my friend."

"Yeah, I understand that one," I said laughing. "Paradise to paradise isn't a bad plan though, man. You still fly?"

"Yeah, here and there. Usually small private planes for folks. I have one or two clients here and I island hop them around a bit. One even has a sea plane. I love flying that thing."

"What about you, Mike. What brings you down here?"

I filled him in on the details of the job and a bit on how I knew Larry. After I was done, he looked at me with a stern expression and concern in his eyes.

"I've heard about your buddy, Larry. He's a shady character. Lots of folks around here don't like him. He throws his money around and acts like some big shot but has little to back it up but a big mouth. I'd be careful, man, that's all I'm saying."

"I've known Larry a long time. Kim has too. I know how he comes across and we certainly butt heads often enough, but he's a decent person. He was there for me a long time ago when my life was in a bad place. A lot of people turned their backs on me, but not him."

"Well, a man died in a boat fire not long ago. He was a leader against the project and there's a lot around it that seems suspicious, most folks say."

"I knew Dave. We were great friends once. He actually worked for me in Miami. And I know Larry can be a bastard sometimes, but he's definitely not a killer. I have all but shut down projects of his and he has been fuming with me, even sued me once. But he'd never kill someone."

"Maybe not – Well, still. You seem like a good guy, but folks won't see it that way when they find out you're working on this damned marina project. Nobody I know wants to see it built."

"I totally understand that man, but look, it'll get done either way. The way I see it is, if I'm here, I can make sure it has the least impact possible."

"Sure, on the environment maybe, but what about the locals, the magic of the place, the lifestyle we all love here. How can you protect that? This will destroy all we know and love about this place."

"I know, man, I really do, and I struggle with that. But I can't do anything about that. I wish I could. Honestly."

He rubbed his face with a heavy sigh. "I want to say you're wrong, brother, but I guess I know you're not. It's just sad. I mean, what would your buddy Dave say?"

"He was fighting against it. Obviously, he hated it."

"No, I mean about you working on it."

"Same answer. He was always a hardliner and challenged everything, which is what made him so valuable. He always pushed me to dig deeper and think differently. The last project we worked on actually cost me my company because I didn't listen to him. It also cost me his friendship. This is actually the first project I've been on since then and I plan to think like him and use his opposition to dig and think deeper."

We sat quietly for a few seconds. Kahuna stared into the water. "Well, man, let's talk about fishin', or women, or anything else. This is getting me heated. You, I like. And I appreciate that you are fighting the good fight and sometimes that means keeping company with the devil I guess."

"Sometimes it does. But yeah, let's change the subject," I replied.

We sat for another hour and traded fishing and sailing stories, tales of the Keys and the islands and found we had more than a few mutual acquaintances. We finished the last of the Kaliks and decided to call it a night.

Once Kahuna was back onboard his tender, I untied the bowline. He reached up and shook my hand, in his was a business card.

"Be safe man, and if you get in trouble, call me. Brothers in arms."

"Will do, and thanks."

***

I was sitting on the fly bridge with my feet on the helm thinking about what Kahuna said. I gazed out into the clear, warm night. Behind me Island Blues was still roaring. In the dark sky, a building cumulous cloud was illuminated by lightning and the boat shifted on her mooring with a heavy gust of wind.

CHAPTER 8

SECOND WIND'S TENDER SLID EASILY THROUGH THE WATER. The morning air was crisp and fresh from the storm that passed during the night but was already becoming thick as the sun started to warm the island. As I approached the dock, I could see that Larry was already there waiting. To my great surprise, Kim was with him.

"Good morning," Larry said as I tossed him the painter line.

"Good morning – You're dressed up pretty nice today," I said.

"As I told you, I have business in Tortola," he replied and extended his hand to assist me.

"And good morning to you too, Kim. Come to see me off?" I asked.

"No, I decided to go with you after all."

"Why the change of heart?"

She looked to Larry. "Well, Larry and I went to dinner last night and he spoke highly of you. He insists that you're nothing less than a gentleman. Besides, I know it'll be fun. Just don't get any ideas," she said, lightly punching me in the arm.

"Really, what else did he tell you?" I asked.

"Just more about how y'all know each other. And a little more insight into what happened to you in Miami."

"Did he now?" I said, peering towards Larry.

"Look, Mike," Larry said, walking towards us. "I could see that you were hitting it off and I could tell at dinner that she likes you. I know this one pretty well. And as she said, I told her, you're a good guy."

"And the Miami stuff?" I asked.

"All I did was fill in some blanks from what was already said at lunch. Nothing specific. It was more about my end of things."

I took a deep breath and smiled at Kim. "Well, if it means you're coming, then I guess it's OK."

"Oh good," she replied.

In the distance the low drone of outboard four strokes broke the silence of the morning. "Ah, here is our ride now," Larry said motioning to the incoming boat.

It was a black rigid inflatable boat and as it met the dock two men jumped off. One secured the lines while the other tossed our bags onboard. Larry climbed on immediately. "Well, let's go, I've got a busy day."

***

Coming out of Coral Bay the twin 300 HP outboards had us skimming over the water. The man at the helm seemed to have little regard for the other boats or people on them as he weaved in and out of the mooring lines, rocking every boat in the bay. A few came out to share their thoughts with clinched fists in the air and words of scorn. I offered a doleful but well intended wave in apology.

Kim had settled onto the aft bench, out of the wind. I was standing next to Larry, near the helm.

"Where are we going?" I asked over the roar of the wind as we passed Long Point and made a heading towards Flanagan Island.

Larry leaned over and said, "Privateer Bay."

"Norman Island. What in the hell are we going there for?" I asked.

"Because that's where the boat is," he smirked.

As we pulled into the bay the only boat in sight was a blue Sea Ray Sundancer 510 with *Silver Linings* was written across her stern and was trimmed with a touch of grey. She wasn't set on a mooring or anchor, the engines hummed, and the exhaust gurgled as she bobbed in the water.

"She must have just arrived. I made sure to have her provisioned for your trip," Larry said, more to Kim than me.

We pulled alongside and Larry tossed a line to a man who emerged from the salon. He quickly tied us off and our bags were transferred by Larry's men.

"Alright, let's get moving. I need to be underway soon," Larry said.

As we entered the main salon, Larry retrieved an envelope from the table. He turned to me, speaking quickly as he handed me the envelope.

"Here is your pay and a company card for any business expenses. The number for Miguel is written on here for you. Call him once you're underway tomorrow then again when inside Vessup and he will guide you to the fuel dock. This boat cruises nicely around twenty-five knots, so don't push her too hard.

The Moorings Marina is in Christiansted, about fifty miles from here so it'll take less than two hours. The exact location is entered into the GPS and the lat/long are written on here as well as the number for the harbor master. They are expecting you. My slip is F-18 but just dock it and they will clean and gas her up. Also, I told the marina that whatever you order is on my account. Enjoy yourselves. I'm hoping when you get back from St. Croix we can get down to business. We have lots of work to do."

"Where is your place?" I asked.

"Just up the road from the marina at Pelican Shoals on the east end. My jeep has been gassed and cleaned. François, the yacht club valet, will bring it around for you when you arrive. The address is in the GPS under home. If you need anything, or anything comes up, call me immediately."

Larry shook my hand "Thank you again for doing this, Michael."

He turned to Kim, hugged her and kissed her cheek then slapped me on the shoulder as he headed to the companionway. I walked onto the aft deck behind him as the mate was untying the lines. Larry shouted back at me as they pushed off.

"If you get stopped you, all the paperwork is in the helm station. Just have them call me if there are any issues. Let me know once you're at the cottage."

Larry signaled to the driver to go. A second later the twin outboards roared to life and the small boat jumped on plane towards St. John. The morning was quiet again. The only sound was from the dull idling of motors below and the lap of the water on the hull.

I walked up the starboard side to the bow and looked around. The day was getting warm, but with the breeze it was comfortable. The skies, as blue as the Caribbean Sea, were clear to the south and east. To the west there were some clouds building on the horizon. The wind blew gently, and a few gulls played on the breeze, their laughter like calls drifting with them as they headed south. I smiled, took a deep breath of salty air, then headed aft.

As I sat at the helm station familiarizing myself with the console, Kim emerged with a tray of fruit, croissants, a bottle of Veuve Clicquot champagne, and a carafe of fresh orange juice.

"Looks like Larry sent us off in style," she said as she took a seat. She popped the cork on the bottle, added a little triple sec into the belly of the glass, a generous pour of champagne, then topped it with OJ.

I nudged the throttles into gear and pointed her out towards open water as Kim made a second mimosa and arranged our breakfast. I smiled and pushed the throttles forward. The two diesels roared to life bringing us quickly on plane and to twenty knots. I adjusted course to south-southwest towards the east end of St. Croix, set the auto pilot and sat back, looking over the bow as we glided smoothly across the water.

Kim handed me my glass, leaned across and kissed my cheek, then raised hers to offer a toast.

"To new opportunities," she said.

I smiled and tapped her glass. "And all they may bring."

CHAPTER 9

WE CRUISED TOWARDS GALLOWS BAY, passing Protestant Cay to our west. I brought her off plane and grabbed the hand mic to hail the marina. There was a brief pause before someone replied.

"*Silver Linings*, Moorings Marina harbor master. Welcome to St. Croix, Mr. Bennett. Please bring her to the fuel dock. I'll meet you there."

There were several large yachts already tied up and taking up most of the space, but I saw an empty spot. "Roger, looks to be an empty space behind the Emerald Sea, I'll head there." I put her into gear and slowly moved through the busy waters.

The Marina was sprawling. There were six main docks, easily a few hundred feet long that ran perpendicular to the shore with slips of various sizes on either side, filled with an assortment of expensive looking boats. At the end of the equal length piers were the fuel docks.

To the right of the main marina there were three more piers designed to hold the super yachts. That day there were two in port: *La Technique* and *The Bottom Line*, each boat running the length of the huge piers and dwarfing even the largest of the other vessels. They were made fast and on board the crews were busy cleaning every inch of them.

"How great would it be to have one of those boats," Kim said.

I scoffed. "Unabashed, conspicuous gluttony. There's no seamanship in it. I'll take a sloop with a fifty-foot waterline over those monstrosities any day."

She rolled her eyes, but smiled. "Well, that sounds great too."

The fuel dock was directly in front of us, backdropped by dozens of bobbing masts and tuna towers of the vessels tied up in their slips. People were walking to and from their boats, some pushing dock carts full of provisions, some full of fish from a successful morning run. Dozens of dock hands dashed wildly about, dressed in tan shorts, white button-up shirts and brown deck shoes.

I made a course towards the open fueling station on far left of the marina. Turning as we approached, I brought the pier just off our port bow at ten o'clock. I asked Kim to go forward to handle the dock lines. Once I was twenty yards out, I placed the motors into neutral and let her carry us forward a moment before turning hard to port and placing the starboard engine into reverse. *Silver Linings* slowed and we gently drifted into the docks rub rails where two young men were waiting, blue dock lines in hand. I left her engines on and headed aft to receive the line.

"Good morning, sir," one boy said as the other joined him, echoing the same greeting.

"Good morning," I replied, securing the line.

I walked to the helm station and turned off the motors. A silence fell over the cabin as the drone from the engines faded.

From outside I heard a voice call, "Ahoy, Mr. Bennett."

"Ahoy? Good Lord," I said to myself, then replied sarcastically. "Ahoy!"

I picked up my bag and walked to the aft deck. A tall man stood on the dock. He looked to be in his mid-forties, his dark hair was combed neatly, and he was dressed in a pressed short sleeve white button-up with black bands on the shoulders, each embroidered with gold bars and something that looked like military rank. His khaki pants were pressed with a sharp crease. His black loafers were brought to a perfect shine.

The two dock hands now stood quietly with their hands clasped behind their backs like soldiers awaiting orders. He removed his aviator sunglasses and allowed them to hang from the lanyard around his neck. Kim appeared next to me holding her bag. "Good afternoon," I said to him.

"Good afternoon, Mr. Bennett. My name is Johnathan Bitmore. I am the harbor master here. Per Mr. Vincent's request we have everything taken care of and will take the boat from here. His jeep is waiting for you at the valet stand." He looked to the two boys standing quietly to his right. "Boys," he said. The taller of the two spoke up.

"Permission to come aboard, sir?"

I nodded and grinned. "Sure, hop on."

He climbed aboard and grabbed our bags, handing them up to the other boy who loaded them into a dock cart and hurried off.

"Ms. Blackwell," he said to Kim, extending his hand to assist her off the boat. I followed behind. "Welcome to St. Croix," he said.

"Thanks. Some place you got here," I said, shaking his hand.

Someone called his name and he excused himself, walking to one of the larger fishing vessels a few slips down. It flew several pennants from the outriggers to show their catch for the day and the crew was in good spirits.

Kim and I were waiting when a woman walked by, digging through her bag. She dropped a small case. Kim picked it up, calling after her.

"Miss, miss, you dropped something," she said. The woman stopped and walked back, still digging through the large shoulder bag she carried.

"Thank you," she said, taking the case from Kim and continuing to search her bag.

"I'm sorry, but have we met? You look very familiar. My name's Kim Blackwell. I live on St. John," Kim said, extending her hand.

The woman stopped and looked up, composed herself and shook her hand. "Sorry… I got myself in a rush and misplaced something. Your name sounds familiar actually. You work for Larry Vincent, I assume?"

Kim and I looked at each other. "How did – how did you know that?" Kim asked.

She nodded to the boat. I know the boat. I worked for Larry briefly a while ago and have seen it before.

"What's your name?" I asked. "I'm Mike Bennett."

She paused, a pensive look on her face. She gaped at me, and seemingly through a held breath slowly repeated my name. "Michael … Bennett?"

"Um … Yeah. I work for Larry too. But I just got started."

"Yea, I'm uh – my name is – my name is Daniele. Well, I have to run, but maybe I'll see ya around. You down here long, Mike?" she asked.

"Till the job's done. Maybe longer. No plans yet," I said.

"Ok, well, yeah. Great. I'll uh – yeah. Maybe I'll, maybe I'll see you later. Bye," she said then turned and quickly left.

"What a strange woman," Kim said.

"The islands draw some interesting people," I said.

Mr. Bitmore returned a few moments later and we followed him towards the clubhouse. He spoke as if giving a tour and gestured with his hand to the marina, then to the club on the hill.

"We are the premier yacht club and marina in all of the Virgin Islands. Only the very best are members here."

"Sounds exclusive," I replied.

He glanced to me over his shoulder. "Very."

We reached the top of the dock. Waiting for us was a long golf cart with the marina logo on the front. The driver stood waiting.

"Please, join us for lunch. You've had a long trip. Mr. Vincent said everything is to be charged to him and you are to have whatever you need. This is François. He is the valet and will handle anything else you may require. He will ensure your bags are secured in Mr. Vincent's Jeep, which will be waiting when you finish your meal."

I looked to Kim. "Hungry?" She smiled and grabbed my hand, leading me as she slid onto the bench seat.

"Splendid," said Mr. Bitmore. He then took his place next to the driver and we made our way around the spiral path to the immaculate building on the hill.

***

After lunch we sat on the terrace overlooking the marina, finishing our drinks. The sea breeze carried the fresh salt air and I took in a deep breath and held it, savoring the stillness, then let the air escape gently.

"You look very content," Kim said.

I smiled at her. "I really am."

She reached out and placed her hand over mine. "Me too," she said, watching my eyes.

I lifted her hand and kissed it, trapped by her gaze.

"So, what's next, Mr. Bennett?"

CHAPTER 10

LARRY'S COTTAGE WAS ON A SECLUDED PART OF THE PROPERTY that only had a few other residences on it. Each sat along the water and were spaced far apart, with wide evergreen trees along the property lines for privacy.

He'd sent someone ahead of us to get the house situated, so the two large double doors were opened. They led into a small foyer before entering into a very spacious room that took up the entire first floor. The full back wall was a series of sliding glass doors that were also opened, allowing the ocean breeze to fill the room.

The area was clearly designed for entertaining with a very nice kitchen in the back corner, a large dining table, and a sitting area with couches, oversized armchairs, and a television on the wall.

The sliding doors opened to a large, covered deck with a grill area and very well-stocked commercial style bar. Outside, we followed the stairs that led to the sundeck above. There was another small, covered bar, sun chairs, and a hot tub near the back overlooking the beach, just fifty feet or so away. We stood and looked out over the water. A narrow boardwalk ran through the sea grapes to the beach.

As he asked, I called Larry to let him know we arrived. The phone rang several times before he finally answered.

"Michael, I was just wondering when I would hear from you. You make it to the cottage?"

"Yeah, we just got here. I'm standing on your top deck. Quite a place here, Larry."

"Yeah, thanks," he replied. "Look, you two have fun and relax. Help yourself to the kitchen and bar. Winters will call you when he's ready to be picked up. He's on his yacht at the marina and runs on his own time, so just be ready."

"No problem at all. I'll take care of everything."

"Good man. Call me when you pick him up and are on the way."

"No problem."

"OK, gotta run. Give Kim my love," he said, then hung up.

Kim went to change into a bikini and lightweight beach wrap. We took a seat in the sun chairs facing the beach and had a beer. "What did Larry have to say?"

"He says to have fun. We have the run of the place, and Winters will call tomorrow to arrange times."

"Well, then, looks like you're off the clock for the night. Why don't we go to the beach for a quick swim then come back to watch the sunset from the hot tub with a couple of nice drinks. Maybe we can go to the marina for dinner."

"Sounds like a plan to me," I replied.

***

The water was perfect, cool and invigorating. Though, we spent more time wrapped up in each other's arms than swimming. Her playfully deflecting my advances, but teasingly always coming back.

Close to shore we were lost in a kiss when a larger wave swept us up and onto the beach. We rolled in the sand, the water surrounding us with each successive wave. She threw her legs over me and fell onto my chest in an impassioned kiss, pressing herself hard against me. A wave broke over us and she sat up. I reached for her, but she grabbed my hand and moved it down her chest, holding it close over her heart.

"Can you feel it?" she asked.

"Yeah, can you?" I said, thrusting my hips upward.

She raised her eyebrows and with a mischievous grin, pulled herself hard against me then leaned in close. Her lips brushed my ear. I waited for a sign of her desire.

"Mike," she finally whispered. Lingering close, I could feel her breath. I tried to turn my head towards her, but she held it gently in place then kissed me on the cheek, stood, and offered me her hand. An amorous look on her face.

"Come on, let's head back. I want to watch the sunset from the hot tub," she said coyly.

As we walked in the sand she reached down and grabbed my hand. Drawing it over her shoulder, she wrapped her arms around my waist and squeezed me tight. I pulled her close and kissed the top of her head as we walked. She let out a sigh.

We were approaching the boardwalk to the house when she suddenly stopped and turned to me. "Mike, what really happened in Miami?" she asked quietly.

I searched her face. Her expression was soft but conveyed more than a simple curiosity.

"Why do you want to know about that? It's the past. It has no bearing on anything."

She sat down on one of the Adirondack chairs and looked into the sand. She seemed to stare off in thought. I pulled the other closer so I could sit in front of her.

"What is it?" I asked, taking her hand.

"I know you don't want to talk about it, but it's precisely what you just said. The past can affect the now and the future. I know. I've lived it. Someone I dated in college also had a successful business that mysteriously collapsed. I was in love with him, and it turned out he was a really bad guy and even ended up in prison. This is all too familiar and I just can't do that again."

"So, you're saying you're falling for me?" I quipped.

She just shifted and sighed, then looked to her feet, digging them deep into the sand.

"What did Larry tell you?" I asked.

She looked back to me. Her face now more stern. She seemed to search my eyes for the answer I was reluctant to give her.

"He said that you were investigated for big crimes, Mike. That you almost went to prison and lost everything. Then what, just disappeared to Key West? I mean, what did you do?"

I got up abruptly and walked away a few steps then turned back. "Kim, if you were so concerned about me, why did you change your mind and come here?"

She got up slowly and walked towards me. Timidly, she took my hands, still searching my eyes and speaking softly. "Because I believe you're a good person, Mike. Larry told me if you weren't he wouldn't have called you down here. He also said that he stuck with you in Miami because he knew you got a bum rap. I just need to hear it from you. Because of what happened to me before, I need to know what happened."

"Look, Kim, it's not bad. It's more embarrassing."

"Why?"

I tried to pull away, but she held my hand.

"Because I was foolish and blind, that's why. I let someone take advantage of me. I let their ego and greed cost me everything I built. It ruined me, Kim. So, I'm sorry if I'm a little reticent to talk about it. Do you understand?"

She pulled me back, her expression gentle and kind. "I do, truly. But, do you understand where I am coming from?"

I squeezed her hands and closed my eyes, taking a deep breath, letting it out with a sharp exhale, then returned to her gaze.

"Yes, I do – Honestly, I do. But, why are you asking now? You knew all of this. You knew you had questions, reservations. Why here, why now?"

"Because I knew if we continued, I'd have to ask you eventually. I just wanted to see what this was first. If it was just a fling while you're here, then I could accept what Larry said without the details. But if I started feeling more, I'd need to know."

I paused.

"So, you're..."

"No. But, there's something here I haven't felt in a very long time. With each kiss I feel it more. Then back there, lying on the beach with you, I could see it. Maybe it never happens, but I know me. It won't if you can't open up to me. I'm sorry if it seems like my feelings come with a price of admission, but it's true."

"I understand," I said reluctantly.

Looking over the water, the sun was going down. The blue sky above turned to a hot white towards the western horizon, which was beginning to smolder orange and red. I searched for what to say and not knowing how to start, I just looked towards the sun and started talking.

"We were considering her for partner in the firm. She was working on a big project that was in danger of failing but working out a deal to save it. The deal would've solidified her position. Her ambition though clouded her judgment."

"What did she do?" Kim asked.

"She falsified permitting documents. She made a risky, and ultimately illegal play to save the deal.

"So how was that your fault?"

I let out a heavy sigh.

"We were seeing each other romantically, and my feelings for her didn't allow me to see what was right in front of my face. She knew what she was doing and brought me papers to sign off on when I wouldn't have time to read them over and waited until the last minute to get them to me.

"Even if I had just quickly skimmed the documents, I would've seen it. But I had other deadlines I was trying to meet. My firm was on the verge of really making it and I had too much happening at once. I lost everything to a few words whispered in my ear and a pretty smile."

"They forced you to shut down?"

"No, there were several investigations and a ton of legal fees to keep me out of jail. That and some hefty fines was more than my budget could handle. After insurance and liquidating all of my business and personal assets I had just enough money to pay it all off and buy my little sailboat so I wasn't homeless. My reputation was ruined, so there was no starting over. Not in Miami anyway."

"What happened to her?" Kim asked.

"She somehow got some high-priced lawyer who blamed it all on me. Even though no criminal charges were filed against me personally, the judge ruled that it was my responsibility as the owner, and she walked. I am not sure where she went after that. Don't really care."

I was quiet and stared off, my anger building as I thought about it all for the first time in what seemed like forever. Kim came to me, demure and compassionate. She put her arms around me and pressed her head to my chest as she hugged me.

"I know that was hard to talk about, and that you didn't want to. But it really means everything to me that you did. It says a lot, Mike. Thank you."

I took a deep breath and rubbed my face, pulling my hands through my hair.

"Well, the sun is setting, and I need a drink. Let's hit the hot tub."

She smiled and grabbed my hand, leading the way.

***

Kim had gone to make us a couple cocktails. I sat staring at the horizon. Lost in thought I didn't notice her slip into the tub next to me. She slid in front of me, submerged in the warm churning water, her eyes peering up at me through the mist.

Behind her the last fleeting moments of the day were slipping beyond sight and into the sea as she raised herself slightly more from the water, revealing her bare, tanned breast. The intensity in her eyes froze me. I held my breath. My heart raced.

She approached me provocatively and pulled herself onto my lap she took a long pull from the fruity cocktail then held the cup to my lips, gently tilting it for me. She smiled and stood to reach past me, placing the cup on the table. My face pressed against her stomach I kissed her navel and grasped her hips tightly, pulling her close. She tensed and slid back onto my lap.

We stopped, locked in each other's eyes, the tension built with each second and we lingered, allowing it to grow. She let a breath out slowly and reached for me, pulling my face into her chest then running her hands down my back, sliding deeper into the water, grasping my waistband and removing my shorts. She gripped my hair firmly and pulled my head back, kissing me deeply as she rose.

Reaching down, she held me in her hands for a moment. We both held our breath as she slowly settled over me, never taking her eyes from mine. We made love as the final rays of light extinguished into the sea and the day succumbed to the night, as we surrendered to our passion.

CHAPTER 11

THE QUIET BUZZING SLOWLY PULLED ME FROM MY SLEEP. Reluctantly, I opened my eyes, but the sound stopped.

I looked through the open doors beyond the balcony and into the blue and white sky. It was well past dawn. The salty morning breeze filled the room, carrying with it the sounds of small waves lapping at the shoreline and the laughing cries of seagulls.

The large palm frond shaped blades of the ceiling fan pushed the air, causing the bed curtains to flutter around us. Kim was lying with her arm across my chest and her head on my shoulder. I brushed the hair from her face, gently kissed her forehead, then, pulling her close, I closed my eyes and quickly fell back to sleep.

I had just entered a dream when the sound started again. More awake now, I listened and realized what it was. Softly, I lifted Kim's head and slid out from under her. She stirred a little then pulled the covers over her head, never fully waking. I grabbed my phone and sent it to voicemail and quietly left the room, closing the door gently behind me.

The morning sun illuminated the first floor through the large windows. I opened the sliding doors and the curtains flowed in with the breeze. I walked outside then up to the sundeck.

My shorts and a bottle of rum floated in the now still water of the hot tub. Her suit was hung over a chair by the bar. Recalling the night, I smiled, walked to the back rail and looked out over the beach.

The small waves broke in a succession of white lines as they crossed the reef. On the horizon, a large yacht was making its way towards the island and I watched as a flock of seagulls moved in low across the water and settled onto the sand.

The phone rang again. I answered, trying to sound less groggy than I was.

"Larry, good morning."

"Good morning, Michael. Have a good night?"

"Yeah, it was great. I'm just getting up and sitting on your sundeck, enjoying the morning."

"Good. Well look. I spoke to Winters last night. I'm sending a car to pick them up and bring them to the yacht club around noon. The driver will be delivering them shortly thereafter. Bitmore said *Silver Linings* will be ready to go and waiting for you at the fuel dock. We have a big gala tonight and Winters needs to be there and ready well ahead of time. The party starts at eight."

"Who's them?" I asked.

"Sarah is with him."

"OK. Great. So, who is Sarah?"

"Right, you haven't met her yet. Technically, she's our liaison to the governor's office. But she and Winters are ... well they are what they are. Look. She tends to be a big distraction so with her there, this may not go so smooth. Just a heads up."

"I should get to the marina early then. I just need to wake Kim and clean up."

"No need to clean anything, leave it all how it is. I'll have my housekeeper come by. I'll text you Winters' number. Call me if there are any issues. He can be a pain in the ass sometimes and has to feel like he is in complete control, and as I said, she won't help things."

"Super. Well, thanks for the warning. I'll get him there on time."

"Like I said, Mike. I owe you for this one – Oh, one more thing. Do you two have any formal attire?"

"Not with me. I am not sure about Kim."

"It's fine, I'll get you with my guy on St. Thomas and her with the boutique at the resort. I am sure we can find something. On the company.

You should definitely be at the event tonight as well. You've been to enough of these, so you know what it is."

"Probably too many. But, looking forward to it."

"OK then. Ciao."

I sat down in a chair facing the ocean and leaned back, closing my eyes and focusing on the rhythmic sound of the waves.

"Who ya talkin' too?" Kim asked.

I jumped slightly then turned as she came onto the deck dressed in a bathrobe she hadn't fully closed. The breeze offered teasing glances. Noticing my eyes, she playfully turned away and grinned as she handed me a cup of coffee.

"I didn't hear you in the kitchen."

"I set the timer on the coffee maker last night."

"Smart girl," I said and toasted her mug.

She looked around smiling and picked the bottle floating in the hot tub, dumping the water out and setting it on the table.

"I'm sure Larry has a cleaner, but we should probably pick up the evidence," she said as she walked around the deck.

I sat my cup down and walked to her, sliding my arms under her robe and around her waist. She looked up at me, an innocence in her smile, but an intensity deep in her eyes.

"Evidence insinuates a crime. I see only the remains of a beautiful night," I said.

She tried to conceal her grin and with a deep exhale, shook her head as she pulled gently away, continuing to walk around the deck.

"So, what sounds like a plan?" She asked, leaning against the back rail, sipping her coffee.

I looked at her puzzled.

"That was Larry, right?" She asked.

"Yeah, it was. He said Winters is being delivered to the boat around noon, but he has Sarah with him so our time of departure may get delayed."

"Oh God, her?"

"You know her?"

"No, not really. I just know she hangs around Winters and does something at the governor's office. We met once at a dinner. I did not enjoy her company, at all."

"Well, on another note. Larry also wanted to know if you have any formal attire accessible."

"I have one evening gown at home. The rest I left in Georgia. Why?"

"Looks like we're going to a party tonight."

She smiled. "Great. I love Larry's parties. Do we need to go back to get my dress? What about you?"

"No, Larry is going to have us fitted for something. Says he has a guy."

She chuckled. "I am sure he docs. Larry has a 'guy' for everything."

***

I pulled onto the short driveway leading to the yacht club, the gates opened and the guard waved as we approached. François was at the valet stand and greeted us when we arrived.

"Ah, good morning monsieur and madame. I'm told you're leaving us today."

"We are. But first, we're going to have some brunch while we wait for our guests to arrive."

"Mr. Bennett," someone called. I turned to see Mr. Bitmore walking quickly our way.

"Mr. Bennett. Mr. Winters just called and is requesting to be picked up at his yacht."

"But Larry is sending a car for him. He already arranged it."

"Yes, I know. But Mr. Winters called me directly and canceled the driver. He said for you to bring *Silver Linings* to his yacht."

"Why?" I asked.

"I am not sure, sir. He's a very particular man."

I sighed. "Fine, which boat is it?"

He pointed towards the mega yachts. "It's on C-dock. His is called *Bottom Line.*"

"Of course it is," I said, rubbing my brow.

"OK, well, Kim, why don't you get us a table. I'll carry the bags to the boat."

"Mr. Bennett, we will handle all of that for you. S'il vous plaît," François insisted.

"I appreciate that, but I'm a little agitated so the walk will do me good. Just need to cool off."

"You, OK, hun?" Kim asked.

"Yea, I'm fine. I just don't like being treated like an errand boy. I'll get over it though. Nothing a short walk down the dock and a spicy bloody rummy can't cure," I said, then kissed her cheek.

"OK, take your stroll. I'll take care of the rest," she said.

I grabbed a dock cart and tossed our bags in, and despite François's insisting that I allow him to help, headed down the dock alone.

The tide was out so the floating docks were low, and the ramp had a steep decline. Having walked through a puddle from the irrigation system, my sandals were slick, and my right foot slipped, breaking the strap. I took a deep breath and sat the cart down, trying to control my building frustration.

Letting go of the handle to pick up my broken sandal and remove the other, the cart ran the last ten feet of the ramp and crashed into a dock box, spilling over and sending our things onto the deck, and my bag into the water.

"Son-of-a-bitch," I said loudly, then ran towards my bag as it slowly started to sink, slipping on the wet deck as I reached the edge. Thankfully I was able to I retrieve it and tossed it on the deck with a loud thud.

"That was hilarious," a voice said from behind me, laughing.

I gritted my teeth, but didn't look up. "Yeah, real funny," I said as I looked though the bag for my passport in hopes of saving it.

"I thought so," the man replied sharply as he continued on.

I smashed my fists into the wet bag then stood up.

"Fuckin' dick," I muttered under my breath as I slammed the heavy bag into the cart.

Hearing me, he stopped and turned around.

"You have something to say?" he asked in a heavy New Orleans accent.

He was all of six-six and well over 200 pounds with the build of a linebacker, but the pallor of someone better suited for more northern climes. He wore an open shirt with a tank top underneath that accentuated, more than it hid, his muscular physique. I definitely didn't want to fight him.

"Man, you're the one with all the things to say," I replied.

François must have seen my cart go in the water and was already heading down the dock. The man and I were ten feet apart but standing squared off to each other when he arrived.

"Everything OK here, gentleman," he said.

"Yea, all good," I said, snatching another item from the dock and tossing it in the cart.

"Good," François replied. "Mr. Bennett, this is Mr. Joshua. He works for Mr. Winters as well."

Joshua grunted then turned and walked away slowly.

"I'll see you around," he said, looking back over his shoulder with a smirk.

The wheel to the cart looked broken so I grabbed my wet bag and tossed it over my shoulder, soaking my shirt. This time I accepted François's help with the other luggage. He collected Kim's items from the dock, tossed everything into the cart, and followed after me. The wheel of the cart now wobbling.

We dropped everything at the boat and headed back towards the clubhouse. "Thanks again," I said with a handshake and fifty bucks.

"Mr. Bennett, I can't—"

"François," I said, smiling at him firmly. "Thank you."

"Merci, monsieur."

***

As I approached the table, Kim started to laugh at the site of me. I could see my reflection in the window behind her. Me standing there in my bare feet and soaked shirt, a scowl on my face and knee slightly bleeding. I felt like, and likely looked like, a small child, pouting and dripping wet.

"What happened to you?" she asked, getting up to offer me a consoling hug. "It doesn't look like you had a very relaxing walk." Her laughter growing despite her efforts to hold it in. "Come on, sit down. So seriously, what happened to you?"

Overwhelmed by the irony I gave into the humor of it all, laughing at myself and took a long pull from my drink. "I couldn't begin to explain the absurdity of it. Let's just hope the rest of the day goes better."

Chapter 12

FROM THE HELM SEAT I STUDIED THE HORIZON. The ocean was calm and blue, the sky clear. I pressed the ignition button and *Silver Lining's* powerful motors growled as the RPMs briefly rose, then faded to a faint hum. There was a large motor yacht in front of me. *Second Coming* was scrolled across her stern in blue, a golden cross was set back in white clouds behind the lettering.

The yacht was moving away slowly, and not seeing any conflicting traffic, I pushed the throttles forward and we took a wide berth around her, covering the distance quickly to *Bottom Line*. Two deck hands were waiting when we arrived, dressed in dark blue shorts and white polos with the ships silhouette embroidered on the chest. They quickly secured our lines and accompanied us to the long footbridge that ran forward and parallel to the large ship on her port side.

"Follow us, please," one of the boys instructed and headed up the ramp. "Mr. Winters is waiting for you on the aft deck.

At the top of the ramp Kim grabbed my arm, pointing back towards the marina. "My God, you can see everything from up here. Have you ever been on such a large boat?"

"Yeah, once for a party in Ft. Lauderdale. Not nearly this big though," I said, coaxing her along.

Kim peered into every door and window as we walked, stopping to point out different things she found exciting. Finally, we reached the main aft deck.

"Please have a seat and relax. Mr. Winters will be right with you," he said then headed inside.

The forward portion of the deck was covered and had a large teak dining table in the middle surrounded by chairs. A small bar sat in the corner and the whole area was lined with blue and white couches. A rocks glass sat on the table with a finger or so left in it. A cigar burned in the ashtray.

After a few minutes with no sign of anyone, I grinned at Kim and yelled, "Ahoy!" There was no reply, so I called out again, "Hello?"

"Out in a minute," a man replied from inside.

Kim and I walked to the back of the deck, which was not covered, and had a soaking tub and several deck loungers. We peered over the aft rail and looked down at *Silver Linings* bobbing in the water. From the deck of the massive ship, she seemed like an insignificant toy.

We strolled around a few minutes, admiring the view when Charles Winters came out. "Sorry to keep you waiting," he said.

He looked to be in his mid-sixties and, besides a small belly, seemed to be in decent shape. He wore white linen pants, a blue button up shirt, and brown loafers. The smell of his cologne wafted over us before he was in arms' reach.

"You must be Michael Bennett," he said, extending his hand. "I'm Charles Winters. Welcome aboard."

"Mike," I replied, shaking his hand. "This is Kim."

He turned to her. "We've met before, I think. Aren't you Larry's girl?" he said, shaking Kim's hand as well.

"Yes, we met briefly a couple times. But no, I am not, Larry's girl. Just a friend."

"OK, well, nice to meet you again then," he replied.

"Helluva boat you have here, Chuck," I said.

He shot me a disapproving look. "She's a yacht. Not just a boat. And you can call me Mr. Winters, or just Winters. I do not respond to pedestrian diminutives."

I lifted my hands in apology. "Mr. Winters. I didn't mean any insult. That was a misstep. I'm sorry if I offended you."

He looked me over once and offered a grin and nod. "Well thank you. No insult taken. I just don't care for the name, 'Chuck'," he said with disgust. Now, I need to go get Sarah, she's sunning on the front deck. If you'd like, follow me and I'll show you a little of my darling," he said, turning and moving inside.

The main salon was opulently adorned with nautical paintings and classical sailing tools in display cases. The back wall and hallway were filled with pictures of him with various celebrities of music, screen, and business.

"Yes, in my business I get to associate with truly great people," he said, glancing over his shoulder, ensuring we noted the images.

"You have this beautiful boat. Why not just bring her over to St. Thomas? She's nicer than any resort, that's for sure," I said as we walked.

He stopped and turned to face me. "Again, Michael, she's a yacht. And once she's here she stays here. *Silver Linings* is much better for getting around quickly. Plus, our base of operations is at the resort. So, it's important for me to be there." He turned and continued walking.

We made our way through a few more rooms, all as ornate as the rest, before coming to a shaded deck overlooking the expansive bow. There, on full display, was his crowning ornamental piece.

Her bikini top was draped over a table to her left and her bottoms expressed little modesty. Her blond hair contrasted sharply against her bronzed skin and gently rested on her shoulders. Her face was young looking and beautiful, yet clearly as hand sculpted as her breast.

He saw the look on my face and grinned as he called to her. "Sarah, darling. Mr. Bennett is here. Why don't you come meet us on the aft deck."

She raised her hand to shield her eyes from the sun. "OK, Charlie," she replied. "Make me a drink and I'll be right there."

He turned to me and paused. "She's something isn't she?"

"That she is, sir. One helluva yacht. Seems to have everything."

He grinned then headed aft.

I turned to follow but lingered for a moment to look back to her. She caught my gaze and waved with a sly grin as she sat up and reached for her top.

Kim had stopped to look at some pictures in the cabin and was just coming out as we were heading back. "How's the view up here?" she asked excitedly.

"Not bad," I said, continuing on. "Check it out."

A few moments later she was at my side. "Not bad?" she said, pinching my arm playfully. I just shrugged and smiled.

We returned to the back deck and had a seat at the table. Winters excused himself then went inside just as Sarah was coming out. She'd wrapped a lightweight sarong around her waist that revealed far more than it covered.

I leaned over to Kim. "They're not much for subtleties on this boat it seems."

"Or modesty," she whispered, looking her over as she approached.

"Mr. Bennett, nice to meet you. Welcome aboard," she said with a pleasant smile, extending her hand.

"Thank you, this is Kim," I replied. "And please, call me Mike."

"Very well. Mike … Kim," she said nodding to us as she took a seat at the table. "Nice to meet you both. My name is Sarah."

She pulled her hair into a ponytail then gracefully crossed her legs and hung an arm over the chair next to her. Her attention focused for a moment on the soccer game on the bar television. Kim was watching her and adjusted her own posture.

"Such a beautiful yacht," she said to her.

Sarah looked at Kim and grinned, then returned her attention to the game. "Yes, she is."

"You work for the governor, right?" Kim asked.

Sarah smiled and adjusted her position to face us more directly. "I do."

"The politics here can be, well, 'exciting' sometimes. It must be an interesting job," Kim said.

"It's never boring, that's for sure," Sarah replied.

Winters returned, followed by a deckhand carrying a tray of cocktails. "Sarah here is actually our liaison to the governor's office," he said as he sat down next to her. "She does far more for us than she gets credit for."

I watched as the cocktails were being handed out. "Mr. Winters, we should probably get going. Larry was adamant about getting back as early as possible," I said.

"Well, it's a good thing I'm the boss. And I feel like a cocktail before we leave," he replied.

"It'll be fine, Michael, don't worry about Larry," Sarah said, lifting her glass and looking at it with disgust.

"Charlie, what is this?" she asked.

"It's a hurricane. Stephan made them. You always love his drinks," he replied.

"I'd really prefer a rosé. It's too early for rum drinks."

"OK, I'll call for him to come back," he said pulling his phone out.

"Charlie, I don't feel like waiting. Why don't you go get it for me."

He started to reply, glancing to his phone, but stopped and smiled. "OK, my darling. I'll get it."

He walked to the small bar and pulled a bottle from the wine fridge.

"So, Mike," Winters began, "Larry tells me you're the guy that'll get us past this permitting hurdle."

"Charlie sweetie, I'd really prefer the Whispering Angel," Sarah said.

He looked at the bottle then to her, and with furrowed brow shook his head and returned the bottle to the fridge.

"Excuse me, I'll be right back," he said.

"Thank you, dear," Sarah said.

He turned a blew her a kiss.

"He's really great," she said.

"You two been together long?" Kim asked.

"Not too long. We met when he was here scouting this project then again at a dinner with the governor. He treats me like a queen, and I love it."

Winters returned, placing a glass in front of her. "Here you are, my dear," he said, kissing her forehead."

"You're the best," she replied.

He sat down and took a drink, then looked to me. "So, Mike, as I was saying. Larry speaks very highly of you. He really made a strong argument to bring you in."

"Yea, I've handled a few difficult projects before."

"I know. You have a very impressive track record. Larry said you were a star on the rise."

"Once upon a time."

"It's too bad it ended so unceremoniously," he said.

"Well, I'm glad Larry told you so much about my life."

"Larry only assured me you were the one for the job. When I asked why we didn't bring you in from the start, he explained a little of your fall from grace. But not too much, honestly. I know more of your story because I looked into you."

"What do you mean, you looked into me?"

He moved his glass and leaned closer, resting on his elbow. "Michael, in this business, I know everyone and keep my finger on its pulse. That's how I'm so successful." He sat back and picked up his glass. "I even know your dad," he said, taking a drink.

"You know my father?"

"Well, we've never officially met, but our businesses have worked together before and we've had a few phone calls. He seems like a good man. And he's clearly a hell of a businessman."

"Oh, yeah. He's great. Just ask him."

He chuckled. "Well anyway, let's hope you've still got it."

"We'll know more once I can look at the reports and access the site. I have to say though, this is a unique job for me."

"How's that?"

"The social aspect of it is something I haven't had to navigate before. There seems to be a lot of folks against this project."

"There are always detractors," Sarah said, "but they'll come around. The governor especially has been a great supporter. He sees the potential to really elevate Coral Bay and the entire island.

"And if the locals don't share his optimism or buy into the vision?" I asked.

She smiled. "Good thing it's not up to them. But as I said, they'll come around. A rising tide lifts all boats, as they say."

"Look, Mike, that is all PR and nothing for you to worry about. We have people who handle all of that. I've dealt with this type of thing many times. You just focus on getting us those permits."

"I'll do what I can," I said.

"Good," he said. "And just know, we always take care of those who get things done. And working with Bowling Green, well that's the kind of thing that makes careers, and atones for a lot of sins of the past."

He grinned and sipped from his drink slowly, his eyes set on me. "I can see it in you. I've been in business a long time and know when I'm talking to someone who is naturally an upper echelon kind of person. This could get you back on top."

I liked what he was saying. It felt good to hear that and I couldn't help but smile.

"Just the thought of it has you perked up," Sarah said. "I bet success looks really good on you."

Winters was watching me, so I returned his stare. "Take a walk with me, Michael. I have something I need to talk to you about."

"Secret squirrel stuff?" Kim said.

He offered her a smile. "Just private business matters. We won't be long." He nodded and walked towards the starboard rail. I squeezed Kim's shoulder and followed him.

As we reached the rail, he turned and, as if searching for the answer before he asked it, studied my face. He let out a heavy sigh and held up a hand, a finger placed lightly over his mouth as he found his words.

"I have to ask you something. As I told you, I keep my finger on the pulse of this business and everything that touches it. So, I also know about your relationship with Dave Blankenship."

"Yeah… he, used to work for me in Miami. Dave was a great man and a dear friend."

"He was also a staunch environmentalist and vehemently opposed to our project here."

"I know. He was always a hardliner."

"I also know your business model was making construction greener. Which doesn't always mesh with my approach. Are you following me here?"

"Look, I know you have far too much time and money invested in this project just to let it go. If I fail, you'll keep going until you find someone who can get it done. If it's me, at least I know I'll do my best to make it all work together. But Larry assured me you were willing to work with me and listen to my ideas."

"And we are, Michael. But you have to do the same. This is an investment venture, and we have shareholders to answer to."

"I understand that. Look, you know one doesn't get to the level I was at by working against people. If I was the guy always saying no, nobody would've hired me. I got where I was because I was able to work with, not just the people, but their vision. There will undoubtedly be concessions, but the net results will be positive, or I failed. And I'm not known to fail."

He smiled. "Man, I love being right."

"About what?" I asked.

"Seeing it in you. Being able to pick a winner."

"Well, thank you."

We started to walk back, but he grabbed my arm. "Hold on. One more thing I need to say."

He again seemed to search for his words. I waited.

"Mike, it's no secret Dave wasn't a favorite person of mine. He and his group caused us a lot of problems. But knowing he was close to you … Well, I'm sorry for your loss. Please don't ever think that I hold a person's death as a positive thing. It was a tragic accident."

"Thank you. That means a lot," I said.

He patted me on the shoulder and we continued to walk. "Good. Well, I think it's time we get moving."

CHAPTER 13

IT WAS LATE AFTERNOON AS WE APPROACHED THE MARINA AT RED HOOK. The seas were calm, only slightly stirred by the ever-present trade winds, so the passage back to St. Thomas went smoothly. Larry was waiting on the dock when we arrived.

He faintly smiled as he greeted Winters and Sarah, motioning to the car waiting near the marina ship store.

"That's a good man you have there, Larry. I have a feeling he'll do just fine," Winters said, nodding to me.

Larry glanced to me and smiled. "Glad to hear that," he said. "You two have your own car, we'll ride in the SUV."

Winters followed Sarah up the dock as two marina staff arrived and were loading the bags into a dock cart. Larry greeted me as I stepped off the boat.

"How'd it, go?" he asked, shaking my hand.

"I got here as fast as I could. He refused the car and insisted that I pick him up at his boat. When we arrived, he wasn't waiting but had us come aboard. We wasted over an hour just so he could flaunt his 'yacht' and show off Sarah."

"I told you he can be a handful, man, and that she wouldn't help. You did what you could though, and I appreciate that. Sounds like you hit it off though."

"In a business sense, sure. Don't think we'll be going out for beers anytime soon, but it went well. Seems he dug into my background and was definitely feeling me out, especially because of my friendship with Dave. But I know how to handle that kind of thing."

"You know that I know that. But, come on, let's get going. Enough time has been wasted." He placed his hand on my back and we began walking towards the parking lot. Sarah was standing on the seawall.

"She definitely has a power over him," I said motioning to Sarah. "Funny given how assertive he is. But he bends to her will pretty quick."

"Yeah, she knows what she's doing," Kim said from behind us.

"Well, despite the hang-ups, you both really came through. Tonight is very important to our project. We have a lot of potential and current investors here, so everything has to go smoothly. So, thanks again."

"No problem," I replied.

"I was just along for the ride, but thanks, Larry," Kim said.

"Well, I hope you enjoyed yourself," Larry said to her. "So, look, everyone is staying at the Paradise Palms resort. That's where the event is, and I have arranged a room for you. I imagine you can stay on the boat in Coral Bay when you're there, so for now, while you're on St. Thomas, that's your place."

"Wow, Larry. Fancy," Kim said.

"Well, one of Bowling Green's companies manages it, so it's easy."

As we approached the waiting SUV, a large West Indian man stepped out of the driver's side. His size, demeanor, cleanly shaven head, pressed dark slacks and polished black shoes gave him an austere but professional appearance. His loose blazer was left open, subtly revealing the pistol under his arm.

The man moved to the passenger side of the vehicle and opened the back door for Kim then motioned for me to follow. Larry climbed into the passenger seat. As the man reentered the vehicle Larry briefly introduced him.

"This is Ahmad."

He peered into the rearview mirror. "Nice to meet you folks," he said in a deep voice.

"Larry, do you need a security guard?" Kim asked.

Larry was reading something on his phone and answered without looking up. "I haven't yet, but I'd rather not wait until I do."

Placing his phone back into his pocket and speaking quickly, he turned to Ahmad. "Let's go." He then turned to face us as we pulled onto the street and sped off.

"Kim, as I explained to Mike, tonight is very important for our project, so I need you both to be on your A-game. Tonight, is a formal black-tie event. Kim, the resort has a nice boutique for you to find an evening gown. I've already made the arrangements. Mike, since we don't have time to do a proper fitting, I have my man Mr. Oliver meeting you in your suite. He will have several options and can make minor alterations on the spot."

We drove quickly for a few more minutes down the typical island roads, most of them badly in need of repair, before turning down what looked like a freshly paved two-lane side road. After a few hundred feet, the road widened and there was a large gate flanked by two marble palm trees. *Paradise Palms* was scrolled in golden letters on the arch above the gate. As we approached the guard house, the gates opened.

The short road leading to the resort was lined with Royal Palms and wound through a well-manicured landscape of golf course quality grass, shaped hedges, and tropical vegetation. The road ended with a driveway that circled a massive pineapple palm before leading to the valet station. The main resort backed up to a small cliff that overlooked the ocean.

As we exited the vehicle Larry was immediately greeted by a small group of men all dressed in business suits. After a brief conversation, he gestured to a woman wearing a polo with the resort logo on it. Larry excused himself from the group and walked to us. The woman from the resort was there a second later.

"OK, I have to tend to some business. Kim, this is Lisa, she will get you whatever you need. I will see you in the ballroom at 8."

He placed his hand on Lisa's shoulder. "You're in good hands." Then he turned and quickly left.

Lisa signaled to the maître d' and instructed him to ensure our bags were delivered immediately to our room.

"Mr. King here will show you the way to your room," she said to me, then turned to Kim with a smile. "And you and I will be heading to the boutique."

The maître d' signaled for a baggage cart which was promptly delivered by one of the bellboys who loaded our bags. Kim kissed my cheek then strolled off with Lisa.

Mr. King led the way to the suite, which was in an isolated area of the resort atop one of the higher cliffs. The front door opened into the living area. Towards the middle of the room a TV was mounted to the wall. A large white linen couch sat on the opposing wall with a coffee table that resembled an old chest. Along the back wall were two sets of French doors that led to a patio which overlooked the cliff and the ocean. A hammock was slung between two palm trees in the small grassy area. Just inside was a small but well-stocked bar.

A cart was situated in the middle of the living area. It had a few tuxedo jackets and pants hanging neatly from hangers. A sewing machine and small sewing kit were on the table nearest the window. Mr. King called into the bedroom "Mr. Oliver?"

"I will be right out," said a voice with a heavy British accent.

A moment later a small, frail looking but well-dressed older man entered the room. "Ah, Mr. Bennett, so nice to meet you," he said as he crossed the room and shook my hand.

"Nice to meet you as well, sir."

He took a step back and looked me over, studying me for a few seconds and then smiled. "I think I have just the tux for you."

"Is there anything else I can do for you, sir?" asked Mr. King.

"I don't think so," I replied and handed him ten dollars.

"Thank you, sir. If you need anything else, simply ring the front desk and ask for me."

"Will do, and thanks again."

"Thank you, Mr. King," Mr. Oliver said as the door closed. Then, turned to me. "Well, let's get to it."

He walked to the bar and grabbed two glasses. Opening one of the two doors below he scooped out some ice, dropping several cubes into each class then poured two fingers of Talisker 25 into one of the glasses. Looking back at me he asked if I was a scotch man. "Rum," I replied.

He smiled. "Ahh, I do love my rum. But I always drink scotch while I'm working on a tux."

He lifted a bottle of Clément XO, gesturing to me. "That will certainly work," I said.

***

The French doors were open allowing the sea breeze to fill the room. A short distance away I could hear the waves crashing on the rocky cliff face. I stood in the mirror as Mr. Oliver made a few marks on my slacks.

It had been a long time since I had worn a tuxedo, I had almost forgotten how good it felt. Mr. Oliver walked to the stand and retrieved the jacket. I set my glass down on the table next to me and he slid it over my shoulders. Adjusting my posture, I pulled the jacket forward by the lapel, buttoning the top button.

Mr. Oliver placed his hands on my shoulders and smoothed out the material. I picked up my glass and took a long pull as I studied my reflection. It was an image of me I hadn't seen in a long time. I grinned over the rim of my glass and shot myself an approving wink as I finished off the last half ounce of agricole rum.

"I don't think I need to adjust the jacket at all, dear boy. And the pants will only take me a few minutes to bring in a little," Mr. Oliver said.

I continued to gaze at myself in the mirror. "Great," I replied as I handed him my glass, "Why don't you refresh our drinks, and I'll change so you can finish up."

He nodded slightly and took my glass. "Very good, sir," he replied.

***

I put on a terrycloth bathrobe and left the tux on the bed. Mr. Oliver was sitting in the armchair on the patio. On the table were our glasses, freshly poured. He looked up as I walked outside.

"Well, I'll get to it. I'll be done in just a few minutes," he said as he stood up to return to the room.

I sat and watched some seagulls riding the updraft from the cliff, suspended in the final moments of the day. The winds that carried them flowed over the ledges, caressing the palm trees as they swayed in the breeze. The sun was beginning to set, and the sky was filled with pinks and oranges as the last rays bounced off the low-lying clouds.

I heard the door open and turned to see Kim, beaming as she floated into the room with a glass of champagne in her hand. She was followed by Lisa who pushed a bell cart with a couple small bags and a garment bag hung neatly. Lisa went into the bedroom and placed the items on the bed, thanked her, then left.

I walked into the living room and Kim threw her arms around my neck, kissing me. "I'm going to start getting ready." She glanced to Mr. Oliver. "And we both need to shower," she said with a smile.

Mr. Oliver cleared his throat. "Sir, madam. I will just be another couple of minutes if you want to begin getting ready. I will leave everything on a hanger in here."

Kim smiled then turned and walked into the room, closing the door behind her.

Mr. Oliver, looking intently at what he was doing, spoke again without looking up, sewing pins between his lips. "Seems to me, when a beautiful woman invites you into the shower, you go." He glanced up to me over the rim of his glasses, a stern grin on his face.

I laughed and in my best British accent, replied. "Right you are, good sir. Right you are."

Chapter 14

THE BALLROOM WAS THE CENTERPIECE OF THE MAIN RESORT. The highest point on the property, it was an extension of the luxurious five-star restaurant, simply named, *Pearl*. The tall wooden doors opened to a large room with a high ceiling. At the center a large artificial pineapple palm tree sat in a shallow lighted pool with several small fountains at its base. A chandelier moon hung above it.

A large bar occupied the right side of the room and a stage and dance floor were set against the adjacent wall. The back of the room had several large doors that opened onto a terrace that overlooked the pool and on to the ocean.

It was just a few minutes past eight when I arrived and the room was filled with chatter and energy. The bar was stacked two deep, and the band was just getting started with "On the Sunny Side of the Street." Larry was speaking with a small group of people and noticed me as I walked in. He gestured towards the back of the room.

"Looks like the magical Mr. Oliver came through again," he said as he approached, slapping me on the shoulder and shaking my hand. "You look damned good, Mike."

"Thanks," I replied.

"Where's Kim?" he asked.

"She's just a few minutes behind me. She told me to go ahead while she finishes up."

He laughed. "I am not surprised. I've never known her to be on-time for anything. Not to worry though, this is just a cocktail hour meet and greet. Come on, let's grab a drink out back while we wait. I have something I want to discuss."

We walked to one of three bars situated on the terrace for the event. The night air was warm and thick, but the breeze from the ocean made it tolerable. Larry ordered us two glasses of *Macallan 18,* and we moved to the back rail. He sat his glass down on a small high-top table and pulled out a cigar. He was focused on the stogy as he cut the ends.

"So, what's the purpose for the party tonight?" I asked.

He looked up at me and smiled as he placed the cigar between his teeth and flipped open his Zippo. The end burned red as he lit it, his face briefly concealed in a cloud of smoke with each puff. Closing his lighter he turned his head skyward, blowing the smoke into the night. He stared off into the crowd for a moment then turned to me, gesturing with the hand holding the cigar.

"This is all for them. Most of the people here have invested in projects with us before, but some are new investors. Tonight, is the wine and dine portion of the sell. Later is the big reveal and presentation. After that, there are a few more days of schmoozing and showing them a good time before we hit them up for any real money."

He picked up his glass and pointed towards me with it. "There is a lot of potential here that can lead to some very good things for you in the future." He raised his glass to take a drink, pausing a moment and speaking over its rim.

"For us."

He swallowed the scotch, took a long drag from his cigar, then continued.

"Mike, while you were on St. Croix some things changed. I need a C-suite level position filled. I need someone who knows this work."

I chuckled. "And let me guess. You want me?"

"You were raised in this business and know it better than anyone. Anyone but me of course. I already talked to Winters, and he agrees."

"I don't know, Larry," I sighed. "I left corporate America twice. Not sure I want to go back. Life is simpler now, and I kind of like it that way."

"This is different."

"How's that?" I asked.

"You owned your business. That's stressful. Mike, this could make up for the Miami incident. Get you back where you should be."

"And where is that?" I asked.

"Back on top, man," he said gripping my shoulder.

He took another long drag from his cigar, then holding it out as if to study it, blew smoke on it. "$200,000 per year to start, plus benefits."

I let his words roll through my head and looked out into the night sky. He watched me patiently, waiting for a response. I took a deep breath, exhaling slowly as I looked at him.

He held a hand up before I could reply. "Just – think about. It's all I'm asking for now," he said.

Someone called his name from across the room. He looked to see who it was and then looked back to me. "Time to get back to work. We'll catch up later." He greeted the man then disappeared into the crowd.

I turned and gazed into the dark towards the sound of the crashing waves on the nearby cliffs. The clouds mostly obscured the stars, and a crescent moon hung in a pocket of clear sky, a white halo surrounded it.

There was an eruption of laughter behind me and I turned back to the terrace. Leaning against the rail I watched the interactions of the small groups. Some seemed engaged in serious conversation, but most laughed and looked to be enjoying themselves.

Then, scanning the crowd, I saw her. My heart stopped. Kim smiled and turned once to show off her dress. Modestly cut on the chest, but deep on the back. Black with hints of shimmer, classic and understated. It was long with a slit to reveal one leg as she walked. Her loosely curled long black hair gently danced around her shoulders as she walked towards me with all the elegance and grace of royalty.

The world seemed to stop and fade away. It was only us on an empty terrace. I sat my glass down as she neared and reached for her, wrapping my right arm around her waist and pulling her close. She took in a quick breath and seemed to hold it. Her hands gently rested on my back. I placed a hand behind her head and softly kissed her. Her body relaxed in my arms.

We broke, our faces still close. She sighed, and moved her hands to my waist, pulling me closer. Her lips near my ear, she asked, "What was that for?" Her voice just a whisper.

"It was the only way I could think of to express how I felt when I saw you."

"Well," she began, then gently cleared her throat. "Thank you. And do hold onto that thought."

"I don't think that'll be a problem," I said.

We were both lost in the eyes of the other, not saying anything. We didn't have to. I smiled and she lightly bit her bottom lip.

"Well… should we head inside and join the party?" she said, her face still close to mine. Her smile poorly hidden.

"OK, let's go," I replied.

"Yeah," she said. "We should."

We stood there a few more seconds allowing the moment to gradually subside with each passing breath, searching each other's eyes.

I stepped back and offered her my arm.

***

Inside, the party was well underway. Swing music poured from the bandstand of men dressed in classic 40's era attire and led by a beautiful woman in a red dress. A crowd near the stage danced and as she pointed the bell of her clarinet to the ceiling at the climax of her solo.

The crowd roared with applause.

Glancing around the room I noticed Larry huddled with several others standing around a presentation board. Stretching his neck so he could see us above the crowd, he waved us over.

"You look absolutely stunning, my dear," Larry said to Kim as we approached. "Ladies and gentlemen, this is Michael Bennett and Kim Blackwell. Kim lives on St. John. Mike here is from Key West and is handling the environmental permitting side of things for us. He and I have worked together a long time. But, he may be coming onboard at a higher level."

Kim pulled my arm. "What's this now?" she asked.

"Well, nothing is set in stone yet, but Larry here made me a nice offer. He drives a hard bargain," I said.

He smiled. "You haven't seen anything yet."

"So, Larry, what are you looking at here?" I asked, referencing the large presentation board.

"Well, Mike, this is our project. Most of this was in the packet I sent you. We just added some artist renderings and diagrams showing the projects in stages from concept to completion."

"Oh, excuse me hun," Kim said. "I see a friend from St. John. I'll be right back."

"I'll be here or at the table," I said. Then turned back to Larry.

"So, what's the holdup been?" I asked, studying the maps.

Larry continued. "But, as you know, there are some protected species of seagrasses and corals in the area that could be impacted. But we have a plan in place that will use mitigation banks to offset those impacts. It'll cost a lot of money, but the R.O.I. will be worth it in the end. We just need to get the permits approved. That's where you come in."

"Yea, as soon as I looked at the reports you sent, I knew this wouldn't be easy. And mitigation banks, you know my dislike for those," I said. "Plus, if the plan is destructive to sensitive marine life, it'll be difficult to get passed. But this isn't unlike a different project I worked on in Tampa. Although I'd need to do my own assessment, looking at the channel and water depths on the bathymetric map, we may be able to make some changes to the plan."

"What kind of changes?" a nearby man asked. Larry introduced him as Kazuo Tojo, a Japanese real-estate developer and investor in the project.

I started to describe a few options to them, pointing out areas of concern on the map, and some possible alternatives. Many included a reduction in pier lengths, and numbers of slips as well as limiting boat sizes based on the channel depths and the use of different materials. As I spoke a small group formed around us, listening.

"I have to say, Mike, those would cost a lot of money in the form of reduced revenue," Larry said.

"Yes, but they'd be more ecologically sound and easier to pass. How much revenue are you losing now fighting to get this done as it stands, with no clear path to success. Sometimes you have to pivot. You know that."

"He's right," said Kazuo. "There's a difference between tenacity and stubbornness. I think if changes were needed, the board would approve them. I just want to see a return on this before I die."

A few of the people listening in started to speak up, some in favor of changes, others opposed. Larry glared at me, though he looked trapped as he tried to navigate the barrage of questions and comments from the small group.

"Look," I said, holding my hands up to quiet the crowd. "This may be able to get done as is, I don't know that yet. I was just spit balling ideas here with Larry. We've done this together before," I said putting my arm over his shoulder. "Your investments are in good hands."

Larry grinned. "He's right. And Mike coming up with alternatives so quickly is why we brought him in, pulling him out of retirement. This is the guy who will get it done for us all."

"But what if changes are required?" someone asked. "Will that reduce our returns?"

"Look, we want this project done the way we designed it," Larry said pointing to the maps. "But, at the end of the day, Mr. Tojo is right. We have to get something done and move forward. Maybe it means expansions down the road once revenue is coming in or adding other things to compensate for the changes. Friends, this will get done and you'll all be happy with the results, I assure you."

Two short bells indicated that dinner service would begin shortly, and everyone headed to their seats. Larry looked at me and laughed slightly, shaking his head.

"Man, that was unexpected. You saved me there. Maybe we save the whiteboard talk for the office from now on," he said, patting me on the back.

I laughed. "Probably a good idea."

"But look, Mike, I was serious about what I said just then. You coming up with alternatives so quickly shows why I brought you down and why you're the man for that job. You're the best at this stuff."

I squared off to him and lifted my chin slightly, studying his face. He grinned.

"Are you really open to change if needed," I asked.

"Yes. If needed."

"And this would be me doing what I do. Helping get this done with the environment front of mind."

"Of course. The beauty of this place is our bread and butter."

"Well," I said and put out my hand, "If that's the case. I'm in."

Larry smiled and went to shake my hand, but I withdrew mine first. He looked at me questioningly.

"But I've been doing this a long time, I know what this position is worth. Make it $250,000 and you've got a deal," I said and slowly lowered my hand to him.

He chuckled and raised an eyebrow. "And you say I'm the one driving the hard bargain."

He smiled and grabbed my hand.

"Done! Damn it, Mike, I knew you'd make the right decision," he said with a soft jab to my shoulder. "What brought you around?"

"I do miss this a little. The puzzle of making it all work is exciting. And keeping bastards like you from destroying the planet is a bonus," I said, jabbing him back in the arm. "And I'm enjoying myself here."

Kim was walking towards us and Larry noticed me watching her. His expression turned more serious.

"Don't do it just for her, Michael. I know your penchant for falling fast and landing hard. I can't have you running off in the middle of the project because she broke your heart. And she may."

I smiled to myself as I watched her then turned to Larry. "I can't say she isn't a factor. But, I won't. No matter what happens with her, I'll see this through."

"I hope so. I have a lot riding on you." His smile returned.

"You both look happy. What's going on?" Kim asked.

"Your boy here decided to take the job," Larry said.

She jumped up and down then kissed me. "Oh my God, that's great. We need to celebrate. Let's go for a sail tomorrow."

Larry shook his head. "Unfortunately, I have work tomorrow. And since Mike is now on board, so does he."

"Well, I guess we'll have to celebrate tonight then." She smiled and grabbed two bottles of champagne from the ice tub on the bar. "Let's make it a private party, get away from the crowd and head back to the room. The hot tub sounds perfect right now. We can order food in."

I looked to Larry. "Go ahead," he said. "But Mike, tomorrow morning, my office, 10 a.m."

"Where's the office?" I asked.

"Magen's Bay."

"Are you sending a car, or should I take a taxi?"

"No, that doesn't work in the long term. I have something I think you'll like that I can loan you. Give me a second."

He pulled his phone out. "Miguel. Bring *Bianca* to Paradise Palms tonight. Leave the keys with the valet for Mr. Bennett.

OK, great. Thank you." He hung up.

I grinned "Bianca?"

"Trust me. She's a great car and fun to drive. You'll enjoy it. Just keep her on St. Thomas."

"Oh my God, that car is gorgeous," Kim said.

"It'll be here in the morning. You two have fun," he said, shook my hand again, then hugged Kim and headed off.

"So," I said, taking the bottles from her. "Hot tub?"

She picked up two champagne flutes and grinned. "Lead the way."

Chapter 15

I'D NEVER BEEN ONE FOR SLEEPING LATE. That morning though, all I wanted to do was stay in bed with her. Our plan was to have breakfast together before I left to meet Larry, so I slipped quietly out of bed and put on a pot of coffee. The aroma quickly filled the room.

Sitting on the bed next to her I gently ran my hand through her hair and kissed her cheek, softly trying to wake her. She smiled without opening her eyes, turned her back to me, and pulled the cover over her head. I lightly tapped her shoulder, and she reluctantly rolled onto her back. Her hair covered her face and with her eyes still closed, she made multiple unsuccessful attempts to blow it away.

She tried to hide her smile, groaned and pulled the sheets up over her head again. I lightly drew them back down just below her chin. With a smirk on her face, she opened her eyes slightly, sleepily glaring at me then held my arm and turned away, pulling me into bed close behind her. I had intended to start the day, but it's hard to argue with such a persuasive argument. So, I kissed her just behind her ear and laid my head on the pillow with her, and before long, drifted back to sleep.

***

An hour passed before I woke again. I had to leave in 10 minutes to meet Larry so I hopped out of bed. Kim watched me as I was getting dressed.

"This shouldn't take long," I said to her. "Let me know what you decide to do, and I'll come find you when I'm done."

She got out of bed with the sheet wrapped around her and walked over to me, kissing me on the cheek. "Have fun today," she said, then dropped the sheet to the floor and ambled towards the bathroom. A second later the shower came on. I stood there for a moment to collect myself before heading out. My mind, and my heart, were racing.

Chapter 16

"WHAT CAN I DO FOR YOU THIS MORNING, SIR?" the valet asked.

"Good morning. My name is Michael Bennett. Larry Vincent had a car left for me."

"Yea, a very sexy car. The person who dropped it off insisted it stayed covered," he said handing me the keys and gesturing behind me.

The car sat on the edge of the driveway. I walked over and with the help of the valet, removed the cover.

"Well, hello, Bianca," I said as I looked the car over.

She was a pearl white 1965 Chevy Malibu SS coupe with a white leather interior and polished billet aluminum wheels.

"Larry really hooked me up," I said.

"You'll definitely make a statement around here with that," the valet said.

"I think this car would make a statement anywhere," I replied.

The valet opened the door and I climbed in, adjusting the bench seat. He stood and watched, waiting for me to start the engine. Then with the turn of the key, she came to life with a throaty growl you could feel in your chest. I nodded to myself in approval and revved the engine a little, smiling at the valet.

"In lieu of a tip, you can give me a ride later," he said.

"You got it," I replied as I dropped her into first gear and pulled away, slowly cruising down the elegant driveway towards the gate, an arm resting on the door. I smiled and put my sunglasses on as I pulled passed the guardhouse.

For a nicer drive I took Mandal Rd, traveling just over the speed limit at first. In the turns I pushed her harder. The sway bars kept her steady and the tires gripped the road like an Indy car. With each turn I became more comfortable at the wheel and pushed the speed higher to feel the pull of the centrifugal force. I came to a straightaway and put the peddle down, sailing past a safari taxi and topping out at 85 just before a turn where I slowed again.

I had made up some time on the drive so it was right at ten when I got to Larry's office near Magen's Bay. When I reached the third-floor suite, the desk outside his door was vacant aside from a coffee cup from the University of the Virgin Islands. The office door was open. I knocked, peering inside around the door.

Overlooking the beach, the sliding doors along the back were opened and the room was filled with salt air and a faint hint of coconut oil, carried in on the breeze. Larry and Winters were sitting at a large conference table with scrolled maps, blueprints, and various other papers scattered about. Larry looked up.

"Perfect timing. Come in," Larry said then began clearing some papers from the table and placing them into a folder.

"So, Mike. I hear you took us up on the offer," Winters said, shaking my hand.

"Yea, and I appreciate it. Like I told Larry, I kind of miss putting the puzzle together. Plus, it's not like I'm starting my own business back up. It's one job."

"Well, my boy, what if could be more?" he asked.

"What do you mean?" I said. "I'm not really looking to relocate to the islands."

"Well, you wouldn't have to. Have a seat, Mike," Larry said.

"A project of ours in Key West is moving ahead and we'll need someone there to manage it. There will be some overlap with the end of this project, plus I have some other things in the works here on St. Thomas. So, I can't do both. That's where, hopefully, you'd come in."

"In what capacity?"

"As director of operations," Winters said.

"What's the project?" I asked.

"Another Marina project. Twice the scope of this one though. We also want to create an entire resort-style neighborhood based around this new yacht club," Larry said.

"Where?" I asked.

"Stock Island. There's a large area coming up for sale that is perfect. We're just waiting on a few details to get worked out. Your pay would all but double, and there'll be some stock options involved."

"Wow. That is a huge offer."

"You're right," Winters said. "And it's a huge responsibility. Obviously, it's contingent on your performance here. Larry's worked with you before, but I haven't. And since I'm the one that has to make the recommendation to our CEO, you can look at this project as a tryout for Key West."

"It all works out perfectly, Mike," Larry said. "I had no idea you lived in Key West until I called you about this job. At the time that project was on ice, but if this new development pans out, we'll need to start filling positions soon."

"Is my getting this job contingent on taking that one?" I asked.

"Not at all," Larry said, sliding a stack of papers to me. "This is your employment contract. Your title here will be our operations director, and your salary is as we discussed. It's all pretty boiler plate type stuff. The final page is very important. It's a pretty binding and detailed non-disclosure agreement. Due to the various companies and investors, it's required for everyone. As for Key West, sleep on it. Nothing is certain yet. We just wanted to put it on your radar."

"OK, I'll think about it," I said scanning the documents.

Winters pulled the papers from me, flipped a few pages then slid it back. "While you do, consider this as well. These pages outline your compensation package for this job. Your salary is on the top as Larry told you. But, you're eligible for a fifteen percent bonus annually, a twenty-percent bonus once the job is done, and a vesting schedule we've applied retroactively to start on January first of this year. You get a ten percent signing bonus, but that'll be applied to your vesting schedule. That all equals a lot of money for this job. Imagine doubling it in Key West."

I sat back and looked at them both for a long moment. "This is a helluva hard sell, gents. Almost seems too good to be true. So, I have to ask. Why me?"

"Because of that right there," Winters said, hitting the table with his hand. "I told you that I can pick a winner, and I see that in you. Aside from the glowing endorsement of Larry and what I found, Larry told me about last night. How quickly you came up with alternatives and how you handled the investors when they started getting riled up. And I could see the wheels turning just now when I was laying this all out to you, just as they are now. You're sharp. You're a natural, my boy. So honestly, it's selfish for me. I can see where you'd make my life easier."

"I agree with him," Larry said. "But for me, it's not all selfish business matters. We have a history, one that to me is a bit unsettled."

"What do you mean?" I asked.

"I can't help but feel partly responsible for what happened in Miami. I pushed her pretty hard to make that project work then had to distance myself from you when it all came crashing down."

"So, this job is to what? Make you feel better for guilt you have from that?"

He laughed slightly and shook his head. "No, my friend."

"Larry, you didn't make her do what she did. That was her choice. And, I understand why you took a step back. Plus, man – you were still there when most others abandoned me completely."

"Thank you, Mike," Larry said.

"OK, enough of the sappy personal stuff, boys. This is business and we have a lot of it to get to. I'll finish getting together the reports and documents you need, Mike. I just need ten minutes. Finish signing those papers so we can get moving," Winters said.

I read through the papers and signed everything. My new salary secured and position solidified, I closed the folder and laid the pen down. The act was impactful. I felt like I was finally closing a chapter of my life and starting a new one. I looked through the open doors towards the horizon. A sense of excitement, nervousness and anticipation washed over me.

***

The sound of the large accordion folder hitting the table snapped me out of my daze. "OK, Mike," Winters said. "This is everything that Apaté did including the submissions to the Corps, correspondences, reports – everything."

"Apaté? Is that Elizabeth Bathory's firm?" I asked, as I thumbed through the folder and pulled out a site survey.

"You know of them?" Winters asked.

"Yea. They're a shady group of *biostitutes* who take shortcuts and payoffs to push projects through."

He quizzically raised an eyebrow. "*Biostitutes?*"

"A sham scientist who'll sign off on anything for the right price," I said.

"Hmm. Yea, well they were Larry's idea," Winters said. "And all they did was cost us money in fees and the fines they got from whatever BS they tried to pull off. I finally fired them."

"Well, I'm happy to be your second choice," I laughed.

"Mike. You were more like my hail Mary," Larry said. "I really didn't think you'd be interested."

"Yeah. Larry was about to follow them right out the door," Winters said. "But he made the hard play for you."

He turned to Larry. "Last resort or not. If you feel you owe him for Miami, you've repaid that debt in spades."

I spread from the pages from the survey out in front of me. "So, we know they found sensitive species in the work area." I said.

"Some. But you and I know, there are always impacts on the environment."

"True, but if these reports are right – like I said at dinner the other night – just looking at the maps and your plans… Gents, we really may need to make some big changes to the plan. But I'll need to dive the site and see what's there for myself," I said.

"Well, the fire marshal assures me the site can reopen tomorrow or the next day, so you'll be able to start then," Winters said.

His phone rang. "Hello," he said answering it. He glanced to me and nodded then walked onto the back deck.

"Well Larry," I began, "The first steps here would be for me to look over all of this work then dive the site to verify the reports and get updated pictures and assessments of flora and fauna in the area. Then we can reconvene and formulate a plan forward.

"Larry," Winters called from the balcony, "come out here a second."

He sighed. "Excuse me a second, Mike."

Larry joined him on the balcony and I started to look over the report. A few minutes later they came back into the room.

"Mike," Winters began, "I need you to do me a favor. I need you to go to St. John and pick up Sarah. We have plans tonight but turns out I'm tied up with other business. Larry will call and have the boat ready for you."

"Can't she take the ferry?" I asked.

He starred at me intently. "Yes, she could. But I'd like you to get her on my boat."

I just smiled and nodded. "Sure, no problem, Mr. Winters."

Larry motioned to the door as he walked. I met him in the hallway. He spoke as we walked to the elevator.

"Thanks, Mike. I know this isn't what you thought you'd be doing today. But we got the important stuff out of the way anyway. I'll text you Sarah's number in a few minutes. Just call her and coordinate with her if you would."

"OK, Larry. No worries," I said. Then motioning to the empty desk. "Is that desk mine," I jested.

"No, we'll get you a proper office soon. Your position wasn't planned for, so nothing's ready right now."

"All good, Larry. Just teasing."

"Good man. I'll be in touch soon. He said as the elevator doors closed.

***

I received the text with Sarah's number before I left the building and called her as I walked to the car.

"Hello," she answered.

"Sarah, this is Mike Bennett. Seems Mr. Winters is tied up today and he asked me to come and pick you up."

She laughed. "I'm sure he is."

"Well, when is a good time for you? I'm free now."

"Any time after three will be good. But I've had a long day and could use a drink. Park the boat at the ferry dock and meet me at Woody's. The governor's St. John office is over near Quiet Mon, so I'm close. I'll call the dock master and tell him it's official business."

"OK well I'm at Larry's office and it's after twelve now, so I'll just head that way."

"Great. See you soon." She hung up the phone.

***

I pulled onto the road and started heading towards Red Hook. How quickly everything was happening, yet how relaxed I felt having some real income for the first time in what seemed like forever, was all running through my head. Edging back into corporate life was an unforeseen turn, but I promised myself, as I had promised Larry, that I would see this through to the end, no matter what. I thought about Kim and how great everything was going with her. Maybe, I thought, this could be the second wind I needed.

I turned east onto Mandal Road towards Sapphire Beach and Red Hook as a text came through from Larry.

Silver Linings is ready and waiting.

Sorry you're playing errand boy.

Last time.

Thanks again.

A second text from Larry came through a few moments later.

Damn glad to have you on board, Mike.

The Doobie Brothers "Listen to the Music" came on the radio. I pushed on the gas a little and felt the wind through my hair. I took a deep breath of the island air and thought of all the parts of this that caused me stress. I slowly let my breath out and imagined all of that going with it, lost in the breeze and salt air, dissipating into nothing and left behind me as I sped forward.

I couldn't help but smile.

Chapter 17

A SQUALL HAD COME THROUGH CRUZ BAY and the water evaporating from the roads made the air thick and humid. Inside Woody's a crowd of tourists were loudly celebrating, so I opted for the outside heat with a cold beer over the A/C and noise.

The ferry had docked, and people flooded the streets. Tourists looking for a bar and hailing cabs blended with locals heading to and from work or home. Their sounds melded with the notes from someone lazily playing piano at the nearby church and were carried by the wind down the streets. The people blended into a homogenous stream of bodies and sounds as they moved.

I was watching the spectacle go by when I noticed her walking towards me. She was striking in her contrast to those around her, both in her appearance and the way she moved. The droves of people faded to a muted background. Only she stood out.

Her blond hair was pulled tight into a ponytail and she wore a mid-length skirt, heels, and a light blue blouse. Professional attire, but on her, it bordered on provocative. She walked with confidence, a self-assured expression, and a steady gate. The people seemed to move around her.

"Good to see you again, Michael," she said as she dropped her Versace purse on the table. Sitting down she gazed into the street and let out a heavy sigh as she released several buttons from the top of her blouse down to the gold clasp in the middle of her black bra. She pulled the tie from her ponytail and shook it loose. Her golden hair fell around her shoulders. And with that, her thin air of the office professional vanished.

I could feel myself staring at her but couldn't find any words, even to simply reply to her. She glanced at me from the corner of her eye, a small grin formed on her lips.

"These meeting days are the worst," she said, still looking out to the street, brushing her hair. "They last all day, and I have to put on this veneer."

She turned in and leaned on the table, resting on her forearms and ran one hand through her hair. "Thanks for coming to get me," she said with an alluring smile.

"No problem at all," I replied, sliding her a beer.

My gaze drifted and her eyes were on mine as I looked up, catching my glance. She smirked and leaned back in her chair. I felt my face turn red.

"So, that's not your typical work attire?" I asked, sitting straight and taking a long pull from my beer, resting an elbow on the table to appear causal.

She continued to gaze at me. Her grin drifted to a contented smile. "No. I usually dress more comfortably. One of the perks of working in this office instead of on St. Thomas. But The Governor needed me to dress more formally today."

She received a text message and looked down at her phone. "So, has Cindy been sent back home?" she asked, not lifting her eyes.

"Who's Cindy?" I asked.

She turned to me and raised an eyebrow. "Really, you don't know?"

"No."

She leaned forward with an impassive expression. "Charlie's wife," she said flatly, her face unchanging, letting the words hang in the air.

"His wife?" I asked.

She watched my face then sat back, a roguish grin on her face. She sipped from her beer then started to dig through her purse, pulling out a pack of cigarettes and a lighter.

"So, you're his mistress?" I asked.

She crossed her legs then lit the cigarette and took a long drag. "Hardly," she replied as she blew smoke into the air and watched it dissipate above her head.

"Then what would you call it?"

"I'm a woman in waiting," she said as she turned back to me.

"And what does that mean? Waiting for what?"

"The man I love. Cindy is just a minor obstacle we have to navigate. – For now, anyway."

"And you're OK with that?"

"For now, I have to be. I mean, she was there first. Sometimes it takes sacrifices to get what you want." She looked into my eyes with a lingering smile then turned her gaze to the street, taking another long drag from her cigarette.

A man walked by and his eyes fell to me then quickly back to her. "Have a good night, Ms. Dobson," he said as he moved quickly down the street.

"You too, Gary," she replied. "Tell your lovely wife I said hello."

"Was that the governor?" I asked after he passed.

She just nodded. Her eyes fixed on mine, leering.

I shook my head. "How do you keep all of this separate?" I asked.

"Michael. Come now. Don't let that imagination of yours run away with you. I simply work for him. If he thinks there's a chance of something else and wants to entertain that fantasy, well then that's on him."

"And you don't benefit from that fantasy?"

"Don't be naïve," she jibed.

I leaned across the table. "I am far from naïve," I said firmly.

She laughed. "Don't get uppity, Michael," she said, leaning in as well. "Don't you understand? Life is just a big game and if there's one thing I know for sure, there are no innocents in this life. There are just winners, and losers. And I intend to be the former.

She sat up and grinned at me. "My, my, you're a bold one, Michael Bennet."

"How's that?" I asked.

"Making allegations and questioning me on my personal life when we only just met. Especially knowing who I am to your boss."

"Hey, you're the one that put all of it out there. I was just responding."

"Yeah, but not like most would."

"How's that?"

"It was bold. But boldness shows strength. And you'll need it.

"Well, we should get going?" I said, standing up. "Mr. Winters will be expecting you."

"Have a seat. There's no rush," she said, leaning forward and smiling up at me. "Besides, I'm enjoying our time."

"Well anyway, I'd like to get moving. I have things to do." I said, then stood and walked to the bar.

From behind me I heard her laugh. "Yeah, you'll do just fine here, Mike."

I paid the tab, glanced to her as I walked by, and hailed a cab. "As you wish," she said.

CHAPTER 18

THE FIDDLER, AS HE IS KNOWN, AND HIS BAND WERE SETTING UP for the night's gig at Latitude 18 on St. Thomas. I got a table near the water and waited for Kim to arrive. Slowly sipping on my rum & Coke I watched a small storm roll in and blanket the bay in a light rain. Across Vessup I could just make out *Silver Linings* in her slip.

I was nearing the bottom of my drink as the ambient glow of the sun was fading, the days light turning a blueish grey through the sheets of rain which fell harder as night neared. *Silver Linings* finally lost from sight in the fading dusk and haze of the storm.

"Bring you another one?" the waitress asked.

"Make it two," Kim said as she sat down. "And an order of conch fritters, and a towel if you don't mind."

Kim was soaked from the rain but seemed in high spirits. Her smile beamed.

One of the other servers brought her a towel. "So, how was your day?" she asked as she started to dry her hair.

"It started off great. I met with Larry and Winters and signed my employment contract. Turns out I get some stock interest in the company as well. Plus, they pitched another job to me. This time in Key West."

"That's great. Doing what?

"Essentially the same thing Larry does here."

"Well, I hope that comes with a similar paycheck to his?" she said with a grin.

"Actually, they said it would essentially double what I'm making now."

She smiled and reached for my hand, squeezing it. "It's so great how everything is working out. So unexpected, but really amazing."

"Mostly… yeah. Well, so far anyway."

She gave me a sideways look and a sarcastic grin. "Mostly? You said the day started off great. So, what happened?"

I took a long pull from my drink and leaned across the table. "Get this. Right after I signed my contract Winters sends me off to pick up Sarah, who very cavalierly tells me how Winters is married but they are in love and how his wife is just an obstacle they both hope to get past. Plus, she seems to be leading the governor on for whatever nefarious reason she has there."

"Wow. What a piece of shit," Kim said. "I'd seen him and Sarah before. Never his wife though. He must keep her tucked away out of sight."

I sighed and leaned back, staring at the ceiling fan overhead then closed my eyes. She touched my hand softly.

"You OK, hun?" she asked.

I looked down at the table then out over the water, focused on the faint green glow of a flashing channel marker through the dense curtains of rain.

I looked back to her. "I have to be honest with you," I said. "This day has really thrown me. On one hand I am excited for this new opportunity. Hell, I was in high spirits when I left the meeting, despite the errand I was sent on. But I can't respect somebody like that. How am I supposed to work for him?"

I leaned back across the table. "And for the life of me, I can't imagine why in the hell Sarah would just spill all of that to me. She's obviously a devious person. I just can't help but wonder what the angle was."

Kim moved to my side of the table, I turned to face her and she put her hand on my shoulder. "Well, I don't know much about her, but I've heard she loves to play with people's minds and assert herself quickly. She was probably just seeing how you'd react."

"That's a big secret to let out of the bag," I said.

"Well, yeah. But as we've seen, subtly isn't their thing. And Winters seems arrogant enough to assume nobody would dare cross him. My dad had a friend like that. But he got his. I'm sure Winters will too."

"It wasn't Winters who told me. She did."

"I doubt Sarah would do anything to mess up what she has there. If she said all of that, she knew it was OK to do so."

"Not that that helps any," I said.

"Fair enough. But luckily, he isn't here too often and when he is, it isn't for long. So, it's really just you and Larry."

"Sure, but if Larry knows all of this and still works for him, what does that say about him, and about me for that matter?"

"It's their personal lives, Mike. There are plenty of successful businesspeople who are not good people in their personal lives. Seems to almost be a prerequisite," she said with a gentle smile.

I sighed. "Yeah, I know. I've been around people like this a lot in business. Just never had one as a boss."

"Well, if it makes you feel any better, between us, Larry can't stand him. I think he just placates him so he can move into his position one day."

"Yeah, I got the feeling Larry didn't like him. Maybe he has something up his sleeve. I guess I can find some solace in that. For now."

The waitress came back, and we ordered some food for dinner. The band took the stage and The Fiddler went into a long intro solo that seemed to draw the attention of the entire place. When he knew he had everyone's ear the band kicked off into an up-tempo version of *Orange Blossom Special*. The dance floor immediately filled with people. Kim grabbed my hand and we joined the crowd.

She laughed and danced and I did my best to keep up with her as we spun across the dance floor. The third song ended and I dipped her. She held on with one hand around my neck, the other held above her head, she breathed heavily from dancing. I lingered a moment in her eyes, then kissed her and pulled her back to her feet, holding her close.

She looked into my eyes and let out a sigh. Smiling she simply shook her head yes, kissed my cheek, and headed towards the table and our waiting food. The music and the energy helped to wash away the latter part of my day and I felt my positive mood start to return.

***

After dinner we went back to the resort. The storm had passed and it was far too beautiful a night to go inside, so we decided to make a couple drinks and lay in the hammock for a while. The moon was directly overhead, obstructed only by the palm fronds swaying peacefully in the warm island breeze and the occasional low flying cloud quickly passing by. Kim's head was on my shoulder and the wind blew her hair, gently brushing my face and sending goosebumps running down my neck. I put my arm around her and pulled her close.

The hammock rocked gently with the swinging of my leg and the salt air enveloped us with each gentle breeze. Kim twitched as she drifted to sleep. Looking into the night sky, my mind started to drift and I thought of how my life had changed since leaving Miami. Once it was full of excitement, travel, and fulfillment. But since, it had become just a series of moments with no real continuous theme. There was little bad about it, but there was also little spark to it anymore. I was adrift, just existing in time, but not really living.

Moments like the one that night in the hammock added enough light to fill the void. But they were sparse, so like a candle I had to carry them with me through the mundane until the next flicker of light appeared.

I knew I had a rare and unexpected opportunity in front of me to regain the flame that once fueled my life. So, I decided then to focus only on the future that was unfolding and the good things, letting go of the negatives and not letting others stifle that. Winters and Sarah were simply unpleasant evils that I could work around. Plus, I trusted Larry. If he could work with them, so could I.

Kim woke briefly and kissed my cheek, bringing me back to the moment and the woman lying in my arms. I let everything else fall away and gently dropped my glass into the sand below us, kissed the top of her head, and soon fell asleep.

Chapter 19

I WOKE IN BED WITH THE DAY BEFORE RUNNING THROUGH MY HEAD. I knew I wouldn't be able to go back to sleep, so I made some coffee and moved to the patio. The pre-dawn darkness was still, warm, and humid.

As the dawn was breaking through the night the eastern sky began to turn orange and blue at the horizon, fading ever darker and back to night to the west. I sipped my coffee and watched as the sun rose gradually higher into the sky and the last stars faded from sight.

Finally, the new day fully arrived and sunlight began to fill the room. Inside I could see Kim through the window, wrapped tightly in the blankets, fast asleep.

Around 8am, my phone rang. It was Larry. In the background I could hear him rustling with papers and the hurried opening and closing of drawers.

"Good morning, Larry," I said.

"Mike. Good, you're awake. We have a busy day today. I just got word that Audrey Stein is coming and wants to do an aerial survey. She's the CEO of the parent company of *Bowling Green* and has controlling interest in this project so we have to do it. I need you to be to the airport by ten. I'll meet you there with Audrey."

"OK, Larry. Sure. But, we need to talk first."

"Make it quick. I'm just getting ready myself."

"Why didn't you tell me about Cindy?" I asked.

The noise stopped and the phone fell silent.

"Shit… Mike… Honestly, it never occurred to me. I'm sorry. I'm just – I'm so used to it. It's, it's no secret around here. Though Winters thinks it is. Honestly, I don't think it's really a secret to Cindy anymore either. I'm guessing Sarah said something."

"Oh, she did more than that. She seemed to flaunt it like some kind of vulgar display of power with him and the governor eating from her hand. But Larry, me being sent to fetch his mistress while he sees his wife off… That makes me complicit in it. I won't do that again."

He let out a heavy sigh and was quiet for a long moment.

"I know man, I'm sorry. I should have sent Miguel," he said.

There was another long silence.

"What did you mean about the governor?" he asked.

"She wanted me to meet her at Woody's for a drink. He walked by and acted really strange when he saw us. She denies anything is going on between them, but after seeing how he acted and knowing what I do of her – I don't know, man. I don't know if I buy that."

"Jesus let's hope not. Despite his infidelities, Winters is viciously possessive over her. He'd never stand for that."

"Yeah, as if they aren't enough of a glaring conflict of interest already." I paused and took a deep breath.

"Man, you and I have dealt with some morally questionable people in the past. I know it's kind of just part of the business sometimes. But I'll be honest with you, working for, rather than with him… that's harder to swallow."

"I know, Mike. Me too. But, he's the boss and it's his personal life. There's nothing I can do about that."

"Sure, there is. You don't have to work for him."

"It's not that easy, Mike. I wish it were. But look, man, he's leaving soon and likely won't be back for a while, and when he's gone, Sarah isn't around. So, stick with me and let's get this thing done. I'll insulate you as much as I can from them."

I stared into the morning sky and pulled in a deep breath. Holding it, I closed my eyes and listened to the rustling of the palms in the breeze.

"Come on, man," Larry said.

I slowly released my breath but paused before replying. "OK, Larry," I said in a sigh. "You were there for me and you gave me this opportunity. I won't turn my back on that."

"I owe you one, or well, another one," he said.

"Alright, well… I'll see you at the airport."

"OK. Take the same gate you did before. They know the car and I'll let them know to expect you."

***

I didn't want to wake Kim so I left her some water by her bed with a note.

Good morning, Bella.

You looked so comfortable I didn't want to wake you.

I Have to do some work with Larry.

I'll call you later. Have a great day. XOXO

I kissed her cheek lightly and she grinned in her sleep then rolled over, pulling the covers over her head.

***

The valet just pulled up in the Malibu when Winters and a woman close to his age came through the doors. He paused a moment when he saw me and I hoped he wouldn't come over, but he motioned to the valet and walked towards me with the woman reluctantly in tow.

"Damnit," I said to myself.

"Michael, this is my wife Cindy," he said. "My dear, this is Mike Bennett, he's works for us."

I clenched my teeth hard and smiled. "Cindy, very nice to meet you. So, you're the woman behind the man."

"We all have our roles to play," she said and returned a faint smile, offering me her hand, which at first felt frail. She lingered a moment in my eyes then squeezed my hand firmly. It's nice to meet you as well, Mr. Bennett."

"I have a busy week so Cindy has to head home," he said. "But she'll be back. Perhaps you and Kim can join us for dinner one night when she returns."

"Well, safe travels home," I said to Cindy. "And I guess I'll see you at the survey," I said to him, then turned and headed off as their town car was pulling up.

I sat and stared into the dash and let the engine idle. In my silence I knew was guilty, but if I said anything, a man like him would make it his mission to destroy my life.

I started to question my promise to Larry.

As their car drove by the driver honked. Winters nodded to me. I offered Cindy a wave and a tepid grin, but she seemed to stare through me, into the distance, over the cliffs, and out to the horizon.

Chapter 20

AS I APPROACHED, THE ROTOR OF THE HELICOPTER WAS ALREADY CHOPPING THE AIR in a steadily increasing cadence as the blades gained speed. Larry was standing next to a black S.U.V. parked nearby and talking to a tall-slender woman with long blond hair pulled into a ponytail through her white Nautica hat. She was dressed simply in trail shoes and a blue button up shirt tucked neatly into khaki shorts.

I couldn't make out what they were saying over the noise from the engines winding up, but she stood directly in front of him and seemed to be speaking with purpose. Larry stood obediently. As I approached, he motioned, and she turned to greet me.

"Mrs. Stein, this is Michael Bennett," Larry said over the noise from the engines.

She smiled and gripped my hand firmly. "Very nice to meet you, Mr. Bennett. Welcome aboard."

"Nice to meet you as well, Mrs. Stein, and thank you," I said.

"Please, just call me Audrey. No need for formalities."

Larry nodded to the helicopter. "Come on, let's get this done," he said.

Keeping low, we headed towards the chopper's open side door. Winters was already sitting next to the pilot, so we all climbed into the back. Larry sat in the middle and picked up two headsets, handing them to us. "Good morning," the pilot said once we all had our headsets on. "I'll have you over the site in just about ten minutes."

A few moments later the chopper lifted off.

"So, Larry. What are we doing?" I asked as the pilot banked and headed east.

"We're going to do a quick aerial survey of the work site then we'll do a walkthrough. We need to get some up-to-date photos of the area for planning and investor presentations. The chopper is outfitted with a highspeed camera, so we get a lot of shots just flying overhead. As we get going, this will happen about once a month so we can have a kind of time lapse presentation. It'll be one of your responsibilities."

"Any updates on the fire investigation?" Audrey asked.

"It's all been cleared. Just an electrical fire," Winters said. "But just to be sure, thanks to the Governor, I have two men on special detail from the police department to beef up security. They're V.I. detectives and have clearance to work in both the U.S. and British islands., so they'll be extremely helpful. They'll meet us there."

We flew straight over Charlotte Amalie, over the sound, and towards Cruz Bay. The sky was a deep blue and the waters below us seemed calm as the ferries cruised back and forth between the islands, small power craft jetting around them, and sailboats lazily making way to destinations unknown.

We flew over Cruz Bay then followed the ridge, flying just over Centerline Road before dropping down towards Coral Harbor. The pilot followed the valley, flying low over Kings Hill Road. As we came out over the waters, he broke into a high bank over Fortsberg before wrapping south over Coral Bay.

I looked out over the island as we slowly drifted above collecting our images. The winds sent the crystal blue Caribbean waters crashing onto the rocky eastern shore. In the bays, lines of boats on their moorings faced into the wind. The island roads were all but hidden beneath a canopy of trees that revealed only secretly the houses and buildings of her inhabitants further up the hills from the bay. It was awe inspiring and beautiful.

It was paradise.

In my headset I heard Audrey's voice. "I've never seen the island from this vantage point. It really is beautiful."

"I couldn't agree more," I said.

"Well, let's get this project done, but make sure it stays that way," she said.

"You're the boss."

"Yes, I am. This one learns quick, Larry. Maybe you two could take a lesson from him," she said, reaching over and patting Larry's knee.

Larry glared at me. "I think we have all the photos we need. Let's get on the ground. With your permission of course, Mrs. Stein."

"Don't be a smart-ass, Larry. But yes, let's get going."

***

The chopper touched down and with the pilot's go-ahead, we exited and moved away from the propwash and noise as a black SUV pulled up.

"Ah, here is our new security detail now," Winters said.

The SUV parked and the men inside exited. Both were tall, muscular, and imposing. One was a local East Indian and wore golden earrings and a thick gold chain around his neck. His arm was bandaged. The other I recognized immediately from the marina on St. Croix. It was Mr. Joshua. They both stopped side by side and crossed their arms as Winters introduced them.

"This is Randy and Joshua. Our security detail."

"Good to see you again," Joshua said to me with a haughty smile.

"You're a cop?" I said. "You've got to be kidding me."

"Run your mouth some more and you'll find out," he fired back, stepping forward.

Audrey stepped in front of Joshua. "OK, enough. Put 'em away, boys. Let's not get the yardsticks out just yet," she said, patting him on the chest with a disarming smile. "We're here to work, and we will work together. Or, you can go elsewhere. Am I clear?"

Joshua shot me a final hard look them smiled at her. "Yes, ma'am."

She looked to me. "Michael."

"No problem here," I said, returning his stare.

"Good. Well, let's take a ride around the—"

"Mr. Winters! Mr. Winters!" a man yelled in a heavy Boston accent from a golfcart as he quickly approached, almost falling as he hopped from the moving cart while trying to set the brake.

"What is it, Tommy?" Winters asked the man.

"These Muthah fuhckahs. They put sand in the fuhckin' tanks," he said.

"Calm down, Tommy. Who did? What tanks?" Winters asked.

"I dunno fuhckin' know, these sons' a bitches! They put sand in the fuhckin gas tanks of the fuhckin machinery. They're all deahd where they sit."

"OK, first," Larry said, "there's a lady here, Tommy. So, let's chill out on the language. Second, which machinery?"

"Gahd, I'm sahrry miss," he said to Audrey. "But I been a fawman fuh fawty yeahs an' nevah had anything like this. A trailah fiyah, now sand in the tanks'a the machinery," he said pointing to the several large bulldozers and frontend loaders at the corner of the property.

"An electrical fire huh?" Audrey said sternly. "I don't believe in coincidences. Who's doing this?" she asked sternly, looking to Winters then Larry.

Larry took a deep breath. "My money's on this damned conservation group. They've opposed us since day one and have been nothing but a pain in the ass since. Writing to the Corps and submitting appeals to hold us up, holding protests, whatever they can do."

"I doubt that, Larry. Sabotage and vandalism seem pretty extreme," I said.

Larry spun around and quickly walked towards me. "Well, who the hell else do you think it could be, Michael?"

I put a hand against his chest. "Take a step back, Larry. Relax. I'm on your team here."

"You bastards are going to destroy this place!" a voice shouted. We all turned to see who it was. Out in the water a man was on a small dinghy circling and shouting unintelligibly over the noise. The gunwales were draped in white cloth, disguising the boat. His clothes and cowboy hat were solid black, his face obscured in white paint. He stopped thirty yards out and stood in his boat with a bullhorn.

"You masters of exploitation, you grim reapers of the land and culture, you slayers of magic and time. You know the real value of nothing!" The man shouted then turned hard, spinning the little boat in a tight circle.

"Who in the hell is that?" Audrey said.

"One of them," Charles replied.

The man stopped and stood, bringing the bullhorn to his mouth and raising his fist into the air.

"Our land, our culture, and our people are all connected and will be destroyed by your myopic dream as you fill it with masturbatory vessels of the rich, leaving nothing but a caricature of what was and choking the life from this place until it's a whitewashed soulless, shell."

He pointed towards the machinery.

"But your great machines, like beasts in hibernation, waiting for their moment to devour the land. Do they lie silent? Just as silent as your demon consciences at night."

Randy and Joshua ran towards him, shouting at the man to identify himself and come to the shore. He just laughed and resumed steering the small boat in tight circles and shouting indistinctly over its motor then again stopped and shouted to the shore through the bullhorn.

"You may have the police and government in your pockets, but not the people!"

He slid a piece of PVC over the throttle handle of the motor to extend it then moved to the center of the boat. He held onto the bridle with one hand and steered with the other, moving as if on a chariot, taking a wide berth away from shore before circling back, passing just ten feet out, slowing and shouting as he passed.

"If your tyranny is supported by law, rebellion is our duty. We will go on to the end. We will never surrender!"

The man quickly moved off and made a few more tight circles then headed towards the far end of the bay, laughing loudly. We all stood in shock as Randy was on the phone trying to find an officer to assist. He walked back to us, shaking his head.

"There's nobody close enough to track him and who knows where he'll come to shore," Randy said.

"Get the damned chopper in the air," Winters demanded.

The pilot shook his head. "She's totally powered down. By the time we get airborne he'll be gone."

"Goddamnit!" Winters roared, stomping off.

Larry leered at me as he approached. "Still think it wasn't them?"

"Sorry, Larry, maybe I was wrong," I said.

"Maybe?" Winters barked then turned and marched towards me, stopping just inches from my face. "I thought you were sharp, Michael. A crazy man shouting at us, all but admitting to sabotaging our equipment and speaking of 'we' and 'our' rebellion. That was all but a declaration of war!"

He turned and walked away with his hands on his hips then stopped and looked towards the ground, seeming to speak to himself. "Well, if they want a war. It's not one they'll win," he said, then strode to the chopper and took his seat.

"Well… I've had enough excitement for one day," Audrey said, smiling at Larry and me. "Boys, Charles and I are leaving tonight. We have other projects to look in on. Let's get to the bottom of this unpleasantness, and fast."

"We will. Mike and I are on top of it," Larry said, patting me on the back.

"You better be," Winters snapped from the chopper. "Your futures depend on it."

Audrey sighed softly and smiled. "Always the hot head. Well, come on, let's get going," she said.

***

Two Town Cars were waiting when we arrived back on St. Thomas. The drivers were leaning against one car talking. Larry was waiting for the pilot to retrieve the image files from the camera so Audrey asked me to walk with her.

"Well, it was nice meeting you," I said to her as we walked towards her car. Winters walked ahead and stood at the door of his car, staring at Amos, his driver, until he walked over and opened it for him. Amos closed the door, shaking his head.

"Don't worry about him," Audrey said. He's passionate. But that's what makes him good. He'll cool off. You've dealt with people like him before, I'm sure."

"How do you know that?" I asked.

She stopped short of the car, touching my arm softly. "Where do you think he got all of his intel from," she said with a subtle grin. She handed me a business card. "If you need anything at all, don't hesitate to call me."

"Will do," I said, tucking the card away.

"I'm serious, Michael. I can see that what the man said over there shook you and I know from reading a couple interviews you did, where your thoughts probably are. This was eye opening for me too. This group is obviously very passionate about this. As they should be.

"I'll reach out to them and arrange a meeting to see if a middle ground can be met. If they agree, I'd love for you to be part of that. You have the background for it and can speak to all sides."

"Thank you, Audrey. And I'd love to be in on the meeting. I think I could really help there."

She motioned to her driver and he opened the door. "Good, well I'll be in touch soon then."

She climbed in and the car pulled away, sounding two short honks.

Larry approached Winters' car and tapped on the window. He opened the door. "Get in, we have to talk," he said.

I started to move towards the car and Larry leaned in briefly then stood and met me halfway. "You don't want to ride with us, Mike. I told you I'd keep you away from him as much as possible. Let me deal with him alone and I'll call you later or tomorrow. Just stay available. Besides, the Malibu's here."

"OK, Larry. Well, good luck. And thanks."

"Yeah, the joys of the job," he said, patting me on the shoulder.

I started to walk away, but Larry grabbed my arm. "Mike. Hey, I'm sorry for getting heated with you back there. But look, it's important you and I are a united front to both Winters and Audrey. But especially him, OK? Next time, if you have an issue, save it and we'll talk it out in private. As you see now, it's really just us here doing this."

"I understand," I said.

"Good, I'll be in touch."

Chapter 21

THE HOTEL ROOM WAS STILL AND QUIET and filled with the orange glow of the late afternoon sun. The AC was turned low, causing condensation to form on the windows and the aroma of shampoo and perfume hung faintly in the air. I called to Kim, but there was no reply. Looking around I noticed a note on the table in the living room.

Mike, I ran into some friends from STJ.

They are leaving for the season soon so I

decided to head back home for a couple

days to hang out with them.

I tried calling to let you know but

didn't get an answer.

I hope all is well.

Let me know when you get this.

Can't wait to see you,

Kim XOXO

"I don't remember her calling," I said to myself. I reached in my pocket but my phone wasn't there. I went out and searched the car since that was the last place I used it, but to no avail. It was gone.

Frustrated it was missing, and even more so that I missed Kim, I decided to decompress and have a drink while I tried to remember where I left it, so I went to the tiki bar near the pool and ordered a Ting Wray. The high proof Jamaican rum and grapefruit soda quickly relaxed me and I struck up a conversation with a couple on their honeymoon. After an hour or so and several more cocktails, I was feeling quite at ease and in better spirits.

I headed back to my room and took a shower then laid down on the sofa. I was lost in my thoughts as I ran the day's events through my head when a knock came at the door. Only being in my boxers, I grabbed the bathrobe, tying it as I opened the door.

"Hello, Michael," Sarah said. She was leaning casually against the wall in a low-cut black dress that fell just above her knees. Watching my eyes, she smiled.

"Mind if I come in?" she said as she walked by me.

"Sure. I guess – come on in," I said and closed the door.

"Aww, Mike. You're a little drunk," she said with a grin.

"I had a few drinks, but I'm fine."

Looking me over she smiled with the same expression I'd come to know from her. Seductive, confident, and dangerous.

"What are you doing here, Sarah? Is there something I can do for you?"

"Plenty, I'm sure," she said then turned and walked towards the bar. She poured a finger of rum and gestured to me with the glass.

"I'm good, thanks," I said.

She drank it down and sat the glass on the bar then slowly walked towards me, her eyes set on mine, a mischievous grin on her face.

"You don't like me do you, Mike?" she said.

"What ever would make you think that?"

"Let's just say you wouldn't be much of a poker player… Too bad – I can't say I feel the same way," she said, rubbing my shoulder as she circled behind me.

I turned my head towards her. "Really? And what would you want with me?"

She moved in front of me and took in a deep breath. "I can think of a couple things," she said, running her hand down the lapel of the robe, pulling it open.

"No thanks," I said, staring into her eyes.

She just smiled back at me then pulled me to her by the belt on my robe.

"Are you sure?" Her lips brushed my ear as she spoke, causing the hairs on my neck to stand up, paralyzing me in place. "I'm not so sure you are," she said as she untied my robe.

I moved away, taking a deep breath. She glanced down and smiled to herself, then walked after me. I put my hand up, unable to find any words. She grasped it gently and placed it on her breast.

"Just do what you so obviously want to do, Michael. Don't worry so much about everyone else and their feelings. There are no innocents in this life. So don't waste yours trying to be one."

I stepped away again. She scoffed at me and squinted her eyes. They were alluring and terrifying, filled with an intensity and raw passion she seemed able to conjure on demand. She moved closer. I tried to take a step back but my back was against the wall. I felt frozen in her stare and I could feel my heart start to race. I took a deep breath and swallowed hard, trying to maintain a sense of disregard.

She grinned and bit her bottom lip, then whispered in my ear. "I bet I can convince you," she said, letting her dress fall to the ground then pushing the robe from my shoulders. Pressing her breast against my chest she ran her hand up my thigh, grasping me gently.

I closed my eyes and held my breath.

She stood on her toes, her cheek pressed against mine and whispered. "See. Your words say one thing," she squeezed lightly and I let out a sigh as I released my breath.

"Ahh… but your body is telling me something else."

I placed my hand lightly on the small of her back and looked into her eyes with gritted teeth.

She stopped and grinned.

"I thought so," she said then stepped back and picked up her dress. "You're no innocent, Michael Bennett."

"Why, why did you….?"

"Just testing the waters," she said and gently kissed my cheek then turned and started towards the door, her dress in her hand.

I stood there, motionless, watching her every move. She stopped at the mirror to put her dress back on and admired herself for a moment, smiling with satisfaction, then opened the door and looked back to me.

"Don't forget to breathe, Michael," she said, then walked out and gently closed the door.

CHAPTER 22

THE BEDSIDE PHONE RANG OUT, STARTLING ME AWAKE. I rolled over and grasped at it, knocking the base from the nightstand and spilling my water onto the floor. I pulled on the cord to lift it as I lay back in bed, clearing my voice to answer.

"Hello," I garbled into the phone.

"Are you still in bed?" Larry asked.

"Yeah. Why, what time is it?"

"Late enough you should be up and working. Just because you lose your phone doesn't mean you get the day off. Especially after yesterday."

"How did you know I—"

"You left it in the helicopter," he said. "The pilot just dropped it off to me. Look, I need you to get moving and get to the office ASAP."

"Sure, Larry. I'll be there as quick as I can. Sorry about—"

"Look, it's fine, Mike. I just need you here. I'll see ya soon."

The line went dead.

***

I drove quickly towards Magen's Bay, trying to piece together the day before. Between the crazy man on the boat, sabotaged equipment, Winters blowing up, and Sarah trying to seduce me, it was dizzying. Larry's voice too sounded anxious. What had happened in the car with Winters, I wondered. He was pretty hot when they left.

I made good time and hurried to the office. Larry's door was opened when I arrived and I could hear him speaking to someone over speaker phone. I stood out of sight and listened.

"I told you, don't worry. It'll get it done," Larry said.

"You'd better. Don't forget, it's not just your ass on the line here," the other voice said, then hung up.

I stood there a moment so it didn't seem as if I was there and listening, then knocked on the door.

"Yeah, come in," Larry said.

"Bad time?" I asked.

"No, just dealing with more shit from Winters."

He tossed me my phone. "Kim tried calling you a few times."

There were two missed calls from Kim about twenty minutes apart. The last one was a five-minute call.

"I answered and spoke to Kim when she called again today," Larry said. "She's on St. John. I let her know you forgot your phone."

"Thanks," I said. "Did she say anything else?"

"No, that was it."

I looked at Larry for a moment, then put the phone in my pocket.

Larry stood and walked to the bar and poured some rum into a glass, slugging it back in one shot. He pulled a second glass from the bar and poured another few ounces into each one.

"Mike, I need a favor from you, but you aren't going to like it."

"What do you need?" I asked.

He walked over to me, handing me a glass and sitting on the corner of the desk. "I've got a lot of pressure on me from investors and from Audrey. Some are threatening to pull out because of the delays. If they do, this whole thing tanks."

He put his hand on my shoulder and looked directly into my eyes as he spoke. "Mike, I have everything riding on this one. If this fails, I'll lose more than you could imagine. But it's not just me. Others stand to lose a lot too. And, a lot of this depends on you getting us over this hurdle. So, in light of that, I convinced Winters to make some adjustments to your hire dates to better your position with the vesting schedule.

"He also agreed to give you a better signing and annual bonus and to apply those towards shares in the company. Now, once this project is done, we have a guarantee to buy the resort from a major cooperation after one year of profitable operation, provided certain requirements are met. That means a lot of money for everyone invested. Including you now."

I sighed. "Thank you. But – that was one hell of a sales pitch. This must be a big favor."

"Smart man," he said then took a sip from his glass and stood up, walking towards the doors along the back wall. "Well, as I said, our time is running very short in some ways so we really need to go full speed ahead on the environmental permitting stuff since that is what's holding us up."

"OK, easy enough," I said. "I'll get to work on it right away. Just need to get some gear and dive the site so I can start my reports."

"See Mike, that's where the problem lies. We're up against some pretty strict deadlines, so we don't have time for all of that. I really need you to review everything Apaté did, make what changes you feel necessary and get it turned in."

I stood and moved to the conference table, sitting my glass down. "Larry, man – I'm sorry, but I can't do that. I have to assess the site myself. Apaté is a shady group. Plus, signing off on others' work is what sank me in Miami. I really have to start from square one."

Larry moved quickly to me. "Mike, we don't have time for by the book right now. No risk, no reward. Just – get us past this one hurdle and we'll start moving again, which will let us meet our deadlines and assuage the concerns of our investors. You can handle all of that detailed stuff later. I really just need you to do this for me so we can move forward."

"Larry, I…"

His expression turned stern and he grabbed my arm. "Mike, in Miami I was there for you when you needed me. When everyone else turned their back on you, I was there. I need you to be here for me now. Just please, get this done. Whatever you need to do."

I pulled away from Larry's grip, walked a few steps, then turned and looked at him. He followed me with his eyes. His jaw was clinched and brow furled. He didn't move, just stared. I looked away.

He turned and walked to the bar, filled his glass half full of rum and opened the French doors quickly, causing them to slam into the walls, the white curtains blew in with the warm air that quickly filled the cool room as he walked onto the balcony.

I sighed, picked up my glass and stepped out beside him. He was leaning against the rail, staring into his glass.

"I need you here, Mike," he said, looking up and staring out over the bay.

I let out a heavy sigh. "All right, Larry. Look. I'll go do a very cursory assessment of the site and take a look at everything from Apaté. I'll make adjustments to what they have and get the application in. While they're reviewing it, I can do a more in-depth assessment and file an amended report later if needed. It still makes me uneasy, but that's the best I can do to get us moving again."

He stood and took a long pull from his glass then turned to face me. With a half grin he said, "I guess it's all I can ask for, Mike."

He glanced out over the bay once more then turned back to me. "Well, it's only early afternoon – but I've already had one hell of a day. I have business off island tomorrow so that'll be a good day for you to go over. If you need to buy or rent any gear, use the card."

He held up his glass, I returned the gesture. The glasses clinked and Larry finished his in one pass. I drank half of mine. "Thank you, Mike," he said. "You're a good friend."

***

I drove out to the beach and walked along the shore for a while. I tried calling Kim on the way, but she didn't answer. I was running everything through my head. I thought about what Larry had done for me and what that could mean for my future. I also considered what he was asking me to do and the immense stress he must be under. The weight of it all pressed down on me.

I sat in the sand and looked over the water. The wind was picking up, making small ripples as the they moved across the bay. A hard gust blew in carrying the smell of rain. Far off on the horizon I could see showers sweeping lazily across the Caribbean, its flat, calm blue waters turned grey and menacing with building seas. From the beach they looked like rolling hills in the distance. Closer to shore, but beyond the bay where the water wasn't protected from the wind by the hills, there were whitecaps beginning to form.

CHAPTER 23

THE GLOW FROM THE COMING DAY WAS BARELY ILLUMINATING a small strip of the horizon as I brought *Silver Linings* off plane at the mouth of Coral Bay. If I was going to get it done, I needed to have plenty of time to dive the site and get as much data as I could in one day, so I decided to be ready to go at first light.

I set anchor, launched the dinghy, and grabbed the underwater camera then headed off, gently maneuvering the tiny boat through the mooring field, avoiding lines and always alert for unlit boats buzzing through the early dawn.

The jeep was right where I left her. It took some coaxing to get started, but it finally came to life with a billow of black smoke from the tail pipe, the backfire echoed through the early morning, sending resting birds into flight and startling a couple loading their little rowboat.

The drive to Fortsberg was less than a mile so I was there before the day had fully come. As I waited for the sun to get up a bit higher so I could see underwater, I took some general photos of the land area using the surveyor stakes for reference so I could tie them back to the map.

After a short time, the sun was high enough, so I made my way to the shore. I slid into the water and swam a u-shaped pattern across the proposed site of the piers, photographing corals and seagrasses below and shots above to reference for location. The entire area was a healthy and biologically rich ecosystem based around an expansive sea grass bed, with several isolated stands of threatened species of coral scattered throughout. Endangered sea turtles were lazily feeding, and many juvenile fish took shelter in the protective shadows of the grass as I neared.

***

After the dive, I sat on the shore and looked out over the bay. The sun was high and the heat of the day was coming on. My heart was heavy, and my mind stirred. I knew there was no way to avoid impacting this area. The shade from the docks and boats as well as sediment from props in the shallow water would cut the seagrass and corals off from the sunlight they depend on. The dredging that would be needed for the larger boats would forever kill the grass in those areas. Within a short time, the vast meadow would be reduced to sand and rubble, the fish and turtles without their essential habitat would move on or die, vanishing from the bay, leaving nothing but an underwater desert.

I watched as the couple I spooked earlier with the jeep's backfire rowed back towards the docks, a small dinghy pulled alongside them and slowed for a moment, both parties greeting the other jovially, then they laughed and waved as they each carried on. Out on the bay someone was being hoisted in a bosun's seat up the mast of an older looking schooner.

I stared into the water, hypnotized as I watched the light dance across it, reflecting off the ripples like thousands of tiny lights. I thought about the deeply imbedded and vibrant community there, some having been there for decades, if not generations. A family of people from all walks of life living simply, and peacefully in their place in the sun. In so many ways it's a place time forgot, hidden from the rat race and degrading progress that was swallowing the rest of the world.

But now, I was helping to usher it in.

A sadness fell over me and I laid back in the grass, watching the clouds. I didn't want to let Larry down, but I knew, if this could be done at all, it would cost far more than money. Echoing from the past, I could hear Dave's voice as I closed my eyes.

"All you have to do is the right thing, my brother. It's that easy."

Chapter 24

THE NOON AIR WAS STILL, THICK AND HOT. Aside from a few people eating lunch and the sounds of Bob Marley in the background, skinny Legs was quiet. My head pounded so I Pressed the cold beer bottle to my temple, closed my eyes and took a deep breath, focusing on the music.

"Mike Bennett?" a woman's voice said. I could feel her move next to me but she seemed miles away. I squeezed my eyes tight and took a deep breath, opening them and focusing on my reflection in the mirror over the back bar then turned to her without speaking.

"Are you, OK?" she asked, a look of concern on her face.

I took a long drink of my ice water and sat silent as the noise of bar slowly became clear and distinct again. I let out a sigh.

"Yeah, I'm OK. Thanks," I said. "Do I…?"

"It's Daniele. We met on St. Croix around a week ago."

"Right. You used to work for Larry."

"Yeah. And sorry for rushing off like that. I had a lot on my mind that day. I'm sure I seemed odd."

"Hardly noticed," I said.

"You're very kind. But hey, I'm glad I ran into you. I'd hate if that was our only interaction."

"Yea, well… another fortuitous meeting," I said then took a long pull from my beer.

So, are you working or taking a break from Larry," she said with a grin.

"Right now, just taking a break. I did a little work here this morning but am going to stay the night. I'm on a boat here in the bay."

"Great. I'm just up the road a bit. Staying at a friend's house for a night before heading out."

"Where to?" I asked.

"North. Maine maybe."

"Well, want to join me for a drink or some food? I was about to order lunch. Love to hear about your travel plans." I said.

"I hate to make this a pattern, but I have to run. I just ate and I need to secure a few loose ends. I saw you and just wanted to say hi again. But maybe I'll see you around later."

"Sure. I'll be around. Is there anything going on tonight?"

"Island Blues has a great band playing," she said.

"Perfect. Maybe I'll see ya there."

Daniele left and I called Kim and Kahuna and arranged for us all to meet later at Island Blues. Kahuna was on a charter and Kim was at the pool with some friends. They'd both be there around sunset, which was perfect. After my early rise and stressful day, I needed a nap.

Chapter 25

ISLAND BLUES WAS PACKED AND THE PARTY SPILLED OUT ONTO THE STREET. The music from the band mixed harshly with the sounds of several stereos blasting from the nearby store, and street bikes racing up and down the road. I bought a beer and was walking outside as Kim arrived with a friend. Kim said something to her and pointed to me as they approached.

"So, this is your mystery man," her friend said as she put her arm around my shoulder.

Kim smiled. "Mike, this is Michelle, Michelle, Mike."

"You were right, Kimmy. He is sexy," Michelle said then stepped in front of me. Her eyes smiled and glinted with wine, her lips lazily grinned. "You seem to have stolen our girl's heart there, Mike. You better treat her right, be good to her," she said, lightly poking my chest.

I looked to Kim. She was covering her now red face. I smiled at her. "You have my word."

"Good," Michelle said, then kissed my cheek. "Then I approve."

"There y'all are." Kahuna's voice boomed from the crowd.

"Well, who is this?" Michelle asked, walking up to Kahuna as he approached.

"They call me Big Kahuna," he said to her, kissing her hand.

She patted his chest. "I bet they do. Very nice to meet you," she said then walked over to Kim, leaning on her shoulder and feigning a whisper.

"My my, Kimmy. You have quite the pair of good-looking men here. Good thing I have one of my own tonight, or we'd have to flip a coin."

Kim just smiled and Michelle kissed her then slid off into the crowd, laughing.

"Well… that's Michelle," Kim said.

Kahuna seemed to strain to follow her with his eyes. "Too bad she couldn't' stay," he said.

"She's a great friend, but trust me, she's also a big ball of crazy."

He smiled. "I'd be counting on it," he said. "But hey, why don't you both find us a quieter spot by the water, and I'll get the first round.

"You actually going to come back out, man? You haven't stopped scanning the crowd since she left," I said, nudging his arm.

"I won't leave y'all hanging, man," Kahuna said.

"There're some chairs down there," Kim said, pointing to a tree. "They look far enough away we'll be able to hear ourselves think."

"Great. Secure them and I'll be there in a few."

***

"So, what did you do today?" Kim asked as we sat down.

"I came in early and swam the work site. Larry really needs me to get this moving so I'm trying to speed it along as much as I can."

"How'd it go?"

"The swim went fine. But after what I found… I don't know how this can get done."

"So, the marina can't be built?"

"Well, it probably could, sure. But not easily and not without really impacting the marine life. Even then, it'll be really tough to get it through the Corps. Larry and Winters are going to have to make a lot of concessions to the plan. And even then…"

I stared off as I considered my words.

"Even then, what?" Kim asked softly, putting her hand over mine.

I sighed. "There may be a path to get this finished and even if they agree to the modifications, the reality is that this will still really have a huge impact on the life here. Above and below the surface. I just don't know if I want to be a part of that."

"Tell ya what, brother," Kahuna said as he sat down and handed me a beer. "This is likely going to happen. Big money always seems to trump everything else. Me, I'd feel better knowing you were working on it instead of someone else who may not care as much as you."

I looked up at him and smiled.

"Your words brother. And, I have to say, I agree," Kahuna said.

"I appreciate that man. I'm not making any decisions yet. I just need to get my mind around it is all. Maybe I'll find a better way after it rolls around for a while. I've never been one to give up."

"That's right, Bubbah. Don't give up the fight. It's like having a man on the inside with you here," he said leaning over and tapping my beer with his."

"Yea, hun. Don't let it get you down. Sometimes the most important things are also the hardest," Kim said.

"I thought the whole thing was sunk after Larry was implicated in your buddy's death a while back," Kahuna said.

I sat up then leaned towards him. "What are you talking about? Larry was accused of killing Dave?" I asked.

"Shit man. I told you that the day we met, sitting on the deck of your boat."

"You said a man died and people felt he was involved. You didn't say he was actually implicated in anything," I said.

"Maybe I didn't. But, I thought you and Larry were tight. He never told you that?"

"OK, enough," Kim said. "That was all a bunch of bullshit and almost cost Larry his job."

"What the hell happened?" I asked.

"Look, Dave and Larry got into a heated argument at a meeting, and it got out of hand. Things got physical, but it was quickly broken up," Kim said.

"So how does that lead to him being arrested for Dave's murder? Knowing Dave as I do, I'm sure that wasn't the first person he's pushed that far." I said.

"Because the Coral Bay Alliance kept pushing the murder theory and as the face of the company for this project, Larry was their target. But it was all a lie," Kim said.

"How do you really know that, Kim?" Kahuna asked.

She stood up. "Because I was with Larry at the time of the accident! And he probably didn't tell Mike because, well why the hell would he?"

"OK, calm down. I didn't mean to upset you," Kahuna said. "I know Larry is a friend of yours. I'm just offering an outside perspective."

"I believe Kim," I said. "Like I said that night, Larry is a lot of things, but I can't imagine him resorting to murder over a project. We've butted heads a lot, but it was always just business."

"I hope so, man," Kahuna said, standing up and walking to Kim, offering her a hug. "Come on now, don't be mad at me. Just looking out for our boy here."

She hugged him back. "I know. That was just hard to see Larry go through all of that. It really got to him that people would think that about him."

"Hey y'all. Mind if I join you?" a voice said.

It was Daniele. She was holding four beers. She held them out as if an offering for the seat.

"Of course, grab a chair," Kim said.

"There's a chair right over here," Kahuna said, gesturing to the one next to him.

Daniele passed out the beers as she spoke. "Well, I wanted to say a proper thank you to Kim. As I told Mike earlier today, I had a lot on my mind when I saw you on St. Croix. I know I was acting odd."

"When did you see Mike?" Kim asked.

"I was having lunch at Skinny's and she stopped by. I told her we'd be around," I said.

"Well, I'm glad you did," Kim said. "I have to say, you were acting a little strange. I was hoping everything was OK. You seemed nervous."

"Everything's fine. Just an off day," Daniele said.

She took the seat next to Kahuna and told us of her plans to sail to Maine which thankfully led the discussion away from the project and Larry and into us all sharing stories of sailing the islands. Daniele had sailed the world and had some fascinating tales. Kahuna shared some of his flying stories from deployments and interesting clients he's had fishing. The hours passed as did the rounds of beers, with the occasional shot of rum. Inevitably, the topic of the marina came up again.

"So, you worked for Larry?" Kim asked her.

She sighed and nodded. "Yeah, for a couple years."

"Why'd you leave?"

"It was just time," Daniele said.

"What'd you do for Larry?" I asked her.

"I was his personal assistant."

"Is that your desk outside his office?" I asked.

"It was. Yeah."

"You went to U.V.I?" I asked.

"No, why?" Daniele replied.

"I saw the university coffee mug on your desk. Thought it was yours."

She paused, took a breath, and closed her eyes. "It was given to me by a dear friend."

"So, what do you see this place looking like if Larry's project gets done?" Kahuna asked her.

She gazed into the night over the waters and was quiet for a long moment then spoke, gesturing with her hands widely.

"This will all change. Ferries, buses, maybe a damned cable car strung from Cruz Bay over the hills, will bring in droves of tourists to walk around a Disneyesque caricature of what was. All of them falsely believing they experienced the island, yet never really knowing it. Maybe a few of the old guard will remain and tell stories of what was, singing mournfully the requiem of their home and way of life. Then as they leave or pass on, slowly the memory will fade, and the new existence will become the new soul of the place. Though empty, and devoid of substance or meaning. It will choke the magic and color from this wonderful place and whitewash it into a monochromatic imitation of life."

After she finished, we all sat silent for several moments.

"Damn," Kahuna said. "That was beautiful, but sad."

"It's from an op-ed I wrote for the paper opposing it. I just hate all of this." She began to cry and her head dropped. We all sat silent. Kim moved to sit on the arm of her chair, putting her arm around her.

"You, ok?" she asked her.

Daniele sighed heavily, shaking the tears from her eyes. "Yea, I'm OK. It just makes me sad to think about. I've lived most of my adult life here. But I guess it couldn't last forever."

"So, why Maine? You from there?" Kahuna asked.

She sat up and composed herself. I handed her my handkerchief and she wiped the tears from her eyes. "No, but there's a great spot near Rangely, a little island on a lake. I have a cabin there I haven't seen in years. I think a summer there will help me reset and decide what to do next."

"Never been to Maine," I said.

"You should go. It's beautiful," she said.

"Well, I'm going to go find Michelle. I want to get back home tonight. We have a farewell party tomorrow for some friends leaving the islands."

"Oh come on, stay with me on the boat. I'll run you back to Cruz in the morning," I said.

"Are you coming back to Coral Bay?" Daniele asked me.

"Yeah. I may stay another day and go back to the site once more before heading back to St. Thomas."

"Well, if it's not too much trouble, and Kim doesn't mind, can I catch a ride? I need to pick something up in Cruz before I leave. It won't take but a few minutes, I promise. It's really very important."

"Well, I guess I can stay," Kim said. "And yea, that's fine with me if it is with Mike."

"Sure, sounds good. Let's meet at the dinghy docks around 10," I said.

***

Lying on the trampoline of *Second Wind* I watched the clouds pass slowly in front of the moon. I knew what Kahuna said was right. They'll find a way to get the project done with or without me. *All I have to do is the right thing*, I thought. And walking away wouldn't be doing that. I just had to figure out how to do it, and fast.

Chapter 26

"LOOK AT THINGS THROUGH FRESH EYES TODAY," KIM SAID. "With all that Larry and Winters have said about you, there's a reason you're here."

"Thanks… I'll figure it out. I always do," I said with a smile, then kissed her cheek.

She turned to Daniele and hugged her. "It was so great to meet you. Hopefully we'll see you again."

"Thank you. It was great meeting you too," Daniele said and handed Kim a piece of paper. "This is my phone number. Give me a call if you find yourself in Maine."

"Sounds like a plan. I love the islands, but I do miss getting into the woods," Kim said.

"Well, where do you need to go?" I asked Daniele. "Since I'm staying another day, I need to run into the Dolphin Market to grab a few provisions."

"That's perfect. The place is close to there. I'll just walk over while you're shopping."

I gave Kim another hug and climbed into the Jeep. Daniele saw me watching her as she walked away.

"You're really in love with her, hu?" she said.

I turned to her. "I haven't known that long… but I can't deny it… I feel something."

"I can see it in your eyes. Even if you don't know it yet," she said, patting my knee.

I let out a sigh and shook my head. "God help me," I said with a grin as I put it into drive and pulled away towards the market.

***

I finished shopping then sat in the Jeep, waiting for Daniele to return. Twenty minutes or so passed and I had the seat leaned back and was drifting off when she opened the door, startling me.

"Oh, was I gone that long?" she asked.

"No, I've just learned to catch little naps when I can. You all set?" I asked.

"Yeah, I have everything I need," she said as she climbed in. She placed a small shoulder bag on the floor then looked to me with a faint smile.

"Would you mind taking Northshore Road? I don't know the next time I'll be here and I really love the view on that drive," she said as I backed out.

"Sure — it's a beautiful day for it," I replied, putting the Jeep into gear.

***

We wound along the shoreline road. Daniele was leaned back in her seat, her head turned, watching the bays and beaches as we passed, her hand resting on the door and her fingers lightly playing in the wind as she stared out the window.

She let out a heavy sigh and closed her eyes.

"Gunna miss it here, hu?" I said.

She opened her eyes and seemed to scan the horizon for several moments before turning to me. Her forced grin did little to mask the sadness in her eyes. I handed her my hankie as a tear fell. She turned her head to again face the shore as we made the bend passing Cinnamon Bay.

She took a deep breath then turned back to me. "Can we stop at Maho for a few minutes? I know you have a lot to do, but I'd really appreciate it. Just a couple minutes – I promise."

137

I smiled at her. "Sure, no problem at all."

I turned into the parking lot and stopped under a palm tree. We both sat quietly for a moment and stared out over the water.

"Do you mind if I have a few minutes alone?" she asked, wiping tears from her cheek.

"Are you OK?" I asked.

"Yeah. I just need a few minutes. Leaving here is hard for me."

"No problem," I said. "Just wave when you're ready if I'm not back.

I got out and walked for several minutes down the shore. I watched the waves as they ran up the beach, circled my feet then pulled sand and shells with them as they retreated back to the sea, slowly shaping the coastline, changing it forever with each wave and each tide. I thought about how I'd never walk on that same beach again and how even my footprints, though quickly washed away, in some small way, have forever changed it.

I stopped and walked into the water up to my knees. The baby blue sky didn't have a cloud in it, and the water was clear and cool. I watched a sailboat come into the bay, turn into the wind, and drop her sails before gracefully catch her mooring.

I thought again about what Kahuna said the night before. Eventually, they'll find a way to get the project done. So, better me than someone else that doesn't care. Maybe there's a way I can influence changes that will help both the environment and the people, I thought. The question was, how?

I closed my eyes and felt the warmth of the sun on my face, and somewhere in the wind I found stillness and clarity. I still didn't know how I would do it, but I found the confidence that I could.

I walked a little longer to give Daniele some more time then slowly made my way back. Looking down the bay as I walked, I saw her sitting under a Seagrape tree, looking out over the water. She saw me and waved.

***

As I approached, she turned to me. Her eyes still carried tears that she tried to hide behind a veiled smile.

"Ready to go?" I asked softly.

She looked up at me, staring into my eyes for a long moment as if searching for something. "Will you sit with me for a minute, Mike? I have something I need to tell you."

Her voice was gentle and calming but somehow carried with it a seriousness. Unsure of what she was going to say, I felt a knot form in my stomach.

I sat down next to her and she turned to face me, then reached into her bag and pulled out a large manilla envelope. She laid it in her lap and stared at it for a moment, her hand delicately covering it.

The expression fell from her face, and she looked up at me, the tears were rolling down her cheeks, her smile, gone.

She tried to say something but choked on her words then closed her eyes and took a deep breath, held it for a moment, then let it out slowly. Fighting her emotions, her breath trembled as she exhaled. She looked up to me again and spoke, slowly and calmly.

"Dave and I were lovers. We'd been together for a couple years before he…" She stopped and cleared her throat to maintain her composure. Her voice quivering now as she continued.

"He always spoke so highly of you and really regretted letting everything that happen in Miami come between you. He planned to call and make amends… He really loved you, Mike," she said, swallowing hard to fight back her emotions.

My heart dropped.

"I – uh… me too. God – I didn't talk to him too much since he left Miami, and we had our falling out. I remember once he mentioned having a girlfriend. I guess I just forgot your name – or never connected the dots… I don't know."

"Well, that's because my first name isn't Daniele. That's my middle name. My name is Tiffany. When I ran into you on St. Croix, I was nervous because of seeing Larry's boat. I was actually about to sail north. But when I found it was you… I had to stay. I had to get you this," she said looking to the envelope. 'Dave's Files' was written in pen on the front.

"Why did feel you had to hide your name from me?"

"Because you were working for Larry. It had been a while since Dave saw you, and people change sometimes. I needed to be sure you were still one of the good ones, as Dave always said about you."

"And working for Larry calls that into question? Dave and I both worked with him in the past. What were you scared of?"

"I know. But it's different this time, Mike."

She took another deep breath and exhaled hard. She inched closer and looked into my eyes, searching or trying to convey something to me. She put her hand on my knee. Her expression was soft and caring, but her eyes reflected concern and pain. She looked down at the envelope again. A single tear fell, causing the blue ink to run.

"Mike, I have to tell you something. It's hard for me. So, please just listen."

The tone of her voice surprised me. Soft, but urgent. She stared at me, waiting for an answer.

"Yeah – OK, I'm – I'm listening," I said.

"Look — I don't believe that Dave's death was an accident."

"What do you mean? You – you think he was murdered?"

"Yes. I do. He was a whistle blower. He did his own study of the site and called the project manager at the Army Corps to report his findings. He also sent emails with all of it to alert the governor. We thought he really had them nailed too, because shortly after that he was approached by an FBI agent. Seems the Corps alerted them, so they were investigating the project.

"Someone must have found out. Which is also why I was so scared. I still worked for Larry, so we were both feeding him information. If Dave was killed over this, and if Larry or Winters were involved, they may also know that I was working with the FBI too. Which is why I was scared."

"That's a big accusation, Tiffany. I've known Larry a long time, and though he's stressed and has a lot riding on this, I don't see him killing anyone. And Winters, he's all talk."

"Maybe you're right. Agent Jones said the same thing. But he hasn't taken anything off the table either. So please, keep your eyes open and do the same."

"What does this agent Jones think?"

"I don't know. After Dave died, I talked to him the one time but was so scared, I just left. I turned off my phone and sailed to Sint Maarten. I only stopped on St. Croix on the way back through to provision and rest. That's when I ran into you."

"Are the detectives that work for Winters aware he and Larry are being investigated by the FBI?"

"I don't think so, but I'm not sure. Agent Jones said not to say anything to anyone, which is fine with me. I don't trust those two anymore than I trust Larry or Winters. Just do me a favor, if you do contact agent Jones, just say that you saw me on St. Croix, and that I was leaving that day but didn't say to where. I just want to leave all of this behind me. My new number is in the envelope. If they really need me, you can call me. But don't give it to them."

"I won't – But, if you think all of this is true, why come back here? Seems risky."

"Because, I had to give you this," she said, handing me the envelope. "Dave would have been angry with me for taking the chance, but he would've wanted you to have it."

"What is it?" I asked.

"Maybe the reason Dave's dead. Inside is a thumb drive with all his reports and notes. He always kept it at my place as a backup in case his computer crashed. All but the last one are there. Those reports, the ones not on the drive, he said would be the death blow to the project. Agent Jones has those though.

"There's also security videos from the docks from the night Dave was murdered. I was suspicious from the start and had a friend who works there pull the footage to see if there was anything there. It shows a small boat leave, then return a short time later. The times line up with the 911 calls about the fire on his boat."

I looked out over the water as a pelican skimmed just over the surface and glided down the shoreline. I watched it as it lifted into the sky and over the hill, banking high in search of fish. I closed my eyes and took a deep breath.

She touched my hand. "I'm sorry to drop all of this on you. Maybe it wasn't Larry or Winters, but all the reasons given for Dave's so-called accident don't add up. He was a hell of a sailor and certainly not a big drinker. Something is off."

"It's OK… I'm glad you did. This is just a lot to process. I really don't believe Larry or Winters would've killed him. But that doesn't mean someone else didn't."

She sighed. "Well, there are a lot of people with a lot of money on the line and Dave was pretty public about his opposition. Greed can be a powerful motivator for evil deeds."

***

Standing on the dock near Tiffany's dinghy, she gave me a long hug and kiss on the cheek. She stepped back and smiled, started to say something, then froze. Her eyes fixed over my shoulder.

I glanced back and saw Sarah at the top of the dock, watching us.

"Does she know you?" I asked.

"We never met, but I know who she is. I'm sorry, but I have to get out of here, Mike."

"I understand," I said and helped her into her dinghy.

"What are you going to do?" she asked as I handed down her bags.

"I really don't know," I said then untied her painter from the cleat and pushed her off with my foot. She started the engine then looked back up at me as she floated backwards.

"You know, I was supposed to be on the boat that night. But we got into a stupid fight, so I stayed at home… Sometimes I really wish I hadn't."

"Dave wouldn't want you to feel that way. Sail with him in your heart."

She smiled and waved then turned the small boat and was off. I watched her for a moment then walked to the top of the dock where Sarah was waiting.

"She's cute, Mike. Well done. Who is she?" she said as I neared.

"An old friend. What are you doing here?" I asked as I passed her and walked to the Jeep. She turned and sauntered slowly after me, casually glancing around.

"Oh, just imagining how great this place will be one day," she said.

I grabbed the duffle with my camera and notepad then turned to face her. She returned my stare.

"This place – is just fine how it is," I said.

She casually smiled at me. I stepped around her but she continued to follow me.

"It is beautiful, you're right there. Just think though, how great it will be to be a part of making it even better."

I turned. My teeth clinched, biting my tongue.

She smirked at me. "Yes. What is it, Michael?"

I stared at her, holding back but her passive smile made my blood boil.

"You know what…" I said.

Her expression turned more stern. "What?"

Her phone rang. She looked down at it and smiled.

"Hold that thought," she said.

"Hello darling."

"Oh, just over in Coral Bay chatting with Mike."

"I was here just to look around and ran into him."

"I'm not sure, he was just embraced with a lovely woman."

"Mike, Charlie wants to know if you're here working."

I didn't answer just held up my mesh duffle bag.

"Seems that he is, yes. He has all his tools with him now. But he's in a grumpy mood," she said poking my shoulder.

"I have to go," I said then turned and marched down to the dinghy.

"Have a good day, Michael," she said.

As I pulled away from the dock, I glanced back up to her. She was placing her phone back into her purse. She smiled and casually waved.

***

Back on *Silver Linings* I dumped the contents of the envelope onto the table. Inside was Agent Jones's card, the thumb drive, a key with a tag on it that read, *Larry's Office*, and a small photo.

I picked up the picture. It was a shot of me and Dave at one of the big jobs we did in Miami. That one is what really put me at odds with my dad. I smiled, recalling the pleasure it gave me. On the back of the photo was some writing.

Listen to your brain but follow your heart.

Words of wisdom from Dave

Be safe, Mike.

Tiffany

I plugged the drive into my laptop. It had a folder with all of Dave's files, images and notes. He'd done an in-depth assessment and documented everything. The data he had on the drive alone would've made the job all but impossible. I wondered what else he'd found.

I looked at Agent Jones's card. Tiffany said he had the last assessment Dave did. I just wasn't sure I wanted to get involved there.

I scanned the files and found a folder with saved emails. Several were to Larry and Winters as well as Elizabeth Bathory urging them to cut their losses and suggesting major necessary changes. Through the emails I could see his growing frustration with being ignored.

There were many messages to the governor's office as well. One had a petition with hundreds of signatures to stop the project. Another shared all his work and noted his intention to send everything into the Corps and file a petition with them. There was only one reply from the Office of the Governor thanking him and stating that the matter would be looked into.

The last email was to the Army Corps and was sent on the same day he tried calling me.

I wondered again why he never left a message.

The security footage from the ferry docks at Red Hook was grainy and poorly lit, but as Tiffany said, it showed what looked like two men in a small dinghy-like boat leaving the docks around 1:00am then returning at 1:45am. A few minutes later you can see several boats racing out of the marina towards the bay, including a fire and police boat.

I zipped the files and used my old work email to send them to myself, then pulled the drive from the port and started at the screen. After a few minutes the screen saver came on. I watched the geometric patterns bounce around, my mind was racing and overwhelmed.

Would Larry or Winters have killed Dave — or had him killed? If they did, would they do it again? If they didn't, who did?

I rubbed my face, picked up the picture and stared at it. Reading the words again, I could hear Dave's voice. "*Listen to your brain but follow your heart, brother.*" It was a common saying of his.

My brain told me to leave. My heart though had other opinions. I couldn't just leave as if none of it mattered. Tiffany put herself at risk to get me this for a reason. I had to do something.

I picked up Agent Jones's card and dialed the number.

He picked up on the first ring.

CHAPTER 27

THE SUN WAS SETTING AS I SECURED *SILVER LININGS* IN HER SLIP. An official looking man was standing on the dock nearby. His shoulder-length black hair was tucked neatly behind his ears, and he wore pressed beige slacks and a tight-fitting black t-shirt under a navy-blue button-up, that was left open.

"Michael Bennett?" the man said as I came onto the back deck.

"Who's asking," I said as I quickly moved towards the bow.

"Special Agent, Preston Jones," he said, handing me the dock line.

I secured it and moved aft.

"Are you Michael Bennett?" he asked again, showing me his FBI badge and credentials as I secured the stern and plugged in the shore power.

"Yeah, that's me. Give me a second, I need to kill the motors," I said and moved to the salon door.

"Why don't we both step inside where it's more private," he said.

"Sure, come on in." I said.

"Well, Mr. Bennett, I'm glad you called," he said as he walked in. "You have stumbled into a bit of hornet's nest."

"Look, I don't plan to stick around. I just want to know what the hell is going on," I said.

"Well, in short, your associate Dave Blankenship and his partner had been working as informants for the FBI as part of an investigation against your boss, Charles Winters. Now, Mr. Blankenship is dead. It's the bureau's opinion he was murdered."

"Yeah, that's what Tiffany said too."

"When did you see her exactly?" he asked.

I looked away from him, searching for the right thing to say. "I – I saw her on St. Croix maybe a week ago or so."

"And she told you everything then?"

"No, of course not. If she did, I wouldn't still be working for them."

He squinted his eyes, leering at me, then turned towards the front of the cabin, looking around for a moment before turning back to me.

"So, when did you find out about all of this? Have you seen her since?"

"No." I replied.

"You're not in any trouble here, Mike. Since you work for them, I already have a file on you. You've been cleared of any wrongdoing. I just need to know what you know. She disappeared but may be vital to the investigation. If you know where I can find her, or how to reach her –"

"I don't," I said. "I saw her briefly on St. Croix, she recognized the boat, and we spoke. I told her I was working for Larry. I – uh, I must have mentioned where I was staying because the other day an envelope was delivered for me with a letter, a thumb drive, and your card."

"What did the letter say? Was there a return address?"

"No return address. The letter just said how Dave alerted the Army Corps to possible fraud and that they were working with you as informants against the project and that she thinks Larry and Winters had something to do with it. It seemed like more of a warning."

"And she didn't say where she was going?"

"No. She's scared. She said she just wants to disappear."

He let out a heavy sigh. "Damnit. I was really hoping you could help me there."

He walked past me towards the salon door, pacing a little as he spoke.

"So, you saw her, and she sent you the letter as a warning. Why didn't you open it right away? I mean, a letter from the girlfriend of a deceased friend."

"She didn't mention they were together. She was cagey about everything. She even gave me a fake name when I saw her. I didn't know her name was Tiffany until I got all of this."

"So, if you're leaving too. Why did you call me then?"

"Dave was a good friend, and Larry has been a close associate of mine for a long time. I just want to know what the hell is going on!"

"I'm sure you do. And you deserve to know, but it's an active investigation with a lot of different parts, so I can't say too much more than you already know. But, as Tiffany told you, we have been investigating Larry and Winters for some time now, especially Winters."

"Right, but for what? And do you think one of them killed Dave? I mean, am I in danger here?"

"We've been building a case for racketeering, bribery, forgery – you name it. And we don't know who killed Dave yet, but there're a lot of things that point to Larry. He's our prime suspect right now. But look, Dave was a fly in the ointment. You're on their side as far as they know, so you're safe."

"OK — well fine then. Ya know what, I'm just going to tell Larry there's nothing I can do, and they need to find someone else. If you think I'm safe, I just want to head back to Key West. Hopefully you're good and I'll read about all of this in the paper soon."

He moved to the sofa and sat down. "Have a seat, Mike," he said, gesturing to the spot next to him.

"I'll stand," I said.

"Fine. But look — I have a big favor to ask of you. It would really help us out with finding out what happened to Dave."

"OK — what is it?"

"Forst off, I'm very good at what I do, which is why I'm here. But what I do best is working undercover and managing informants. It's too late in the game for me to try and infiltrate, and to be blunt, with both of my informants gone, I don't have many avenues here. So, you may be the only one who can help us."

"So, you want me to be an informant?"

"Yeah, we'd like you too, if you're willing."

"We?"

"The FBI. I assumed we may need you and already had you cleared in case I did."

"I don't know, man. I'm no spy or anything. Seems risky."

"Look, Mike, as I said, you may be the only one who can help us. All you have to do is keep working, pretend to go along with what they want, and feed us information. Just take notes. I know you're good at that."

"Thanks, but I don't think so. If he was murdered, doing that is probably why."

"Mike, I've been running informants and undercover ops for a long time. I know what I'm doing. Plus, Dave was very vocal about what he was doing long before I was involved. As far as I know, he never mentioned to anyone he was working with me. So as long as you don't do anything or talk to anybody but me about this, you'll be fine."

"I don't know," I said, then walked onto the aft deck into warm night air. He called after me.

"This wouldn't be the first time you volunteered for hazardous duty, would it, Airborne?"

I turned and walked back in. He was still on the couch.

"I told you, I had you cleared. That means investigated. I know you were an infantry paratrooper. I assure you this is far less dangerous than jumping out of a plane into a war zone. If you do as I say that is."

He got up and walked over to me.

"Mike, I'll be frank. Tiffany and Dave were our only real hope of proving the fraud. Because of them, we *almost* have all we need. But I don't have a good avenue to proving who killed Dave. Any evidence was burned up or is on the bottom of the bay. If you don't help us, we may never find out what happened."

I closed my eyes and ran my hands through my hair, but didn't reply.

"Come on. I know you were the environmental warrior. I'll get you the last report Dave sent me. It's clear what they're doing. I just need to tie it to them. And if they killed Dave, we'll get them there too. Bury the bastards!"

I opened my eyes and looked up, meeting his gaze.

"I've never lost an informant until now and I'm making it my personal mission to take down whoever did this. You're on the inside, man. This is a perfect scenario. What do you say?" he said, slapping my shoulder.

"I don't know. This is a lot. Risking my own life won't bring Dave back. And I love this place, but is it worth my life?" I said, walking back outside and leaning against the transom.

"What if I told you Larry's why your business went under in Miami," he said. His words carried from the salon and landed like jab to my chest, almost taking my breath away.

I walked to the companionway and stooped in the door.

"What are you talking about?" I said.

"In our investigation of him we dug into his old business ventures. We found evidence that he manipulated your partner to falsify those documents. He knew about your relationship with her and the promotion she had on the line. He simply used it to his advantage."

"That doesn't add up. When that all imploded it cost him a ton of money too."

"True, it was a gamble that didn't pay off. He had a lot riding on the project and needed to make it work. His gamble failed."

My stomach began to churn. "Sounds like a familiar story," I said.

"Mike, he has a history of doing this. He makes huge bets, takes risks, and bends or outright breaks the rules, and sometimes the law, to make it all work. The difference is, typically he's gambling with other people's money, this time he has a lot of skin in the game. So, here you are again. About to take the fall for him a second time. I don't want to pressure you into this, but I want you to have all the information to make the best decision."

"Yeah, a purely noble act, I'm sure."

"It's true. I have a job to do, and you can help me. But, if it were me, I'd want to know either way."

I stared into the dark and watched the navigation lights of a boat leaving port. It's wake gently rocked *Silver Linings* as she passed.

"Can I think about it?" I said quietly, watching the small boat carry out to sea.

He walked closer and put his hand on my shoulder. "Of course. Just, if you decide to leave, please let me know ahead of time. For now, like it or not, you're my responsibility and I can't have you disappearing. I have enough to worry about."

"Yeah, sure. No problem," I said.

"Great, well look, I need to get going. I have to be in Miami by morning." He handed me a small flip phone. "I know you use Larry's work phone so take this. My number is already saved. Only call me from this number and don't use it to call anyone else. Keep it with you at all times. If I need to pull the plug and get you out, we'll need to be in direct and quick contact."

"No problem. I'll let you know soon… I just need to process all of this."

"Mike, I need you to look at me," he said.

I looked up at him. His expression was stern as he looked directly into my eyes.

"Do not by any means mention me, the investigation, any of it, to anyone. That means Kim too. Larry has a way of manipulating people, as you know all too well, and we don't know for sure where her allegiance would fall. For the sake of the mission and for your own safety, you can't tell anyone. Period. You remember operational security, I'm sure. This is imperative."

"Op-Sec, sure. Got it. I won't."

"Alright, well, if I don't hear from you in a day or two, I'll call you. Think it through, but I do need to know sooner than later so I can make my plans."

***

I walked back inside and poured a few fingers of rum on the rocks then sat on the sofa and took a long pull from the glass. My mind raced. There was no reward for trying to play the hero, not that it mattered really, but the risk was high.

I laid my head back and stared at the ceiling, sipping slowly from my glass.

What *should* I do? Was it all really worth it? The questions were swimming though my mind when my phone vibrated. It was a text from Kim.

"Hey hun, I ran into Larry today.

He's heading back to STT sometime tomorrow

morning so I'm catching a ride with him.

He invited us to lunch at the resort tomorrow.

Thinking of you and wishing you were here with me.

Can't wait to see you. XOXO."

I didn't reply. I just put the phone on the sofa next to me. In that moment, all I wanted to do was convince her to go to Key West with me and get the hell out of the islands and away from all of it. If I explained it all to her, would she warn Larry? Could I trust her?

I didn't know.

***

I went back to the resort, but was unable to sleep, so I sat on the back porch of my suite late into the night. Staring into the black sky, all the uncertainties and unanswered questions ran endlessly through my head. I pulled out the small photo of Dave.

If Agent Jones was right, Larry is the reason we weren't still in Miami building the business together. Looking at it, I was filled with disappointment, anger, and the lingering question of what I really *should* do.

I laid the picture next to me on the table, reclined the chair back and closed my eyes.

It seemed like hours passed, but finally, somewhere in the early dawn, just as the dark sky began to turn navy blue with hints of the rising sun, I succumbed finally to exhaustion and fell asleep.

Chapter 28

THE SOUND OF FARAWAY THUNDER ROLLED HEAVY AND SLOW through the late morning air. A thin layer of sweat from sleeping outside covered my skin but was cooling in the light breeze. I opened my eyes and stared at the fan overhead. The weight of the previous day still sat heavy on my chest as I drew in a deep breath.

I sat up and rubbed my face, nodding passively to a couple walking by. Leaning forward I stared blankly into the sand at my feet, my thoughts an incoherent hum. I stood up and stepped into the sun, tilting my head back and closing my eyes, trying to quiet my mind.

Behind me, my work phone rattled across the small glass table. I picked it up and read the text. It was from Larry, asking me to join them at the pool for lunch. I wished I had more time to think before seeing him, I thought, then put the phone in my pocket.

Looking down at the table the picture of me and Dave was under the phone Agent Jones had given me. I picked them both up and sat down.

"What do I do here, Dave?" I asked aloud, then stared at it as if waiting for a reply.

I sat the picture down and flipped open the phone. The only number saved didn't have a name. I selected it, my thumb resting on the call button.

My stomach turned and I started to sweat, then I gently shut the phone and closed my eyes, taking a deep breath, squeezing the phone in my hands.

Another text came through my work phone.

"Hey hun! We have a table near the pool. Come join us!"

"Be there in a few minutes," I replied, then with a deep breath, got up and headed to the shower, unsure of what I was going to do when I met them.

***

I walked towards the resort's poolside café. Agent Jones's phone was in my back pocket to keep it out of sight. I put my hand on it as I came around the corner. Somehow it offered a sense of assurance.

I stopped where I felt hidden but could see Kim and Larry. Larry was at the table talking on the phone, Kim was sitting with her feet in the pool, watching a group of children playing. She noticed me and waved.

I waved back. "Here we go," I said to myself with a sigh.

Kim ran over with a big hug and kiss on the cheek. At first, she felt good in my arms, but a feeling of sadness formed in my stomach, so I held onto her, squeezing her tight, my head on her shoulder.

"Have a good time with your friends?" I asked, still holding onto her.

She pulled back and cocked her head to the side. "Are you OK?"

"I'm fine — why?" I asked.

"Are you sure? You seem upset."

"I'm fine. I just didn't sleep well last night."

"Work stuff?" she asked.

"Yeah, just work stuff. It's all good."

"Larry's in a funky mood too. But none of that right now. It's time for lunch," she said with a playfully feigned seriousness then grabbed my hand and towed me behind her. I caught up and wrapped my arm around her shoulders and kissed the top of her head.

Larry hung up as we approached. He sat the phone down and leaned back in his chair, stretching with a deep breath then looking to us with a halfhearted smile. He didn't stand but offered his hand.

"Good to see you, Mike," he said.

I smiled and shook his hand. But Larry, always good at reading people, noticed my muted response.

"Everything alright, Mike?" he asked.

"All this work you've given Mike has him tired and all serious today too," Kim said. "I tell ya, you boys are working yourselves too hard."

"Yeah, this one is turning out to be a lot more work than expected. But hopefully you have some good news for me after your site visit, Mike," Larry said.

Kim had already ordered appetizers and wine for the table, and it arrived as we sat down. I did my best to seem at ease.

"Well, man, as you said. This one's hard. I looked over everything you gave me and did a quick site assessment – and there's just no way we can…"

I held onto my words, glancing to Kim then back to Larry, studying his face. The picture of me and Dave flashed in my mind. I locked eyes with Larry.

"Come on, Mike. This one is hard, but we've gotten through worse. Just like back in the old days. We can get this done," Larry said.

I held up my hand. "What I was going to say is, there's no way we can do this with the plan as is. It'll take some major redesigning, which means more time."

"Redesigning I can deal with. Man — I really thought you were about to bail out on me."

"Come on, Larry. I've never quit anything. And like you said, this could make up for Miami."

"Well, can you do some work from St. Barths?" Larry asked.

"Why there?"

"I have to go there for some business, but we can always extend the trip and make it a getaway. I could certainly use a day or two off myself. I am sure Kim would love to come too, she loves it there," he said, looking to her.

"That sounds lovely," Kim replied. "I haven't been since we rented that villa in Lorient…"

She stopped and glanced to me then quickly to her plate, slowly sipping her wine.

"Don't be embarrassed. We're all adults here, Kim. It's fine. Right, Mike?" Larry said.

"Yeah, sure. But we have to meet with the surveyor tomorrow. You set the meeting, remember?" I said.

"Damnit, you're right. Well, I can't miss the meeting in St. Barth's and I feel like you can handle the surveyor. It's not your first rodeo and it's just to go over a couple questions he has. Maybe you can go over some of your thoughts with him and let me know what he says. You OK with that?"

"Yeah, I can handle it. If I have any questions, I'll call you."

"Well, Kim my dear," Larry said, looking at me as he began, then turned to her. "You are more than welcome to come along if our boy here is OK with it. We can go to *Le Sereno* for dinner."

She looked to me. "I'd really like to go. I haven't been in a long time."

I just shrugged and offered a reluctant grin.

"Go for it," I said.

"Great, I'm in," she said.

"Good. Well, the car leaves tomorrow at eight for the airport. We'll be gone two nights."

My stomach turned and I felt lightheaded. I sat my napkin on my plate and slid my chair out.

"Going somewhere, Mike?" Larry asked.

"Yeah. I am not feeling so hot. I think I need to lie down."

"Man, if it bothers you, I can go alone," Larry said.

"Would you rather me not go?" Kim asked.

"It's fine," I said. "I didn't feel well all night and I guess I'm not over it. I just need to lie down."

"OK, babe. I'll be in when I finish eating. Want me to bring you anything?"

"No, I'm OK," I said, then kissed the top of her head and headed back to the room.

***

I was lying on the bed with my hands over my face when the door came open and Kim walked in.

"Are you OK?" she asked, setting a plate of food on the dresser.

"I'm fine," I said rubbing my eyes.

"You don't seem fine."

I looked towards her. "Maybe I'm not then."

"What is it then, baby? Talk to me," she said, sitting down on the bed next to me.

"Like I said before, it's just work stuff, Kim. Nothing I can talk about with you."

"Then go talk to Larry."

"I know. I will. I just need to think."

"I really don't understand. You're upset about work, yet for some reason can't talk to me about it, and you won't talk to your boss."

I pulled the pillow over my face. "Yeah, it's a paradox alright."

We sat in silence for a few moments. She put her hand on my chest.

"Mike, what's going on?"

I threw the pillow and sat up. She stood and moved away, her eyes wide.

I took a deep breath. "Please – just —stop," I said, getting up and walking across the room to the window.

"Whoa… what the hell is that about, Mike? I was just seeing if you are OK?"

"I'm sorry. It's not you."

"Then what?"

"I just — I shouldn't have taken the job," I said.

"Then why did you?" she said, moving closer to me.

I turned and faced her, speaking softly.

"I don't know. The money, a chance to redeem myself… you."

"Me? That doesn't make any sense. You just met me."

"I know," I said walking onto the back porch. She followed. "Maybe I thought an opportunity to redeem myself would make me feel better about everything."

"And now?"

"And now, honestly, I'm reminded of why I was happy to not be in this business anymore."

"So, what do you want to do?"

"Honestly… just to go home to my little boat in the mooring field… But…"

"But what?"

"I want you to come with me. I don't want to leave you here. I took a chance on the job and that was a mistake. But it gave me the opportunity to take a chance with you, and that makes all of it worth it."

She sat down and looked up at me, sadness and compassion in her eyes.

"Mike, I can't do that."

"Can't?"

"Won't," she replied softly. "I need more than that. I love these islands, and I really like you, but we just met. And a tiny boat on a mooring doesn't sound so appealing."

I took a seat in the chair next to her and we sat for a few moments in silence. I put my arms around her and kissed her neck, holding her close.

"Don't go with Larry. Stay here with me. Let's take *Second Wind* and go sailing."

She shook her head and pulled away. "I think you need some time to yourself. You need to figure out just what it is you want to do. But, I can't, I shouldn't, be a part of that decision."

"Please. He's leaving so I'll have time to think about everything. But I want you to stay."

"I'm sorry, Mike. But I'm going to go," she said, standing up.

"Why? You'd rather go with him than stay with me?" I snapped at her.

"Do not, get that way with me," she said, her finger leveled at me, then took a breath and calmly continued. "Even if I didn't go, I'd give you your space. I really think you need it."

"Fine!" I fired at her, walking back into the room. "Go then. Enjoy your date with Larry."

"You're an ass!" she replied, tears forming in her eyes.

She walked into the bedroom and grabbed her bag then walked to the door. "I'm sorry you're having this crisis, Michael, but do not put it on me. I care about you, but I won't be spoken to like that when I've done nothing to deserve it. Figure out what you want to do because I am not sticking around to watch you implode. If you can't do that, just go the hell back to Key West!"

She slammed the door and left.

I stood there, staring at the door. My breathing increasingly shallow and rapid. My face went hot. I grabbed an empty glass and threw it at the door then through clenched teeth screamed, "What the fuck am I gunna do?"

I walked quickly to the door but stopped. I knew if I followed her, it'd only make things worse. I wasn't angry with her. I was however furious with Larry that he'd done this to me, seemingly for the second time.

It would've been easier if I could've just told her everything, but I couldn't. Not yet anyway. Besides, I wasn't sure she'd believe me anyway.

My hand on the knob, I put my forehead against the door. "What am I going to do?" I ask aloud. My voice just a whisper.

I moved back into the bedroom and collapsed onto the bed. I laid there, motionless for what seemed like an hour, just staring at the ceiling fan then closed my eyes and fell asleep.

***

When I woke it was late afternoon. I felt heavy and listless, so I moved to the back patio for some fresh air. But listlessness turned to restlessness then to anxiety. I felt trapped and started to pace the room.

Shit, am I losing it? I wondered. I needed to get out and away from the resort. I needed to talk to someone.

I grabbed my phone and called Kahuna.

"What's up, brother?" he said over the roaring sound of his outboards and rush of the wind.

"Man, you were right," I said.

CHAPTER 29

A STORM HAD ROLLED IN AND WAS BLANKETING THE ISLAND. I was sitting at Duffy's Love Shack, watching the cars slowly roll down the street through the curtain of water pouring off the roof. The crowd was noisy, but I was fixated on the sound of the water slapping the pavement and the voices, music, and laughter blended into an indistinct, muffled sound.

Unconsciously my focus turned to the faint hum from a nearby ice maker. My heart began to pound in my head and seemed to be keeping pace with the rhythmic vibration of the machinery. I could feel sweat running down my face. I opened my eyes but couldn't focus. My heart started to race, and I couldn't catch my breath. I felt dizzy and steadied myself on the bar.

"Hey there, bubba," Kahuna said as walked past me, tapping me on the shoulder. He took a seat at the stool to my left. Without having to order, his beer arrived as he sat down.

"Thanks, Melissa," he said to the bartender.

"Sorry I couldn't talk earlier. I had to get those folks back to the docks before this storm got on us," he said.

"No problem, man," I said.

"Hey. You OK there, cuz?"

I sighed. "You were right, man."

"Oh, hell. What happened?"

I took a deep breath, talking to him but staring at the bar. "After dropping Kim off yesterday, on the way back, Tiffany told me she was not just Larry's secretary but was also Dave's lover. Something Larry didn't know."

"Sorry to interrupt you there bud, but who's Tiffany?"

"Daniele. Tiffany is her first name. She said she was scared so she hid her real name."

"Why, scared of what?"

"Well, that's where this gets really interesting. She told me how Dave was a whistle blower and had called the Army Corps to report the company, accusing them of lying on the applications. So, they called the FBI and were investigating Larry and Winters for fraud. Seems her and Dave were working as informants. She thinks somehow someone found out and had Dave murdered."

Kahuna was silent. He scratched his head and sighed. "Damn, brother. That's a lot."

I nodded in silent agreement then sat back in my chair, hands behind my head. Staring at the ceiling above me, I pushed out a heavy breath to steady my nerves.

"Tiffany gave me the agent's contact and a file with everything Dave had. His own site assessment, pictures, maps, not to mention the emails to the Corps, Larry, and the governor's office."

"Did you call him?"

I turned towards him. "Yeah. I had to find out what was going on. So, we met on *Silver Linings*."

"What'd he say?"

"He agrees with Tiffany. He feels Dave was killed, but he's not sure who did it yet. Though he said Larry's a suspect."

"So, what now?" Kahuna asked.

"Well, he wants me to stay on and be an informant. He swears I'll be safe if I don't say anything."

"I'm sure Dave was careful too."

"Well, no. He was very vocal. I do have the advantage of nobody knowing I'm talking to him and for now, they think I'm on their side."

"What are you going to do?" he asked.

I held up my bottle to Melissa with two fingers. "I don't know, man. Part of me just wants to grab the first flight out of here and head home."

"So why don't you?"

I didn't reply. I just stared off.

He smiled and slapped me on the back. "I get it, cuz. Beautiful women have that effect. Most of the stupid shit I've done in my life has been because of, or for, a woman."

"It's not just her, man. She's a big part of it, but I may be the only one who can do something about it."

"About what? Dave's gone, Bubbah. Nothing's gunna change that."

"What about this damned marina? Dave may have died trying to stop it."

"But if any of those guys *are* involved, that means the lengths they'll go to are pretty great," Kahuna said.

"I know, man. But, there's more. This agent, he says when investigating Larry, they found evidence that he's to blame for what happened to me in Miami. He had pretty explicit details."

"Good lord, brother. What have you walked into?" He took a long pull from his beer. "But look, revenge isn't a good motivator. Trust me on this one, Mike. I know."

"I know, brother," I said.

We sat in silence for a minute, both lost in thought. I thought of my little boat back home then leaned forward and put my head on the bar. "I just want to go home," I said quietly.

"Just go then, Bubbah. It's that easy."

I sighed. "I just feel like I have to do *something*."

Then it came to me. I stood up, grabbing Kahuna's shoulder. "Larry and Kim, they're leaving for two days to St. Barths."

"OK?" Kahuna said.

"That gives me time to dig around. Even if I leave, at least I could get the feds more evidence to bury him with."

"What are you going to do?"

"I have a key to the office. Another gift from Tiffany."

He shot me a look. I held up my hand and shook my head to signal I didn't want to talk about it.

"As long as I know nobody's at the office, I can go look around. There must be more there."

"Brother, I think you should do whatever you feel is best. But man, now you are toeing that line. You get caught snooping, and if these guys are behind Dave's death, you could be asking for some real trouble."

"I know, man. But I have to do something. And this may be the only opportunity I'll have to really be able to dig into it."

Kahuna sighed. "OK, man. I'm in. When do they get back?"

"Day after tomorrow."

Well, if we go tonight, it'll look suspicious. We have tomorrow, so let's go in the morning."

"OK. I'll call agent Jones and let him know the plan."

"What's his name?" Kahuna asked.

"Special Agent, Preston Jones."

"Well, maybe wait on that. Report what you find. I have a lot of FBI buddies and in my experience, the feds have a way of screwing up simple tasks with all their protocols. This won't exactly be by the book."

Chapter 30

WE ARRIVED AT LARRY'S OFFICE AROUND TEN THE NEXT MORNING. The parking lot was mostly empty. Kahuna parked on the far side of the lot under a tree where he could see the front door.

"Once you get inside, give me a text for a comms check. I need to know I can alert you if needed."

"Will do," I said, then headed off.

I made it to the office door unnoticed. Quickly, I put the key into the lock and opened the door. But just as I stepped inside it occurred to me, Larry may have an alarm.

I scanned the walls near the door and looked around the frame for any sign of a sensor but didn't see any. I took a deep breath of relief and looked around. The office was clean. Everything put away and organized. I had to move quickly, but carefully.

I checked all the file cabinets, but the drawers were locked. I scanned the room but didn't see any boxes or files left out. I moved to Larry's desk but it was the same. Everything was put away and all the drawers were locked.

I was starting to feel like this was a waste of time, something I didn't have a lot of. I felt around under the desk, checked the coffee cup full of pens, under his desk calendar, anywhere I could think of for a key to be hidden. Then, looking around I noticed a small vintage looking safe tucked away on the floor. I pulled on the handle and the door seemed to budge. I gave it one more hard tug, and it opened.

Inside was a few thousand dollars in cash and two manila envelopes, one was sealed so I pulled the documents from the other. It was paperwork for a ten-year lease for Gary Edwards at the marina.

My phone beeped as a text came through, startling me and causing me to jump and hit my elbow on the shelf behind me. It was from Kahuna.

"You get in ok?"

"Yeah. Out soon. Who is Gary Edwards?"

"The governor."

I pulled out the phone Agent Jones gave me and took a picture of the lease and texted it to him. *"This is interesting. A lease for the governor at the resort."*

I put the papers back into the envelope and picked up the other one. It was sealed, but looking around, there was a box of similar envelopes on the shelf I hit my elbow on, so I quickly opened it and dumped the documents out, scanning through the pages.

I couldn't believe what I saw. It was a permit application to the Corps for the original plan, but on the maps and report entire segments of seagrass and coral were misreported or outright omitted. The entire thing was all bullshit.

I continued to look through the pages, taking photos of each one as I did.

Then, I came to the last one. And there, under a statement claiming the report was up to date and truthful, is what looked like my signature.

"How in the hell did you get my signature?" I said aloud.

Then I turned to the last page. "What the fuck!" I said aloud. I was stunned and confused with what I saw. There, attached to a report that gave them everything they wanted, was an approval letter from the Army Corps of Engineers.

I took a picture of the page and sat back in the chair. There's no way that plan would ever get approved. The Corps would do their own verification study and shoot this down. But if it was approved already, how, and why have me going through all of this. If the approval letter if fake, then to what end? I wondered.

I sat there, stunned and dumbfounded. Then it came to me. This would all be submitted electronically as well. The originals had to be on the computer. I tapped the spacebar on the keyboard and the screen came on, but it was locked. I tried several passwords, but none worked. I looked all-round the desk, under the calendar, the keyboard, wherever I thought Larry might have written it down, but there was nothing. Larry was too smart for that.

Then, from beyond the door, I heard the elevator bell. It carried like a siren from the far end of the hall. I quickly placed the files into the new folder, sealed it, and placed everything back into the safe, pushing the door shut. As I walked towards the door, stuffing the old envelope into my pocket, the security guard came in.

"Can I help you?" he asked.

"I was just looking for Larry. I had some things I needed to take care of."

"How did you get into the office? The door was locked."

"I have a key. I work for Larry," I said, holding up the key.

"What's your name? He hasn't added anyone to the security list. Let me see that key," he said, then before I could react jerked it from my hand. The tag Tiffany placed on it was still there with her note. I tried to pull my hand back, but he grabbed it. Holding tight to the tag, the small line broke. He looked at me.

I held up the tag. "Just a note so I knew what it was for."

"Mmm hmm," he groaned, looking at the key over his glasses. "What'd you say your name was?"

"Michael Bennett," I said.

Well, Mr. Bennett. This belongs to his secretary. I remember, she brought in the blank because she wanted the dolphins on it."

"Well, she doesn't work for Larry anymore," I said putting my hand out.

"No sir," he said putting the key into his pocket. "She is on the list. You are not."

"I'll have a talk with Mr. Vincent about security procedures," he said, shuffling me outside.

He shut and locked the office door then turned and walked away mumbling to himself. "Lazy ass people, going to cost me my damned job."

He entered the elevator and was gone.

I texted Kahuna. "*Close call, but I'm on the way out.*"

***

Kahuna was at the front door when I came out. "Let's go," I said as I climbed in, slamming the door of his truck.

"Find anything else?" he asked.

I didn't answer. Everything ran through my head.

"Son-of-a-bitch!" I said, punching the dash. "All I wanted to do was get enough info to give to the feds and spilt. Get Kim to come to Key West, leave all of this bullshit behind me and wait for news that the cards all came tumbling down on their greedy fucking heads!"

"Damn, man. What happened in there, Bubbah?"

I took a breath. "At this point, I don't know, man. Larry has a full report, full of lies, and an application to the Corps, all with my signature on it. Not to mention, an approval letter from them greenlighting the whole god-damned thing."

"How'd he get your signature? Is it forged?"

"I don't know, man. If it is, it's a damned good one. Maybe when I was signing all the intake paperwork, he slipped the page in or lifted it. I really don't know."

"What do we do? Time to cut and run?" he asked.

"I really don't know. With my name on this now, I don't see how I can leave. I have to find out what they're up to."

"Well, I'm here with you, brother. I won't leave you strap hanging."

"You don't need to get involved, man. We just met. This is my mess."

169

He looked at me sternly and slapped his chest then mine. "Never leave a man behind."

"Thanks, man, that means a lot. I'd be alone in this without you," I said.

"Brothers in arms, Bubbah. Besides, this is my home, and I know too much to ignore it now."

I returned a light slap on his shoulder. "Thank you," I said.

"So, what's your plan?" Kahuna asked.

"I don't know yet, brother. I need to call Agent Jones.

My phone beeped as a text came through.

"Good intel. I'm still in Miami

but will be back in a few days.

We're getting close, keep up the good work.

Stay close to Larry."

"That's him. Guess we're in a holding pattern," I said.

"So, play it cool. Make Larry think all is well. Be his buddy. You know the end is close," Kahuna said.

"Yea, there's some comfort there for sure. I tell you one thing though, man. My goal at this point is to get the hell out of here as soon as possible."

"I don't blame ya, brother. But for now, where to?"

"Can you drop me at the resort? I need to get some rest, reset and get my mind around all of this. Get ready for when Larry comes back."

"10-4," Kahuna said.

***

Kahuna dropped me off and I went to the pool bar. I ordered a fish sandwich, and a strong rum drink then sat, watching the world around me move forward, all oblivious to my situation. Two children ran around the pool deck, chased by their mother who was yelling at them to stop running. The boys laughed and jumped into the pool to escape, splashing a young couple intertwined with each other near the stairs. I turned back towards the bar as my food arrived.

A group across the bar spoke loudly as they tossed back another round of shots. The blender churned and the calypso music played from the speakers. On the television above the bar, a hockey game was on.

Chapter 31

SECOND WIND'S BOW MOVED CLEANLY THROUGH THE WAVES as I approached Seal Dog rocks near Gorda Sound. I was on a beam reach. Kim was to my left. I waited until the rocks were at my five o' clock then gave the command. "Prepare to come about."

"Ready," she replied. I spun the wheel hard to starboard.

"Coming about," I said.

The bow drug through the water and Kim moved to release the jammer for the port jib sheet as I pulled hard on the starboard sheet.

My line went taught.

"Come on, Kim, get the sheet loose."

"The jammers stuck! The line won't pay out," she yelled.

Second Wind froze halfway through her tack. Stuck in irons, we came to a standstill, the jib lashing violently in the wind. I moved to the port jammer and pulled hard on the release, but it wouldn't budge. I grabbed my knife, trying to pry it open and release the sheet, but it was stuck and my knife tip snapped. I thought a moment about cutting the line but knew that would make matters worse.

The jib continued to lash in the wind. I knew I had to get it under control, so I drew in the starboard sheet until the sail's clew was midship, then brought in the furling line until both sheets were tight. Her bow carried through and brought us onto a weak closed hull port tack. We started to move.

"Mike, starboard!" Larry yelled. "What the hell are you doing?"

My focus on the sails had distracted me from my surroundings. Looking up I saw the rocks now just a hundred feet off our starboard rail, and the distance was closing as the wind pushed us helplessly towards them, the white water crashing over the jagged grey rocks.

I released the main sheet to dump wind from the sail, pushed the wheel hard to port, then reached down and fired the motors, jamming them into gear. We surged forward away from danger.

But seconds later a piercing sound filled the air, and the starboard engine died.

I reached down and again tried to fire the engine, but it didn't respond. "Shit!" I yelled. The rocks were growing closer. I could hear the waves breaking on their jagged face. I stopped, took a breath and calmed myself.

"What the hell is going on," I said aloud. Then it came to me. I spun around and saw the dinghy drawn up close to our stern.

"Damnit!" I yelled.

"What's wrong?" Kim replied.

"We wrapped the damn painter line in the prop."

With just the port motor running, I jammed the throttle full ahead and put the wheel hard to port, glancing to the rocks just twenty feet or so away and getting closer.

"Come on, baby," I yelled.

Then as if from the sky, another alarm pierced my ears, followed by the sound of a loud crash.

My heart sank…

I opened my eyes, breathing heavily and covered in sweat. The fan hummed overhead. I sat up and tried to focus. The phone rang again. I looked to see it laying on the floor next to the nightstand, vibrating with each ring. Then it went silent.

I reached down and picked it up. I had missed several calls from Larry. Still recovering from my nightmare, I lay back in bed. The phone rang again. I put it on speaker phone and sat it on my chest.

"Nice of you to answer, Michael."

"I was sleeping," I said, rubbing my face and noting the line of sweat still on my brow. "What's up, Larry?"

"We'll be back on island at noon. Why don't you meet me at the office around one? I set a spa day for Kim, so she'll be busy for a few hours."

"I have to meet with the surveyor today. You're back a day early."

"I already called him and pushed that to another day. I wanted to meet with you first. We have to go over a few things."

"Yea, OK. See you soon."

"Good. Oh, and Michael, I hope you made some progress while I was gone."

"I did. I think I know what needs to happen."

"Great. Can't wait to see it," he said.

***

I drove to Larry's office, arriving fifteen minutes early. The door was open. As I walked in I glanced around the room, but nobody was there.

"Right on time," a voice said from behind me. I jumped and spun around quickly. Larry laughed as he walked by me into the office.

"Sorry there, Mike. Didn't mean to scare you. I called Jim earlier and had him open the door in case you got here before me."

I took a deep breath and followed him inside. Larry walked to the bar, picked up two glasses and poured two fingers of Bajan rum into each. He handed me one and casually touched his glass to mine, then without taking his eyes off me, took a hard swallow.

His eyes still set on mine he gently rolled the dark rum around in his glass and let out a slow sigh. "Step outside with me, Michael," he said, then turned and walked towards the balcony. I followed behind him, stopping just outside the doorway.

Outside the breeze carried the smell of the ocean and was cooling against the warm, tropical mid-day air. Larry walked to the far end of the balcony and leaned on his arms against the railing. He looked down at his glass and swirled the rum slightly then took another long pull as he stood and looked out over the beach.

I stood quietly. Waiting. My palms started to sweat.

"You know, Mike. Trust is an important thing in life," he said, still gazing out over the people on the beach.

"I agree," I said, shifting in my stance.

He watched me for a second then turned to face me. "You and I, we have to trust each other," he said, pointing at me with the same hand that held his glass then finishing the last ounce of rum.

"Of course. Why, what's – what's going on?" I asked, casually taking a drink from my glass.

"You're on board right, Mike? We're on the same team here?" he asked intently. His eyes narrowed and brow furrowed.

My heart started to race and a bead of sweat ran down my temple to my cheek. I scratched my face, hoping to conceal it. Fighting the urge to look away, I held his gaze.

"Yeah, of – of course I am. Why?"

"What all did you get done while I was gone?" he asked, ignoring my question.

I let out a long huff of air, glancing into the office. "Well, I looked over everything and came up with a working plan. But I need to meet with the surveyor and look over the blueprints to really finalize it."

"You know we have the blueprints here, right?" he asked.

He was challenging me. He knew I was there. There's no way the guard didn't tell him. I took a slow pull from my glass and nodded, "Mm - hmm," I replied as I swallowed the rum. "Yeah, I know. I came by here to get them, but all of your cabinets were locked."

"So was the door. How'd you get in?"

He slowly started to move towards me. I met him halfway and gestured towards the front door with my glass.

"I found a key in the desk outside."

"OK, well, when the cabinets were all locked, why didn't you call me? I could have told you where the keys are."

I looked down and sighed, only raising my eyes to him. "You said you were busy. I was just trying to get things done without interrupting you." With a shrug I straightened my posture and tilted my head back, looking him in the eye. "Maybe surprise you with some big plan. Sorry if that was the wrong move."

"Good initiative, but bad judgment. I have to admit, it all just seemed a little strange to me. But, as long as that's all it was, it's fine," he said.

"That was it, Larry. I swear."

He stepped closer and put his hand on my shoulder, looking me in the eye. "Look, I trust you, Mike, but I have to cover my ass. There's too much at stake here. Next time, if you need something, call me. OK?"

"Sure, Larry," I replied.

He grinned and set his empty glass on the patio table. I sat mine next to his.

"You know, the topic of you running the project in Key West came up again when I was meeting with Audrey. She likes you," he said as he turned and walked back into the office. I let out a sigh, happy the conversation was over, and wiped the sweat from my brow with my handkerchief.

"Yeah. She was nice. I liked her too," I said, then followed behind him.

He chuckled as he sat down at his desk. "Don't let her fool you. When it comes to business, she can be brutal."

He picked up a few papers, quickly looking through them as he spoke. "So, things seem to be going pretty good with Kim," he said, tapping the papers on the desk to form a neat stack. "She certainly seems smitten with you."

"Yea. She's been the best part of this trip," I said, sitting down in the chair in front of his desk.

"She's a special woman. I'm glad you guys are hitting it off," he said, as he slid the stack into an envelope. "She can be a hard one to pin down though."

"I think I'm doing pretty good there," I said.

"Well, I'm pulling for you," he said as he sealed the envelope.

He paused and looked at me as if shocked by a thought that came to him. He sat the envelope on the desk and with a heavy exhale, leaned forward. "Damn it," he said.

"What's up, Larry?"

"I think I owe you an apology."

"Apology for what?" I asked.

"Well, I know you didn't like Kim going to St. Bart's with me. And with our past, I understand that. I know that you two had a little argument over it, but in the end, you trusted not just her, but me. And then I bring you in with these with accusations. We've known each other too long for that. I should have trusted you, just as you trusted me with Kim. In the end, that's all we have, right?"

"Yeah, of course," I said.

"Well, I'm sorry, Mike. It won't happen again."

"All good, man. No worries."

"Good. I'm glad we understand each other then," he said then picked up the envelope and placed it into the safe, closing the door hard and pulling on it.

"This safe is an antique you know. If you don't really close it hard, it doesn't always lock," he said, looking up at me with a flat expression.

I must have stopped breathing because I felt starved for air. A subtle grin formed on his lips, and he started to put a few other things into his desk drawer, then locked it.

"Well, let's get moving, shall we," he said, as he stood up. "I have to meet Winters at the resort."

He walked around the desk, patting me on the shoulder as he walked by me. "But first, I have something to show you."

I reluctantly followed him down the hallway to the next office. My mind running scenes from gangster movies in my head. I imagined plastic laid out on the floor and goons waiting inside to carry me out in a rug. I failed his test, and with an old heavy door of a safe, he let me know it.

"What's this?" I asked.

He unlocked the door and handed me the key. It was the same one Tiffany gave me.

"I had this door re-keyed so that one works on both doors. Just in case you need anything while I'm not around." He pushed the door open. "After you," he said, holding his arm out.

It was a large room on the corner of the building. Each exterior wall had sliding doors that led to a balcony that wrapped around and overlooked the beach. The only furniture was a desk and large chair near one of the sliding doors. Thankfully, no plastic on the floor. I walked in, glancing to my right for imaginary goons.

"My boy, this is your new office," he said patting me on the back. "It just came open, so I grabbed it. We'll get some more furniture for you."

I glanced back to him and nodded then slowly walked in past the desk to the sliding door. Larry flipped on a light and in the reflection, I could see him standing in the doorway. I felt trapped and just stared at the silhouette, then focused on the horizon beyond the image in the glass.

"What do ya think?" he asked. "I probably should've taken this one, but I don't feel like moving all my stuff."

I didn't turn around. "It's great. Thank you, Larry."

"You earned it, Mike. But come on, you can enjoy the view later. I'm sure Kim will be excited to see you."

Chapter 32

I QUIETLY ENTERED THE COTTAGE. The permeating aroma of Kim's shampoo filled the room. She was standing and looking out of the window, tying a sarong around her waist. She hadn't heard me come in, so I stood watching her, trying to put Larry's words out of my mind. I knocked gently on the door.

"Welcome back," I said.

She didn't reply. She just turned and smiled, walked over and put her arms around me and her head on my chest, squeezing me tight. I returned her embrace and gently kissed her forehead.

"Did you have fun?" I asked.

"Yeah, we did," she said quietly. "St. Barth's is always beautiful."

She glanced up briefly with barely a trace of a smile then walked into the living room.

"But hey, I'm headed to the pool. Why don't you change and meet me," she said.

"Are you alright?" I asked.

"Yeah, of course, why?"

"I don't know, you just seem a little distant, I guess."

She came up to me and kissed me. "Oh baby, I'm fine. Just tired after traveling."

"OK, well, I need to relax for a few minutes then I'll be out. It was a long morning with Larry."

"Everything OK?" she asked.

"Yeah, just lots to do."

"OK, well take your time. I'll see ya soon." She kissed my cheek then turned and left.

I walked to the sofa, laid down and closed my eyes. Finally, I was able to breath. I pulled the phone Agent Jones gave me from my pocket, laid it on the coffee table and looked aimlessly around the room. Hanging on the wall near the door was a geometric painting of a spiral. Along the borders of the frame other shapes and patterns floated in the air, a line from each tied to the edge of the twisting figure.

I sat up and stared into the vortex of the painting and it seemed to move, everything being pulled into the starlike center in an endless succession. My mind, a torrid of thoughts and emotions, became quiet and I felt calm and focused. My thoughts more clear, started to fall into place.

Larry gambled with my business in Miami and that's why I lost everything when it failed. Now he's doing it again. And again, it's my ass on the line if it all goes south. And with the Miami fiasco still hanging over my head, all fingers would point to me, including Larry and Winters, I'm sure.

And would Larry kill Dave? I was starting to wonder. With all of this, he's able to smile at me like were friends. Who else but a sociopath could do that?

I felt my anger start to return, but this time it was reasoned and clear. I decided to trust Kim and put Larry's insinuations out of my head.

I needed a plan. I knew Larry thought he had the upper hand, catching me in a lie. I needed to take that from him so as far as he knows, we're all good. But then what? What can I do and how can I end all of this?

I got up and grabbed a beer from the fridge, cracked it, took a long pull from the icy cold brew and let out a deep sigh as I stared out of the back door. With the FBI on my side, I had the upper hand. I just needed to be dealt an ace card.

I turned and was walking back towards the sofa when a knock came at the door.

"Yeah, one second," I said, taking a quick pull from the bottle and setting it on the table.

"Who is it?" I asked through the door.

"Sarah," she said.

What the hell is she doing here I wondered. I paused with my hand on the doorknob and took a deep breath, ready for whatever she had planned.

"I guess I should take this as a compliment," I said, opening the door quickly. But when I saw her, my trepidation quickly faded. It was her, but this wasn't the temptress I saw in the doorway before. She didn't have on any makeup and was dressed only in jeans and a simple top. She still had her confidence, but she had a sadness in her eyes.

"Can I come in?" she asked softly.

"Yeah – um, come on in," I said.

"Thanks, Mike," she said with a gentle smile, lightly touching my shoulder as she passed.

"So, I don't mean to be rude, but why are you here?" I asked, closing the door.

She turned and looked at me. "You're not being rude. You're smart to ask. Given our interactions, I'm just happy you let me in at all."

"Well, your intentions are clearly different this time."

"Yeah… for what it's worth, I'm sorry about that."

"It's fine… I – I guess."

"Well, I almost had you," she said with a feigned smile as she wiped a tear from her cheek. "But it's not fine. And I am sorry."

She turned away from me and walked to the back of the room.

"Are you OK?" I asked.

"Yes, no – hell, I don't know anymore. Can I make a drink?"

"Yeah, whatever you want."

She moved to the bar and dumped a heavy pour of smoky Scotch into a glass then held the bottle up to me.

"I'm good, thanks," I said, holding up my beer.

She sat the bottle down and walked over and sat down on the sofa then took a long drink of the whiskey. "I won't stay long. I'm on the way out but wanted to see you first."

"Me? For what?" I asked.

She looked at me for a long pause. "Would you sit with me?"

I looked at her for a moment. "I won't try anything. I promise. I just need to talk to you."

I nodded then sat next to her. She put her glass on the table and turned to face me. She started to talk but couldn't seem to find her words, her mouth partially open, her eyes searching mine. Then with her lips tight and her eyes closed she shook her head and let out a heavy sigh, seeming to chuckle at herself.

She turned and picked up her glass and delicately took a small sip before turning back to me. Her expression was soft and she smiled as she looked into my eyes. It was the kind of smile you'd want to see on a first date after trying to say something sweet.

"I'm really glad you didn't give in to me," she said.

"Why's that? Seems like it would've been an insult."

"No, it wasn't. I'm glad you didn't because my intention was never to sleep with you. I was just seeing where your moral line was. If you gave in, I'm not sure I would've been able to stop myself." She looked almost bashful then reached for her glass. "Kim's a lucky girl."

"Thanks, but what do you mean you were seeing where my moral line is?"

She shook her head and stared into her glass, tilting it back slightly as if to get a better look. "It was Charlie. He wanted me to test you. I didn't know it at first, but you picking me up on St. John that day was by design. After we were at Woody's, he texted me to, 'use you assets, and see where the line is for our boy scout.' He was testing you.

"Later, I told him I thought I could get you to give in, so he had me get you alone and try. I was with Charlie at the resort when I saw Kim leaving that day, so I saw my opportunity."

I got up and walked away from her.

"I don't understand. Why in the fuck would he do that? Why would you?"

"Mike, you have no idea who he is. I guess I didn't either," she said and trailed off, staring blankly at the floor. "He's a monster and a manipulator," she said, looking up. "To him, if you would've caved, that would show him you have flexible morals and that you have a weakness he could exploit. And trust me, he would. He loves leverage and control."

I was pacing the room, trying to keep calm. "And you?"

"I don't have anything I can say here to vindicate me, Mike. I was being manipulated and used by him. I just didn't see it. But I knew what I was doing, and I knew it was wrong. But honestly, I liked it."

"So why are you here now?"

"Charles is very smart. But so am I," she said and placed a thumb drive on the table.

"What's that?" I asked.

"You're a genuinely good person, Mike. You're not innocent, but you're one of the good ones. Better than these people for sure. In my world, I sadly don't come across that too often. So, this is my apology and my word of advice. Get out of here and away from them while you can. And if you can light a match on the way out, do it."

She stood and walked to me, looking into my eyes and kissing my lips gently. "That's my plan anyway," she whispered then turned and left, closing the door gently behind her. I stood there, and for the second time, she left me speechless.

***

I plugged the drive into my computer and opened the only file. At first there was no sound, so I turned up the volume and moved my ear closer. Faintly, I heard the tapping of quickly moving shoes across a hard floor, then a click followed by a swoosh of gusting wind. I sat up a little but kept my ear turned towards the speaker.

Over the wind I could hear the clinking of glass bottles. Then, a slight thud and the noise stopped. For a moment there was nothing — just the wind. Then, the tapping sound of the shoes returned. This time, moving slower and away until once again, it was just the sound of the wind.

A minute passed and there was still nothing. The blast from a boat's airhorn sounded in the distance and I could slightly make out the cries from seagulls. A minute more… and nothing.

Then, another click. The sound of a door opening and muffled voices. They drew closer but were talking quietly so were hard to hear over the wind and poor quality of the audio. I listened closer, closing my eyes to focus. As they approached, one voice stood out.

It was Charles Winters.

"If you're going to do this, you need to do it right. I can't have anybody thinking we may have been involved," Winters said.

I could hear what the second person was saying, but over the wind it was harder to tell who it was.

"Don't worry, Randy and Joshua will handle the heavy lifting. They're pros at this stuff."

"So, what's your plan?" Winters asked.

I heard a rustling of paper. "This," the other voice said.

"What's this?"

"A newspaper article from last year warning people who live on their boats to check their propane stoves. There were three deaths that year due to people leaving them on. On one, the gas ignited, and the boat burned to the waterline and sank. The authorities weren't able to recover very much from the wreckage. Dave will simply suffer the same fatal mistake."

"And you're sure it'll work?"

"They'll see to it that it does. And the good news is, it'll be them investigating it. It's perfect."

"And what about you?" Winters asked.

"What do you mean?" said the other voice.

"You know what I mean. This isn't just another real estate scheme where you're setting up some schmuck to take a fall for you. I've been down this road before. It isn't pretty."

"No risk, no reward, right?"

"That's true, but just know, we may be in this project together, but this was your idea, so it's on you if it goes south. You understand that, right?" Winters said.

"I know the risks. Don't worry about me."

"OK. Well, when it's done, we'll come back here and open that bottle of Pappy 23 you gave me. But come on, I hear Sarah calling. Let's head back inside before someone comes looking for us."

Their footsteps and voices faded back into the sound of the wind. The click and opening of a door, then silence again. I looked at the screen, there was five minutes left on the recording. I scanned through, stopping to listen here and there, but there was only wind. I got to the end and in the last few seconds I heard the clinking of glass bottles hurriedly being moved around, the sound of hands over the microphone, then it ended. I gently closed the computer.

The conversation ran through my head again as the final piece fell into place, causing my stomach to turn. I ran for the sink, heaving until I couldn't breathe, then rested my head on the cold porcelain, gasping for air. "What the fuck?" I said, wiping my face and looking into the mirror.

Leaning on the sink my arms shook. How could he do this? I wondered, staring into the bloodshot watering eyes looking back at me. I turned on the faucet and closed my eyes, letting it run as I steadied myself. "Fuck this," I said, splashed water on my face and walked back to the desk, grabbing my phone.

Jones picked up on the first ring. I put it on speaker phone and tossed it on the bed.

"Mike, what's going on?"

"I'm out of here," I said, as I pulled my duffle bag out of the closet.

"Whoa whoa whoa. What happened?"

I was stuffing clothes into my bag as I spoke. "Ya know, I thought about what you said. Then, when I went into Larry's office the other day, I found not just that lease for the governor, but also a full report for the original plans, complete with my signature, and — a forged approval letter from the Corps. After that, I was all set on helping you bury the son-of-a-bitch and take Winters down with him."

"Was? What changed?"

"Everything's changed," I said, yanking the phone charger from the wall and walking towards the bathroom.

"Larry and Winters had Dave killed. They had those phony fucking cops do it." I said as I came back into the room.

"How do know – OK, slow down. It sounds like you're running in circles. Just — just stop, take a breath and talk to me so I can help you here."

I picked up the phone but started pacing the room. "I'm listening," I said.

"OK. Where did you get evidence that they had Dave killed?"

"Sarah. She stopped by with a goodbye present. A recording of Winters and Larry planning to have Randy and Joshua kill Dave."

"You and I both know she can be vindictive. You're sure it was them?"

"Yeah. I recognized Winters' voice right away. Larry's was harder to hear. It wasn't until after I thought about it that something he said clicked."

"What was that?"

"No risk, no reward. He said that to me a few days ago when he was leaning on me to file an incomplete report."

"That's a bit shaky for evidence of conspiracy to commit murder, Mike."

"Maybe. But Winters said to him that this would be different than setting up some schmuck in a real estate scheme." I stopped and squeezed the phone as tight as I could. "That schmuck was me! You saw the evidence. You know what he did to me. Who the hell else could it have been?"

I laid down on the bed and closed my eyes. "I'm losing it, man. Get me out of here — I'm done."

He was silent for a few seconds.

"OK, Mike. Calm down. Remember, you're safe. Nobody knows about you talking to me. Everyone knew about Dave's opposition. They still think you're on their team. So, you're not in danger, bud. OK?"

"Yeah, sure. Whatever. Either way. I'm done. I'm out, gone."

"OK. But talk to me first. I need to know everything. Sarah. Did she say why she brought you the audio file? We need to be sure that wasn't a bait for something."

"No. She just said it was an apology and a warning to get out. She said I should light a match on the way out, and that she planned to do the same."

"Seems like you may be that match. But to what end – OK… do you have any proof of the documents you saw?"

"Yeah. I took a picture of them like I did the lease. I just didn't send it yet," I said.

"Great. Send those to me when we're done here. But Mike, we have to be careful with how we use those. You're not a cop and without a warrant, that was breaking and entering and would make those inadmissible in court."

I got up and walked to the window then started to pace the room again.

"I'm fucked here, aren't I? After Miami, those papers could send me to jail, couldn't they?"

"Not necessarily, but they do add a bit more complexity to all of this. I can't promise your immunity if anything happens with that report. If your signature is on it, that's hard to dismiss. And like you said, your past will unfortunately complicate things for you."

My anger boiled over. "Goddamnit," I shouted and slammed my fist through the wood door. Splinters dug into my skin as I yanked it back through.

"What the hell was that?" he asked.

"Larry owes the resort a new door," I said.

"Mike, I'm serious. You need to calm the hell down and trust me. Panic and emotion are what gets people in trouble in these situations. Work with me here, soldier."

With blood now running down my arm I walked into the bathroom and sat the phone down. "Fine," I said, pulling the splinters from my arm and rinsing the blood away. "What now?"

There was a long pause.

"Man, we're so close here. I really need you to stay with me or everything was for nothing. Including Dave's death."

"Don't give me the guilt trip. So, what? Because of my friendship with him, I have some sort of moral responsibility to avenge him? Why not just take what you have right now?

"You don't have any duty here, Mike. But we just don't have any solid evidence yet, and a grainy audio file that was obtained by and passed through questionable hands… well the lawyers they'll get will have that tossed pretty fast."

"So, I don't have a choice then is what you're saying?

"Of course you have a choice. I'm just asking you to stick it out with me a little longer. Nail these bastards."

I didn't respond. I rinsed the sink, watching the blood spiral down the drain then wrapped a towel around my arm, grabbed the phone and walked towards the sofa.

"Come on, Mike. We're so close. You're the perfect ace in the hole. There's no way we can lose. Look, I'm coming down as soon as I can. I'll be there until I slap the cuffs on both of them. Hell, I'll even let you cuff Larry."

I sighed. "Fine. What do I do?" I asked.

"My man. Good – For now, just play it cool and do the job they hired you for. I'll be there soon and we'll come up with a solid plan. Remember, you know more than them."

"Yeah. OK. Sure," I said.

"Well, I got to go. Lots to do before I can head out. I'll see you soon," he said then hung up.

I tossed the phone across the room.

I sat back on the sofa and watched the condensation slowly run down the amber glass of my beer bottle, across the table, and drip onto the floor. The only sound in the room was the ticking of the clock on the wall above my head. I listened to it for a while, watching the water form a small pool on the floor.

Everything seemed surreal, like I was in a dream. I was angry, I was scared, and I felt trapped. The only way out was to do what Sarah said. Light a match. But rather than do it on the way out, I had to burn it down from the inside. I just had to make sure my past didn't cage me in with them.

Then something occurred to me. I grabbed the phone and called one of the few numbers I knew by heart — My lawyer.

"Good afternoon, Offices of Cunningham and Grooms, how may I help you?"

"Courtney, this is Michael Bennett, is John in?"

"Hello, Mr. Bennett. Yes, one moment and I'll connect you."

"Michael Bennett, been a long time. What can I do for you?"

"I need some legal advice on something."

"Are you in trouble, Mike?"

"It's a long story — I'll fill you in later. I just need to know, hypothetically, if there is evidence that Larry Vincent is responsible for what happened in Miami, would there be any justification for re-opening my case to potentially exonerate me?"

"Well, it's nuanced, and I'd want to look at everything, but, yes. In light of new evidence, you can re-open a case. Why, what's going on?"

"I'm working with Larry again in the Virgin Islands on a Marina project. I found evidence that he's setting me up for the same shit he did in Miami. This time though, I'm on to him and working with the FBI, who has the evidence against him from Miami."

"The FBI? Mike, I'm your lawyer but also a longtime friend, why are you just calling me?"

"I know. But this has all happened fast. Honestly, it just occurred to me to call you."

"OK, Mike. I need you to tell me everything so I can be ready for whatever happens here. First, what's the agent's name?"

"I don't have time right now. The agent's name is Preston Jones, but he's not on island right now. So, if anything happens, call Captain Kahuna. I'll text you his number. But I have to go. Thanks for the info."

"Damnit, Mike. Fine — OK. Just — just call me back as soon as you can. I need to get ahead of this."

"Great, thank you."

"Mike, be careful. If you need anything, let me know. Call my cell."

"Will do, and I will. Thanks again."

I finished the beer and headed towards the door. If I could flip this all onto Larry and restore my reputation, it could change my life. I finally knew what I had to do.

CHAPTER 33

I PULLED THE PINS OUT OF THE DOOR HINGES and sat it on the side of the building, hoping Kim wouldn't notice its absence, then dumped my clothes from the duffle bag and put on a long-sleeved shirt to hide the cuts on my arm. I had to play this carefully, so I didn't want to explain why, in a fit of anger, I put my fist through a door.

I glanced around the room. Everything seemed in place, so I headed towards the pool to meet Kim.

***

The sidewalk from the cottages to the pool cut through a wide grassy area with lounge chairs and umbrellas sparsely spread across the field. A few people had towels laid out and were sleeping in the sun, while others read or sipped cocktails. As I came over the small hill near the pool area, I saw Kim standing with Larry at the tiki bar. He noticed me and waved me over.

I felt the unease of nervousness in my stomach and slowed my pace a little. I knew I had to keep my calm and really sell this if it was going to work. You have the upper hand, I told myself. You have the FBI and a damned good lawyer behind you. All he has is thinking he caught you in a lie about the safe. So just tell him the truth.

I smiled and waved back and feeling my confidence return, picked up my pace again.

"There he is," Larry said as I approached, extending his hand. I grasped it firmly in a handshake, looking directly into his eyes and nodding with a smile.

"I thought you fell asleep in there," Kim said.

"Yeah, I did. Sorry about that," I said, giving her a hug and kiss on the cheek.

"Hey, Larry, you have a second?" I asked.

"Sure, Mike. What's up?"

I nodded away from the others at the bar then glanced back to Kim. "We'll just be a second."

"What's going on, Mike?" he asked as we approached an empty picnic table.

"Well, I was thinking about our conversation earlier. It was never said, but when I was looking for the blueprints, I did notice the safe open and dug around for a key. I pulled out the envelopes, looked inside and shut the door when I didn't find anything."

His eyes narrowed and he tilted his head back slightly, placing his hands in his pockets.

"Why are you telling me this now?"

"Well, I didn't want you to think I was hiding something. Especially after what you said earlier."

"Did it seem like I thought that?"

"Not until after I thought about our conversation more. It just seemed like, you drawing attention to the safe may have been you seeing if I'd tell you I opened it."

"So why didn't you say something then?"

"It just honestly didn't occur to me, man. I was in the office. You knew that and I explained why. But it sure seems like it's a good thing I said something."

He nodded his head and sighed. "Well, thank you. I knew when the door was locked that you had been in it and honestly, it was bothering me that you didn't fess up."

I offered him my hand. "It was never my intention to lie to you, Larry."

He smiled. "I should've given you the benefit of the doubt. Alright, now that that's behind us, let's not keep the lady waiting any longer," he said and put his arm over my shoulder, leading us back towards the bar where Kim was waiting.

"You boys done working now?" she said.

"All done, babe," I replied.

"Indeed, we are," Larry said. "In fact, we're taking the next two days off. There's a full moon party at Foxy's tomorrow night and I'm taking *Silver Linings* over with some friends. You two want to go?"

"I definitely want to go," Kim said.

Now, a party wasn't really a priority, and I'd have preferred to be away from Larry as much as I could until Agent Jones got there, but I felt turning down a second invite may seem suspicious. However, I definitely didn't want to be stuck on a boat with him.

"Sounds good to me," I said. "But I want to get under sail, so I think I'll take *Second Wind* over. Besides, it'll give us a little more privacy," I said glancing to Kim. "We'll head to the boat later today so we can get an early start."

"Oh, I love that idea," Kim said.

"Alright. Well, I'll see you over there," Larry said. "But for now, I have some work to do if I want to take off."

"Anything you need me for?" I asked.

"Yes. I need those reports as we discussed."

"Alright, Larry. I'll work on it and have it to you when we get back so we can get moving on this."

"Good man," Larry said, patted my shoulder then walked away.

I turned to Kim. "Well, you seem more upbeat."

She grabbed her glass. "Nothing a few Margaritas can't fix," she said and walked towards a pool side table.

"In that case, bartender, I'll have two shots of tequila, lime slices, and a shaker of salt."

"Anything else?" he asked.

"Actually, yeah. A Red Stripe to wash it down with."

I felt the phone Preston gave me vibrate in my back pocket. I turned away from Kim and opened it. It was a text.

I'll be back on island late tomorrow.

Let's meet somewhere private.

Time to nail this thing shut

I slid the phone back into my pocket as my beer arrived. The bartender placed a small serving of lime wedges and two empty shot glasses next to it then poured the tequila to the rim of each, spilling some on the bar. I picked up one of the glasses, brought it halfway to my mouth and stopped, holding it for a second, then took a deep breath and tossed it back.

"Here we go," I said to myself with a heavy sigh.

"You coming?" Kim said from the table.

I grabbed a lime and tucked it into the bottle, shoved the saltshaker into my pocket, then turned to her and smiled. "I'm on the way."

CHAPTER 34

THE EARLY MORNING WAS QUIET AND STILL. From *Second Wind's* fly bridge I sipped my coffee and looked out over Coral Bay. The only sound was the water gently lapping on the hull. From my right the buzz of a small outboard broke the silence, and I watched as the dinghy slid smoothly across the water towards the docks, the mast of several boats rocked slightly in its wake.

White clouds drifted with the trades as if pushed forward by the sun, highlighted in orange and yellow as it peeked over the horizon and crested the hills. A breeze blew across the water carrying the warm salty air, thick with humidity and aromas of the island after the pre-dawn rain.

The tranquil morning though did little to still my mind or calm my nerves. The weight of the days to come and the uncertainty of it all were weighing on me and my stomach was tied in knots with anxiety. I watched the rising sun as it climbed higher into the sky and the people of the Coral Bay began to stir. I thought back to Miami and that job with Larry. That's really where it all began.

In my mind the story unfolded with a new clarity. Like watching a mystery movie for the second time, you already know the who did it and the how. Now, it's the subtle nuances you notice. Things Larry said to me, his over-confidence in getting things done, how Briana approached me when she needed me to sign off on the application, waiting till I was busy and the deadline just around the corner, rubbing my shoulders and speaking sweetly as she waited, ready with an answer to any questions I had.

It was all clear.

Fast forward. The timing of the phone call from Larry, Dave's death, the absolute certainty they had in my abilities, and the level of responsibility placed on my shoulders to make it all happen. And again, I was distracted by a beautiful woman. So, I had to consider, maybe she was part of it. A femme fetal, a diversion to my thinking, something alluring to keep me in line and wanting to be there beyond just the job.

Larry knew me, and that may have worked. But I didn't believe she was in on it. Besides, they had Sarah, and I doubted they'd play the same card twice. Larry knows my type and Kim fit it well, so if anything, she was an unwilling pawn.

Pawn or not though, I was glad it happened the way it did. I was glad she came into my life.

As the scenes flashed through my mind and the pieces continued to fall into place, my anger grew. Larry and Kim's trip and how I had to stay back, Sarah's visit, her departing words, and the audio file with Winters and Larry plotting to kill Dave.

My blood boiled and my face went hot as the pressure grew. I wanted to scream at the sky, purging it all from my chest and my mind. But that would've woke Kim, and half the bay. Then I'd have to explain my anger — and I just couldn't tell her yet. Even though I wanted to.

Firmly, I gripped the helm until my knuckles went white and through tense lips and gritted teeth, I screamed to myself and shook the helm violently, my eyes tightly closed. Then in a final expulsion of anger and frustration I pulled hard until my muscles strained and I thought the helm would come off in my hands.

I opened my eyes and stared into the water, trying to steady myself then released the wheel, breathing slowly and deeply, trying to push the anger from my body with each breath. I knew I had to focus. I had to be in control of my emotions. Anger wouldn't work for what lay ahead. I had to pull it together.

Staring into the water I drew in a breath through my nose, counting slowly, 1… 2… 3… 4… and held it for four seconds. Then a slow release through the mouth, 1… 2… 3… 4…, pushing all the air from my lungs and pausing for a final count of four. With each round my nerves steadied, my heart slowed, and my mind became focused.

Everything that happened, it already happened. There was no changing that and no use in getting angry. That only makes the bad things worse, I told myself. What I had was that moment. The present time to choose how I let these things affect me, and my actions going forward.

One thing was certain — I had to do something. It wasn't just clearing my name or vengeance for Dave. It was more. I felt, knowing what I knew, they would do this again. Winters even said in the recording. It wasn't his first time. They had to be stopped.

All I had to do was get through this party then link up with Agent Jones. They may get great lawyers to try and toss the audio file, but they don't know about John. He's one of the best corporate lawyers in the country and his partner, Carlton Grooms, is a feared trial lawyer. In my business, when threatened with lawsuits, all I had to do was drop the name Cunningham and Grooms and suddenly negotiations were open again. I had my ace in the hole.

As I thought about what was ahead, I realized that I needed to reply to Agent Jones and let him know I was heading to Jost and let him know about John. I went into the salon and pulled the flip phone from my duffle, but it was dead. Not wanting Kim to see it, I plugged it in and hid it in the navigation desk, freshened up my coffee, then stretched out on the aft deck bench.

***

I don't know how much time passed but what little was left of my coffee was cold when Kim finally came out.

"My, you look pensive this morning," she said as she sat down next to me. "Whatcha thinking about?" She smiled and took a sip of her coffee. I looked into her eyes and smiled back.

"Hey, would you want to go to Key West with me? I have a couple things I need to do since I'm staying here longer than planned. We'd be back in a few days or so. Tickets are on me."

"Absolutely. I've never been. When?"

"Not sure yet, but hopefully soon. But before business really picks up. Maybe in a few days."

"I can't wait," she said.

***

We took our time getting to Jost Van Dyke. Stopping at West End, Tortola for lunch, to clear customs, and a swim in Cane Garden Bay. By the time we arrived, the sun was set, and Great Harbor was full, so we took a mooring on White Bay, then opted to dinghy over rather than take the safari taxi. Luckily, we found a spot on the dock we were able to squeeze the little dinghy into.

It was a humid night, and the air was hot and thick. My white linen shirt already clinging to me as we entered the bar. The speakers blasted dancehall reggae, and the smell of sweat, island barbecue, and ganja filled the air. The dance floor was packed and had overflown beyond the thatch roof. Locals, islanders, and tourists filled the place, their bodies surging, almost trancelike with the tribal beats.

Looking over Great Harbor I could see *Silver Linings*. She was lit up and the deck and bow were packed with people. I felt a nervousness creep in but quickly let it go, reminding myself what Agent Jones told me. If I played it cool, everything would be fine.

I reached back to pat the phone for reassurance.

"Shit," I said out loud. It wasn't there. I stopped and was frantically patting my other pockets when it came to me. I had forgotten it on the boat. It was still charging, hidden in the nav station.

"What is it?" Kim asked.

"I forgot my phone."

"Babe. We're at a party. Do you really need it?" she asked.

"Well — not really. I mean — just in case Larry calls."

She reached in her bag and pulled out the phone Larry gave me. "I grabbed it for you," she said with a smile.

I couldn't let her know that wasn't the phone I meant so I just smiled back. "Thanks, love. Probably better in your bag anyway," I said.

"No problem," she said then tucked it away and kept walking towards the mass of people.

I was mad at myself because I never called Preston to let him know where I was, and he was arriving that night and would surely be looking for me.

Well, if he's good, he'll be able to track down Larry, I thought. He did seem to know right when I'd be coming in that night we met at the marina. He must have a tracker on *Silver Linings*. But either way, nothing is going down tonight anyway, I told myself. You smoothed out everything with Larry so just enjoy the night. You can call Preston later when you get back to the boat.

I took a deep breath and followed Kim who began moving with the music before we even entered, then she sauntered into the crowd with ease. She led me by the hand, and I could feel us being swallowed into the surging mass of flesh, both of us consumed by the energy of the music.

Dancing provocatively, she leaned back against me and placed her arms behind my neck, pulling my face close to hers then guided my hands over her body.

I kissed her neck. The taste of salt on her skin, the vibrations of the music, the crowd, the heat and the sweat, all gripped me tight as we danced, moving as one.

She took a step forward. I grabbed her hand, and she turned, casting my hand off. Her expression, sensual and passionate. Her skin glistened and her chest heaved. A devious smile crossed her lips as she slowly raised a hand, and with one finger, motioned me to her.

I stepped towards her, putting my arm around her waist, pulling her close. She pressed her face against mine and tugged at my belt loop, pulling me tighter against her and kissing my cheek and neck.

What seemed like an hour passed as I did my best to follow her lead, holding tight to her hips, the music flowing through us. Then when the music slowed, and we danced close, she unbuttoned my shirt and ran her hands over my shoulders, blowing gently on my chest to cool me while she looked deep into my eyes.

Her seductive gaze pulled me in and gently I ran my hand through her hair and grasped it, locking into a passionate kiss, then dropped one hand to her waist and dipped her ever so slightly. She relaxed in my arms, both of us letting the kiss linger.

I slowly stood her back up, our faces pressed together, swaying slightly with the music. Her arms rested over my shoulders and my hands around her waist, each lost in the other's eyes, unspoken words left to drift into the night.

The D.J. changed to salsa and the crowd let out a cheer as the energy ramped back up.

"Let's stop and have a beer," I said. "I need to cool off."

She smiled and nodded towards a bar furthest from the crowd. As we broke free from the mass of people even the warm night air felt cool. My shirt was soaked through with sweat and Kim's hair clung to her shoulders. I ordered two cold beers, and we walked out to the beach near the dock where there was a small wooden pram turned upside down on the beach. I leaned against her hull to rest. Kim sat down next to me.

We sat for several minutes, sipping our beers and cooling off. The ringing from the music slowly faded from our ears and was replaced by the faint sound of the waves against the shore and the rustling of tightly packed dinghies on the dock.

I was staring into the night sky and out over the harbor. It was full of boats of various sizes, some with large parties of their own, others dark aside from their anchor lights. Far away I heard the rumble of thunder, so I scanned the night sky above for clouds and lightning. But all I saw were stars.

Kim put her head on my shoulder and leaned against me. I put my arm around her and kissed her forehead. She looked up and found my eyes but not the words for the moment. I hugged her tightly and she nestled into my chest. I squeezed her once more and she let out a sigh.

"Yeah… Me too," I said to her. She didn't look up, just inched a little closer.

The lively squeal from a girl running down the dock ripped us from our moment and the music and heat of the night were again present. She was giggling uncontrollably, followed by a large man wearing only blue shorts. He caught up to her on the sand and placed her over his shoulder. They both laughed as he carried her towards the party, and she playfully punched him in the back.

Kim jumped to her feet and stood in front of me. Smiling, she reached for my hand. "Come on, let's dance," she said.

I was tired but had a hard time saying no to her. So, I followed her back into the pulsing mass. Again, clumsily trying to follow her as she moved. Occasionally she'd offer a patronizing grin, teasingly judging my lack of rhythm. But after several songs, I had enough and was leading her towards the bar.

Kim never stopped. Dancing against me as I leaned on the bar, pleading with me to join her. I just smiled and shook my head as I exaggerated the drink from my beer and rubbed the cold bottle on my face. She grinned and shrugged.

"Suit yourself," she said, and kept dancing alone in front of me.

Before long a space opened around her as her movements became more seductive in her attempts to draw me back onto the floor. Then, a large man from the crowd approached her. He moved to the music as he drew closer and unbuttoned his shirt, letting it fall then tossing it over his shoulder, revealing a massive chest and rippling arms. She raised her eyebrow to him and moved close, but kept her eyes on me, a devilish grin on her lips. I smiled and nodded to her with a nonchalant pull from my beer.

With a shrug she turned then slowly and suggestively moved around the man. He moved with her, but she kept her distance, teasing him with her illusive advances. He stepped forward quickly and grabbed her hand, spinning her close to him. I stood and took a step forward. Kim, seeing me, calmly smiled and held up a hand, telling me to stay where I was.

She never stopped dancing, just gently removed the man's hands from her hips and placed it softly on his chest, smiling and moving backwards, shaking her head and holding up her finger in denial of his advance, then gesturing towards me.

"What is this?" the man said and moved quickly towards her. She retreated to me, and I stepped in between them, pushing him back into the crowd.

"OK, enough," I said. "If you can't just dance and respect the lady, then find somebody else. I'll dance with her."

"Why don't you let the pretty lady dance with a real man," he said, flexing his muscles and slapping his chest. Some people nearby let out a cheer of approval.

"She already has a dance partner," I said.

"Fuck that," he said and moved towards me. I dropped back on my right foot and braced for his impact. But as he neared an equally large man stepped in and grabbed him.

I maintained my stance and watched his eyes. He tried to pull away, but the other man held him firm.

"That'll be enough of that," a voice said from the crowd. Larry approached the man, and removed the cigar from his mouth, blowing smoke in his face as he spoke.

"Now, why don't we all go back to having fun. Find another lady to dance with. That alright with you?" he said to the man.

He looked into the face of the man holding him. "Sure," he said, shaking free as his captor loosened his grip. "I don't want any trouble."

He shot Larry then me a stern look, then turned and walked into the crowd.

Larry approached me with a smile, placing his cigar back into his mouth. "Man, if he'd gotten to you —" he began.

"I can handle myself," I interrupted. "But thank you."

Kim reappeared, clearly shaken. "Thank you, Larry," she said, putting her arms around me.

"I doubt that," said the large man who'd just saved my ass.

I looked up at him. "I didn't know they had bouncers at Foxy's."

"They don't," Larry said. "This is Reese. He's a bodyguard I use from time to time."

Larry leaned across me to an ashtray on the bar, stamping out his cigar.

"Well, do you mind if I dance with this lovely lady? I'll be more respectful than her last partner."

"Of course not," I replied with a smile and a nod.

They moved to the dance floor and soon fell into a familiar rhythm. He held her close, and they moved as one. Dancing in a way only those in tune with their partner's body can do. Her face close to his, he whispered to her. She smiled and stepped away, but he pulled her back to him. They both laughed, moving deeper into the crowd.

It took everything I had to just stand there, watching Kim dance with the man who destroyed my life and killed my friend. Trying to keep my sense of calm, I turned towards the bar and ordered another beer and a shot of rum.

Song after song they danced, never missing a beat. It killed me to watch, but I felt like I had to keep a protective eye on her. To swallow my pride and what I was seeing, I ordered another shot of rum. Then another and two more after that, pulling half a beer down with each one.

The heat and alcohol were starting to take its toll as they danced on. My mind was a torrid of thoughts that ripped through my subconscious.

I'd turned away for a moment and when I looked back, I'd lost them in the crowd. Almost panicked, I started looking for them, weaving through the bodies, then came to the DJ stand and stepped onto the platform to get a higher vantage point.

Just as I set eyes on them, I saw Larry kiss Kim's neck. She pulled away, but he pulled her back as she resisted.

That was all I could take. I walked onto the floor and stepped between them, pushing Larry back and meeting him face to face. Kim, in an attempt to defuse the situation, grabbed my hand and tried to pull me away, but I twisted free from her grip, never breaking my gaze on Larry.

Larry returned my stare. "What the hell are you doing, Mike?" he asked.

"You're a real piece of shit, you know that, Larry?"

"Is that so?" he laughed.

"Stop it, Mike," Kim said. Standing between us. Neither of us acknowledged her.

Others, seeing the confrontation stopped and started to watch.

"It is, actually." I moved to within inches of him. I could feel my face turn red. "I know what you did, and I know what you're doing," I said.

"I'd shut up if I were you."

"Or what?" I screamed at him. Several people stopped and looked towards us. Reese grabbed me, dragging me towards the beach and away from the crowd. Behind me Larry apologized to Foxy as he walked over.

"Please excuse my friend. He's just a little drunk. We're taking him home." He handed Foxy some cash in a handshake. "OK?"

"No problem, Larry. Just get him home safe," Foxy said.

Reese dragged me to a place on the beach away from the others, hidden in the darkness, and pushed me to the ground. Kim came and helped me back to my feet.

"That's a little much, don't you think?" she snapped at him. He just shrugged and took a few steps back as Larry walked quickly out of the shadows and stood near a palm tree, the red glow from his cigar illuminating his face.

"What the fuck is your problem, Michael?" he sneered at me, tossing his cigar into the ocean.

I stared through him, trying to control myself, but I could feel my grasp slipping.

"I can't do this shit anymore, Larry."

"Do what, exactly? What the hell are you talking about?"

"You don't think I know?"

He smiled and spread his arms. "Enlighten me. Just what do you think you know?"

"What you're doing here. I saw the lease for the governor and false reports with my name on them. It's fucking Miami all over again. I trusted you, Larry. I thought you were a friend."

He walked closer. "You mean like a friend who goes through personal files then lies about it with a bullshit admission. Did you just happen to forget you opened, then resealed the folders, Michael? I wonder what reason a 'friend' would have for doing that?"

His eyes burned through me, waiting for a response. But still trying to play my hand, I didn't have a good one, so I said nothing. I just looked away.

He seemed to relax and put his hand on my shoulder, speaking calmly. "Look, I am a friend, and you're drunk," he said. "Why don't you go sleep it off and we can talk tomorrow. Once I tell you what all of that is for, you'll understand. I assure you, it's not what you think. I mean, do you really think after all that happened in Miami, I would put you in that situation?"

Maybe it was the mention of Miami, knowing now what really happened. But with that I felt all the anger I'd held in that morning come bubbling to the surface. Every muscle in my body tensed and I focused on Larry with gritted teeth, trying to hold back.

"Fuck you, Larry. Don't you dare call yourself my friend," I growled, shoving him backwards. Reese moved towards me, but Larry held up hand, still watching me, and listening.

"I know what you did, how you manipulated Briana, pushed her to do it — all while keeping your hands clean. I lost everything because of you! And you expect me to believe you now? You're nothing but a selfish fucking coward."

He stepped closer. An austere look on his face, but subtle smile across his lips. "That's a hell of a story. I assume you have some proof?"

Again, I didn't reply.

He shook his head. "Like I said, you're drunk and need to get some sleep. We can talk about all this tomorrow. I'm sure everything will make sense. And as for Miami, I don't know where you get your information, but you've got something twisted somewhere. Because that just isn't true, my friend."

He looked to Kim, then to Reese. "Kim, take care of our boy, would you? Reese let's go. I was enjoying the party on the boat better."

"I'll call you tomorrow," he said, patting me on the shoulder, then turned and headed off.

As I watched him walk away, all the anger and fear spun around in my head. I broke into a sweat as I fought to hold it back. I drew in a breath...

"I know you had Dave killed."

As the words left my mouth, I felt like I was in a dream, watching it all happen. Time seemed to stop. Everyone, including me, froze in place.

Larry slowly turned around. His expression and demeanor a mixture of shock, concern, and disbelief. He didn't speak at first, just, stared back at me. His eyes squinted and head cocked to the side.

He looked away and shook his head then looked back to me and started slowly walking towards me, Reese followed behind him. As they got closer Larry turned and motioned to him. Reese stopped and crossed his arms.

Larry continued towards me, stopping a few feet away. He seemed to be searching for his words as he looked into my eyes. "Drunk or not, what on earth would make you say that?" he asked.

I let out a heavy sigh, lowered my head and closed my eyes. I knew I fucked up. I had said too much and there was no taking it back. The anger mixed with fear and anxiety in my stomach. I swallowed hard to hold it all down.

"Mike, talk to me," Larry said. "Why do you think that?"

I just stood with my eyes closed tight, breathing slowly. My heart raced and I felt lightheaded. I started to shift slightly back and forth. I had to get out of there. I looked past Reese then glanced to the dark road behind me. I wanted to escape the situation and release the pressure and emotions building inside me. I wanted to run, a dead sprint into the night.

"Mike..." he said again.

I looked up at him. Tears were running down my face and my heart was beating so loud I was sure he could hear it. My palms started to sweat and my mouth went dry. My eyes darted around, looking for a place to run, then to Reese, and back to Larry.

I turned and looked towards Kim. A lump formed in my throat and I swallowed hard again. Her expression shifted from fear to compassion, her hand over her mouth.

Larry reached out and touched my shoulder softly. I closed my eyes. Then, something inside me — just let go.

In pure reflex I wrapped my arm around his, trapping it, and slammed my palm into his chest then tossed his arm off and pushed him backwards. The air forced from his lungs he stumbled but stayed on his feet. Ignoring Reese who was now closing in on me, I took a step forward and landed a kick to his chest, sending him to the sand gasping for breath.

No sooner did I land that blow than Reese closed the gap between us and landed one of his own. A blinding pain shot through my body as his large first landed on my left temple. I dropped to a knee with my arm up to thwart a second shot, but his kick landed square in my stomach, sending me to the sand, writhing in pain. The big man was on me in a second, landing several blows despite my attempts to block him.

"Enough," Larry said from his knees, still trying to catch his breath. Reese stood and kicked me in the ribs once more as he walked over me. I winced and laid back in the sand. The metallic taste of blood ran down my throat.

Larry stood over me. "Pick him up," he said sharply.

Reese snatched me from the ground by my collar then turned me around and held my hands behind my back. I tried to twist free but there was no use. He squeezed tighter and pushed my hand towards my shoulder blades.

"OK, stop!" I shouted. "I get it."

He stood me back up, facing Larry.

"I think we need to go back to the boat and talk in private. You will explain yourself here, Michael," he said jabbing his finger into my chest.

"Fuck you," I said, and spat bloody sputum in his face.

He wiped it off with his shirt. "Hold him tight," he ordered Reese then moved to within inches of me. With his chin raised, he peered down his nose at me, then grabbed my hair, drew his arm back, and landed a hard punch into the center of my chest. I sagged, but Reese held me up. Larry grabbed my chin and raised my head to face him.

"Stop it," Kim yelled as she ran towards us. Reese let go with one hand and pushed her to the ground. She fell hard, hitting her head on a small stump. Sobbing, she pleaded to Larry.

"Please, stop this. If you ever actually cared for me, stop it."

"Goddamnit, Reese," Larry said. He walked over to Kim to help her up, but she pushed his hands away.

"Get away from me, Larry," she shouted through her tears.

Larry sighed, turned and walked towards the water. His hands on his head, he looked into the sky for a moment.

"Let him go," he said.

Reese released me and I fell to the sand. He put a hand on my shoulder, pushing me down. "I'd stay there if I were you," he said with a final nudge, then walked away.

Larry turned back around but kept his distance. He spoke calmly. "Mike — I need to know where are you getting this information from?"

I sat up and wiped my face. "Why would I tell you that?"

He took a few quick steps towards me but stopped. "Because, it isn't true, OK. I don't know what is going on, but I need to know so we can get to the bottom of this. If someone is trying to set me up… damn it, I need to know."

I tried to stand, but Reese put his hand on my shoulder, holding me down.

"Let him up," Larry said.

Reese stayed close. I stood and brushed the sand from my hands and ran them through my hair, then helped Kim up.

"Fine, but were talking over here," I said, walking past him.

"Where are you going?" Larry asked.

I stopped and turned back towards him. "Where there're witnesses," I said, then continued walking.

I stopped at a place I felt safe, near the crowd but out of earshot. Larry was talking to Reese as they approached, who veered away but posted close enough to react in short time.

"This is ridiculous. What'd you think I was going to do back there?"

"At this point, Larry – I really don't know."

"You actually believe I had Dave killed?"

"I know you did!"

"Again, why are you so sure of that?"

"I heard your voice on the recording with Winters. Hell, it was your idea! The newspaper article, the propane on the boat, making it look like an accident, those thugs of his doing all the 'heavy lifting.' Ring any bells?"

My anger was returning, and I started to pace. "He even warned you that doing it wasn't just setting up another schmuck in a real estate scheme. But here I am. Your schmuck for hire!"

Larry looked stunned and sat down on a bench, his hands on his knees and let out a long sigh, staring into the sand.

"I mean damn it, man. You even planned to celebrate when it was done," I said.

He looked up at me, a disoriented and confused expression on his face.

"The bottle of Pappy you gave him. Your celebratory drink. Remember?"

"Mike, I never – son of a bitch!" he said as he stood up.

Startled, I took a step back but to my surprise, there was someone there, their hand tightly gripped my shoulder. I tried to turn, but the man grabbed my arm, pinning it behind my back.

"Michael Bennett, you're under arrest."

I turned my head and saw it was Randy holding me. Joshua was coming in behind Larry. My blood ran cold, and my adrenaline surged. Quickly I tossed my head back into Randy's nose then stepped sideways, plummeting my elbow into his gut then pulled away and took off.

"Run," I shouted, grabbing Kim's hand and heading towards the crowd. She moved fast and was slightly ahead of me as we rounded a picnic table. Out of my peripheral I saw Reese moving fast to intercept us, Randy was close behind. Like herding dogs they closed in, forcing us away from the crowd. We turned and ran towards the dinghy dock but from the shadows Joshua smashed into us, bring all three of us to the ground.

I sprung to my feet, adrenaline coursing through my veins. Joshua had Kim pinned and reached for his cuffs. I took two quick steps and with the force of a goal kicker landed my foot across his face. His snapped back with a spurt of bloody mist and he fell to the ground.

I grabbed Kim and was pulling her up when an arm wrapped around my neck and lifted me from the ground, my eyes bulged and I gasped for breath, pulling down on the muscular forearm to loosen the grip.

Joshua was walking towards me. Rage filled his eyes. I twisted and kicked, but Randy held me like a vice.

Slowly my consciousness faded, and I started to slump. Randy tossed me to the ground and kicked me hard just as I gasped for air.

"Pick him up," Joshua ordered. Randy grabbed me and held my arms behind my back.

"What are you going to do? Kill me like you did Dave!" I shouted.

Looking around I saw Reese had Kim held tight.

"What are you arresting them for?" Larry demanded as he caught up.

Joshua walked over to me. "Besides assaulting a police officer?" he said then landed a hard punch to my face. I sagged in Randy's arms, but he held me up. "That's none of your business. You're not his lawyer." He landed another blow to my stomach and Randy dropped me into the sand.

"So, as I was saying," Randy said. "You're under arrest."

"There something you don't know," I said, spitting blood into the sand, still on my hands and knees.

Randy reached down and stood me up in front of him. "And what's that? Not that it matters. Nothing is going to save your sorry ass now."

I looked to Larry then back to him. "I've been working with the FBI. They know all about you and are about to bring the hammer down on all of you. Killing me won't save you."

He chuckled. "We'll see about that."

Larry was standing next to Reese and said something to him. He released Kim and she started to run away. Randy shouted to Joshua and raised his arm to point at her, exposing his gun. I grabbed it tight and pulled it from the holster, but he seized my arm, twisting it until I screamed in pain, releasing the pistol.

A fist landed in my side, and I dropped, but Randy caught me with one hand then drew his fist back and smashed it into my jaw. I collapsed back into the sand, my ears ringing and consciousness quickly fading. I tried to move — but couldn't.

Through my blurred vision I was shocked to see Larry and Reese struggling with the two cops and Kim running towards me, past the fighting men. She fell to her knees and cradled my head on her lap.

Everything started to fade. I rolled onto my back and looked up at her. She was crying, watching the men and leaning over me as if to protect me.

My face felt numb, and I closed my eyes. As I drifted into unconsciousness the sounds faded far away and seemed to echo through the blackness. I reached for Kim's arm.

I felt her muscles tense and she jumped as the sound of a single shot ripped through the night.

CHAPTER 35

I STARTED TO COME TO AND COULD FAINTLY HEAR VOICES over the idle of a small outboard. With each beat of my heart my head throbbed, and any movement sent a sharp pain throughout my body. My head was in Kim's lap. Her hands rested on my chest and I could hear her crying.

"He'll be OK, Kimmy. Don't worry. Let's just get him to my boat in case they come back," the man's voice said.

The boat shook as someone climbed on board and moved past us.

"Thank you, Tim," she said through her tears.

The motor ground into gear and we drifted backwards for a moment. I felt the bow swing around then we lurched forward as it slid into drive. The RPMs quickly came up and we jumped onto plane.

We made a long right turn, hopping over the choppy water as it started to lightly rain. The water felt cool and comforting.

I tried to open my eyes, but my left eye was swollen shut. Through the blur of the rain, I saw an older man at the stern, navigating the small vessel. His eyes intently focused ahead as we sped into the rainy night. Behind him the lights from the beach quickly faded into the background.

I strained to raise my head, but a pain shot through my body like an electrical current, causing me to gasp. Every muscle in my body tightened.

"Mike, are you OK?" Kim asked, running her hands through my hair.

I groaned in pain and laid my head gently back into her lap and took a deep breath. The taste of blood filled my mouth, and the rain stung my eye. I closed it and squeezed tight then once again, faded into unconsciousness.

***

"Hey, buddy, I hate to do this, but we need to move you."

I looked up and saw a small framed older man with a kind smile. Kim sat next to him.

"Are you ok?" she asked me.

I pushed the palms of my hands over my eyes and let out a slow exhale. "I'm alive — I guess. Are you OK?"

"I'm OK," she replied. "A small bump and headache from hitting my head, but otherwise fine."

"Where are we?" I asked them.

"This is my boat. You'll be safe here for now," the man said.

"Where is *Second Wind*? What about Larry and his goons?"

"Larry saved our lives, Mike," Kim said.

"Wait— what? What happened? I thought I heard a gunshot just as I passed out."

"You did," she said. "When Reese was holding me, Larry told him he was being setup and if they didn't do something, we'd all be dead. When Randy forced you to drop his gun, he never picked it up. So, Reese took down Joshua and Larry managed to get Randy's gun and shot him. People scattered.

Tim saw me covering you and stopped. He threw you over his shoulder and we headed off in the cover of the crowd. A little up the road a safari truck came by. We loaded you in and took off."

"What happened to Larry?"

"All hell kind of broke loose after that, man," Tim said. "A big Sundancer tore ass out of there. Kim said it was Larry. We don't know what happened to the cops. Didn't really want to stick around."

"So, what now?" I asked.

"I'll get your boat over to Cane Garden. They'll think you took off. Nobody will be looking for you on this old clunker."

"What if they find you on my boat?"

"Don't worry about me, son. I can handle myself."

"Thank you so much, Tim. This is huge," Kim said.

"No problem. If you need to leave fast though, take the dinghy. Old Susie here is heavy and slow. But come on, we need to get you onboard."

I groaned as I sat up. Tim offered me his hand.

"How in the hell did you pick me up?" I asked him.

He grinned. "I was raised bustin' broncos out west then spent my life at sea doing just about every hard job you can think of. I can carry a lot more than you. Especially if there's gun fire."

I grabbed his hand and could tell in a second, he was telling the truth.

He patted my back as I sat up. "Do you think you can make it to the deck?"

I looked towards the boat, bobbing slightly in the waves. She was small but right then, seemed like a mountain. Just the thought of moving made me sick.

"Come on, son, I got ya," Tim said.

Kim was already aboard, holding onto the railing and reaching her hand out. "Come on, baby."

I took a deep breath and braced myself on the gunwale of the dinghy, then with all the strength I had left, pulled myself aboard with Tim pushing me. Kim grabbed my hand and helped me as I lumbered into the unfamiliar salon where I collapsed on the sofa. Tim came in and covered me with a blanket, which I quickly pulled over my head.

Kim came and sat next to me. "I'm running back to the boat with Tim to get him underway," she said, rubbing my back.

I pulled the blanket down and looked up at her. "Inside the nav table in the salon is another phone. Please grab it," I said.

"You have two phones?" she asked.

I sighed. "I didn't make up the FBI agent. I need to call him."

"Oh, that was the phone you were looking for earlier."

"Yeah. If I had it, it may have saved us from all of this."

"Why didn't you tell me about him?" she asked.

"I'll explain later, Kim — I promise. Just please, don't answer it if he calls. Just bring it to me."

"OK, hun. Just rest."

"Be careful, Kim."

"I will. I'll back soon."

She left, turning the lights out and pulling the gangway door closed. I heard the dinghy fire up and quickly move off. The sound of the outboard faded into the distance and the small sailboat rocked gently. I turned to face the back of the sofa, pulled the blanket back over my head, and drifted quickly into a deep sleep.

CHAPTER 36

THE SOUND OF THE ANCHOR CHAIN DRAGGING FROM THE LOCKER RATTLED THE BOAT, pulling me from my sleep. I looked around the unfamiliar salon with only a faint memory of how I got there. The engine revved briefly and I felt the tug of the anchor as she caught bottom. I could hear Kim moving around topside, forward, then aft. Then the motor fell silent.

Sitting up I took stock of myself. I seemed to be OK. My head still hurt and I noted that my swollen left eye was able to open a little. With a heavy sigh, I lifted myself from the bench and shuffled forward to the head.

The light was bright, and when it came on, I closed my eyes briefly as they adjusted. Staring into the mirror revealed a slightly better image than I had expected. My eye was indeed black, though the swelling had subsided. I ran my tongue around my teeth once more and was happy to note that all still remained in place.

I stood there staring into my reflection, looking at myself in the eyes then lowered my head and stared into the sink.

"What in the hell have I gotten into," I said.

I didn't notice Kim so I jumped as she slid her arms gently around my waist, placed the side of her head against my back and squeezed me tight.

"You OK, hun?" she asked.

"I'm fine," I said, reaching down with one hand and grasping hers.

"Where are we?"

"I was nervous on Jost, so I moved us over to Manchioneel Bay while we decide what to do next."

"How long was I asleep?"

"About twelve hours."

"I feel like I could use twelve more," I said with a sigh. "Alright, well, I need some fresh air and to make a call. Did you find my phone?"

"Yea. It's in the galley," she said.

"Great, I'll be up in a second."

***

Kim was sitting in the cockpit, staring out over the water. I looked around the boat as I came through the companionway. It had all the makings of a sea gypsy caravan. Cans, buckets and lines hung here and there, swinging and clamoring with the rocking of the boat. Small pennants tied to the standing rigging and flag halyard snapped in the wind above. At a glance it was in disarray, cluttered and unclean. But a closer look showed the vessel of a seasoned sailor. All lines stowed properly, items on deck were secured, rigging and sails were all in good order. Everything was in its place. There was just a lot of it.

I sat across from Kim and picked up the phone Preston had given me, it was off. I hit the power button, but nothing happened. The battery was dead.

"Damn," I said.

"Was it on the charger?" I asked her.

"Yeah. In the nav station. I unplugged it."

"The AC power must have been off to the outlets. Did you grab the charger?"

She reached into her bag and dug around for a second, then pulled it out. I went below and plugged the phone in.

Standing in the galley, my stomach growled with hunger. I grabbed an apple from the net hanging above the table.

"Hey, are you hungry?" I asked, peeking up through the companion-way at her.

"A little," she said with a half-smile, wiping a tear from her cheek as she turned to face me.

I climbed into the cockpit and sat on the deck near her feet.

"What's wrong," I asked, putting a hand on her knee.

"I guess everything is just starting to hit me. What Larry did, I just – I can't believe it."

"I know. Even after I had all the evidence in front of me, it was hard to believe."

"When did you start working with the FBI?" she asked.

"Not long, a few days ago, maybe more."

"Well, why didn't you tell me?"

"I couldn't. Agent Jones said not to tell anyone. Not even you. Dave was working with him when he died, so we had to be careful."

"So, you've known that Larry killed Dave?"

"No, I only found that out just before we came to Jost. Sarah of all people dropped off a recording of him and Winters planning it."

"Jesus, why did she do that?"

"She never said why. But she was upset about something. Told me to get out and burn it all down on the way out."

"OK — I'm trying to piece this all together. So, what made you go to the FBI?" Kim asked.

"Well, you remember Daniele?"

"Yeah, of course," she said.

"Well, her name is actually Tiffany. Daniele is her middle name. Not only was she Larry's assistant, but she was Dave's lover. Larry never knew that though. She and Dave both worked with Agent Jones, so she was scared. She knew about me from Dave but was still feeling me out to see if she could trust me. She only came to Cruz with us that day to warn me and give me all of Dave's files before disappearing. With that was Preston's card. I met him the next day."

"What do you think Larry meant when he told Reese he was being set up? I mean, he risked his life fighting those two cops."

"I don't know. I heard his voice on the recording, but he did seem shocked when I told him I heard it. Maybe he is being set up. It did come from Sarah after all. Who knows what she and Winters are planning."

She shook her head and took a deep breath then leaned back and slowly let it all out.

"I feel sick," she said. "This is all too much."

She laid down and put her head in my lap then gently began to weep. I ran my hand through her hair, trying to relax her.

"What do we do now?" she asked. "Larry, those cops, they're all still out there."

"I need to call Preston, make sure we're safe, then we're getting out of here. FBI escort all the way to Key West. They can clean up this mess."

She let out a heavy sigh. "OK. I just want to be away from here and with you."

***

I powered on the phone and called Preston. He answered on the first ring.

"Mike, I've been trying to find you. Where the hell are you?"

"We're at Manchioneel Bay, southeast side of Little Jost."

"What are you doing there?"

"Look it's a long story. Larry dragged me into going to this party at Foxy's, I wanted to play it cool, so I agreed. I forgot to let you know, then my phone died."

"Well, what the hell happened? I heard there was some huge brawl and a cop got shot?"

"Look, I really don't know what happened. It all blew up pretty fast and I got the shit beat out of me. I'm just now able to move around. But look, Larry knows about you, the tape, everything. Plus, he's the one that shot the cop."

"Jesus fucking Christ, Mike. You call that playing it cool?"

"You can call it whatever you want. Things got out of hand with Larry and me, then these so-called cops showed up and tried to arrest me, but I doubt I would've ever seen a cell. Larry saved my ass."

"OK — well, I'll come to you. Then, we can see if we can salvage this mess."

"No way in hell. I'm done man. Get me the hell out of these islands. Damn it all."

I heard him talking to someone then Kahuna's voice came over the phone.

"Hey, brother, you're on Little Jost?"

"Kahuna? What are you doing with him?"

"He found me this morning, said you may be in trouble and needed my help. We're tied up to *Second Wind* now in Cane Garden, but she's locked tight and her dinghy's gone."

"It's a long story, man, I'll fill you in later. We're the only boat here right now. Green hull, ketch rig with lots of stuff on the deck."

"Alright, cuz. Your extraction team is en route. Hang tight."

***

I was lying down in the cockpit when they arrived and sat up when I heard Kahuna shout to Kim to catch a line and tie him off.

"Damned glad to see you two," he said.

I climbed out of the cockpit and walked to catch the other line. Kahuna seemed to wince when he saw me.

"Damn, Bubbah, what happened to you?" he said.

"I think I may be out of a job," I laughed, causing a pain to shoot through my ribs.

"Next time keep your phone on," Preston snapped.

"As I said — there won't be a next time."

He just smiled. "That's true, this will all be over before the day's out."

"Well, come on. Let's get the hell out of here," Kahuna said.

As we climbed onboard Kahuna got a phone call. He glanced to the screen and walked to the front of his boat.

"Hey man, what's up?" he said.

"Sure – OK."

"Yeah, out near Little Jost."

"Yup."

There was a short silence.

"Son-of-a-bitch!" Kahuna shouted at the phone, turning his back to us.

"OK."

"Red Hook."

"Sure"

"OK, I'll call you later.

"All good man?" I asked.

"Yea — just a charter I missed today and the captain I sent them to called to tell me about the massive marlin he caught off the North Drop a few minutes ago."

"Sorry, buddy," I said.

"No worries, man. Happy I'm here helping you guys out. Plenty more fish in the sea."

"OK, let's go," demanded Preston.

"Sure thing. Mike, Kim, y'all lie down and rest. Those beanbag chairs in the back are super comfortable. Preston, why don't you hop on the other boat and untie us. Stern first please, sir."

Preston did as ask. He jumped onto the little sailboat and Kahuna fired up his motors. I was rubbing Kim's head as she laid in my lap and we were both already starting to fall asleep again, exhausted mentally and physically.

I watched a plane fly overhead, leaving vapor trails in the sky. I let out a sigh of relief knowing it was all coming to an end and soon I'd be heading home.

Preston clearly wasn't a seaman. Unsteady on the little boat, he held tight to the jackline as he moved and fumbled with the lines on the cleat. Finally, he freed the stern, tossing the line into the water. Kahuna quickly retrieved it.

Still crouched down Preston moved cautiously forward. Quicker this time he freed the bow line and tossed it into the boat then slowly moved aft.

Kahuna slammed the throttles forward, the stern of the boat dug in and we quickly leapt onto plane.

Kim and I both sat up, startled by the sudden movement. Preston shouted and tried to jump on as we sped away but tripped over the jacklines and fell into the water.

The motors screamed as we slid over the bay towards Jost.

"Stay down and hold on," he said.

We ran at full speed around Georgy Hole Pointe and headed southwest towards St. John. When we were a few miles off Jost, Kahuna slowed the boat so we could stand but kept a good speed.

Holding tight to the rail I moved forward. "What's going on?" I asked over the wind.

"That call back there was from your buddy John. He called me yesterday. After he talked to you, he was worried. He said he was going to call some people and get more information about what's going on down here. Guess he has friends in the FBI."

"Yeah, his dad was an agent a long time ago," I said.

"Well anyway, he couldn't reach you and when he called, he sounded really anxious. He said don't let anyone know who I'm talking to, asked if I was with you and if Preston was there. When I told him I was and he was there, he just said that whoever's payroll Preston is on, it isn't the Bureau's anymore."

"Damn it to hell! He's working for Larry. That's how Larry knew about Dave talking to the Corps and how he knew I was in his office," I said.

I could feel the anger building in my chest and my face went hot as it all became clear.

"That's why the son-of-a-bitch was so smug when he called me into his office, and why he pressed the St. Barth's trip. All this time, I thought I had the upper hand, but he was toying with me — I walked right into his trap."

I turned to Kahuna. "But why did he come to you looking for me? Larry must have told him where I was."

Kahuna shot me a hard glance. "I hate to think it, but he came to me after your blowout on Jost and you spilled everything to Larry. And he did say this would all be over today. I'm guessing he planned on cleaning house and tying up loose ends."

I sat down hard on the bench, staring blankly into the dash as what he said landed.

"Holy shit… I almost got us all killed," I said, barely able to whisper the words.

I slumped onto the deck and tried to catch my breath. I felt numb and empty. Kahuna seeing me, brought the boat off plane. He and Kim were talking to me, but their voices sounded muffled and distant.

Soon anger and fear overcame me, and I slammed my fist repeatedly into the fiberglass deck, splitting one of my knuckles open.

"Son-of-a-fucking-bitch!" I screamed through my tears. "I never had a chance."

Kim sat next to me and rubbed my back, not saying a word. Neither did Kahuna. There was nothing anyone could say. We just floated in silence.

After a few minutes Kahuna put the boat back in gear and we idled forward. He handed Kim a bottle of water and small first aid kit. She took my hand and cleaned my bleeding knuckle, applied a bandage and sweetly kissed it.

"We need to get going, Bubbah," Kahuna said softly.

"Alright," I said, rubbing my face. "Just — give me a second."

Just as we started to move again, Kahuna's phone rang.

"It's your buddy, John," he said, handing me the phone.

I hit the answer button and put it to my ear. I felt weak and my words labored as I spoke.

"Hey John."

"Kahuna?"

"No, it's Mike."

"Mike. Are you OK? I've tried calling you, but it goes straight to voicemail."

"Sure. Well, I'm alive anyway. But yeah sorry, man, that phone's been off."

"Is Preston with you?"

"No."

"What about Kim and Kahuna?"

"Yeah. They're here.

"Where's Preston?"

"Probably on the beach on Little Jost by now."

"Good. So, you're safe?"

"I'll feel safe when I'm home, man."

"Well look, I have Special Agent Alex Ramirez on the line with us. He knew my dad and is who helped us put all of this together."

"OK. Hold on a second," I said.

I stood, put the phone on speaker and placed it on the dash.

"OK. You're on speaker with the three of us. I hope there's a plan to get us out of here."

"Mike, Agent Ramirez here. Where's Jones?"

I chuckled. "Kahuna left him bobbing in the water at Manchioneel Bay," I said, smiling to him. He nudged me in the arm and returned my grin.

"OK, I'll get someone over there to look for him. For now though, we need to get you into safe custody."

"With whom? The FBI is working for Larry, the two guys that killed Dave and are now after me are detectives, and I've seen proof that the governor is involved. So just who in the hell are we supposed to trust here?"

"Look Mike, I understand you're scared. But Preston Jones has not been working for the FBI. I assure you that. The rest of it right now is a big question mark. Which is why I need you to trust me here."

"Mike, it's John. You can trust him, buddy. Just work with us and we'll get you home."

I sighed. "Alright, what's the plan?"

"I just got off the phone with my D.E.A. counterpart down there and the commander for the Coast Guard. There are two agents on St. John who will meet you at the ferry dock in Cruz Bay. Head straight there. The Coasties will be there for backup on the water and I'll alert them about the detectives and Jones."

"Will do," Kahuna said and aimed us at St. John as he brought the RPMs up a little more. "Probably thirty minutes out."

"Mike, call me when you get there and are with the agents," John said.

"Will do, buddy. And hey, man, thanks. I owe you one."

"OK, Mike. Just be safe. Now get going. Talk soon."

Kahuna hung up the phone and pushed the throttles forward, bringing us back on plane. Kim moved to the front bench and laid down. I stared off over St. Thomas, trying to figure out how all of it happened then closed my eyes and focused on my breathing and the rhythmic movement of the boat through the water.

"Looks like we got an escort," Kahuna said.

I opened my eyes and looked behind us. Just as we were entering U.S. waters a fast-moving police boat moved in with its lights on.

Kim stood up and looked around then glanced back to the boat behind us and waved. I reached out for her hand, pulling her to me. She smiled and turned to sit next to me, then suddenly, pulled back and her grip tightened. I thought she was being playful, so I tugged again, but she didn't move. She was frozen.

"Oh my God! It's them," she shrieked, releasing my hand and ducking behind the helm station.

Kahuna and I turned. Behind us in the police boat, which was now just a few feet off our stern, were Randy and Joshua.

"Oh shit," I shouted.

"Hold on," Kahuna roared as he shoved the throttles to the dash. The two 300 horsepower motors screamed, and the boat quickly picked up speed, seeming just to tip toe across the water as we raced away. The sudden acceleration startled Kim and she just sat down on the deck. I clung to the rails of the T-top.

"Check our 6," Kahuna yelled over the roaring wind.

I turned back expecting to see them fading quickly into the distance, but they stayed with us and were closing in as we careened towards Cruz Bay.

"There's no way I can outrun them in that boat," Kahuna said, tapping on the throttles to get everything he could out her."

"Take her for a second," he said, handing me the wheel. And don't try to turn at this speed, we don't have much steerage."

I slid in behind the wheel and tightly gripped it, my eyes focused ahead of me, scanning the waters, and blasting the airhorn at a few boats moving slowly ahead. Kahuna moved forward, holding tight to the rail. He lifted a seat and pulled out two life jackets, then moved back to me.

"Here, you two put these on, get low, and move to the back."

"What are you going to do?" I asked.

He glanced back to the boat chasing us. His eyes were calm and focused, and his expression stern. "I have no idea man. But you'll know when it happens. Just be ready."

I turned and moved to Kim. She was lying low on the bench forward of the helm station with her eyes closed. I touched her shoulder. "We have to move," I said, handing her the life jacket.

She let out a deep sigh and just stared at me for a second. I nodded to her reassuringly. She took the vest, slowly sliding it on then pulling the straps tight, but just laid back down.

I could see in her eyes she was terrified so I moved closer to her ear so I could speak more softly. "We'll be OK. Just stay with me. I won't let anything happen to you."

She forced a grin and nodded in agreement, gripping my hand tightly.

We moved cautiously towards the stern, holding tight to the rail for support as the boat danced across the water. Before long Randy and Joshua had caught up and were pulling alongside of us, just a couple feet from our rail.

Just as we reached the beanbag chairs in the back Kahuna turned into them. They pulled away but stayed with us.

I had too much adrenaline to stay hidden so holding onto the helm seat, I pulled myself up a little and looked ahead. Near the mouth of Cruz Bay was a Coast Guard FRC and fast response boat. Kahuna was aimed right at them. He grabbed the VHF.

"Coastguard vessels near Cruz Bay. This is Big Kahuna coming in fast from your starboard with a bogie in pursuit."

"We see you, Captain," they replied.

Kahuna crouched low, holding the mic close to his face. "Look, boys, the men in the police boat chasing me are not cops. We need some assistance here."

"We've been advised of the situation, Captain. Maintain your course, we're moving to intercept."

I looked right and saw Joshua, his pistol leveled at us. "Gun!" I shouted and ducked.

Kahuna pulled back on the throttles, turning hard to port and away from them. I heard the snap of the bullet through the air and Kahuna yelled out, grabbing his right shoulder.

"Those motherfuckers shot me," he said then turned and barked at me to "get down and stay down."

I did as ordered and slid back to Kim as Kahuna brought us back to full speed. Peeking over the gunwale I could see the police boat circling back and closing in, Joshua again taking aim at Kahuna. I turned to warn him, but his eyes were locked on the men. I noticed in his left hand he now gripped a Glock 45, his finger rested on the trigger. Blood was pouring from his wound.

He pulled back slightly on the throttles then engaged the autopilot, we slowed a little just as Joshua fired, blowing a hole through the windshield near Kahuna's head. He didn't flinch.

As they flew by us, Kahuna took aim and fired six rounds at the outboards. Randy yanked the wheel to starboard and they almost rolled over as they slid broadside.

I jumped up, moving back next to Kahuna.

"Did you get 'em?" I asked.

"It wasn't my dominant hand, but had to hit something," he said, handing me the gun then grabbing the wheel and disengaging the autopilot.

The agile police boat dug deep into the water as they pulled a tight circle, shooting out of the hole and back onto plane.

"Damn it," Kahuna said, then jammed the throttles back down, the thrust tossed me into the seat.

Snap, snap, snap. Three shots ripped past us, one punching a second hole in the windshield, another struck the throttle control.

"There're eleven rounds left," he said.

I must have hesitated because for the first time he looked angry. "Come the fuck on, airborne. Send 'em down range and get that damned bogey off my tail," he shouted.

I turned aft, glancing down to Kim who was curled into a ball on the deck. Her eyes widened when she saw the gun in my hands, she pulled her arms over her head.

I took aim and emptied the magazine. The men ducked as rounds pierced the windscreen and tore holes in the console. I tossed the gun into the open bag on the bench behind us.

"Oh, come on. Give me a fucking break here," Kahuna growled.

I turned to see him moving the throttles back and forth, but nothing was happening. He pulled a little more and one came off in his hand. "Shit that ain't good," he said, then grabbed the radio mic. "Throttle's busted, coming in hot, boys," he shouted as the smaller coast guard vessel flew past us the other way. They replied, but we couldn't hear them over the wind and screaming motors.

We shot past the FRC at the mouth of the bay. A few men on the deck waved at us frantically. Ignoring the mooring lines, Kahuna took aim at an empty part of the beach.

"Hold on!" he shouted as we neared shore, then pulled the lanyard from the kill switch. The motors stopped and the heavy boat dug into the water, slowing a little but was still carried forward by the weight. We slammed hard into the sand, tossing us all to the deck.

Kahuna jumped up and grabbed his pistol, jamming another magazine into the handle and locking a round into the chamber as he moved aft, taking cover behind the motors. Still in the bean bag chairs Kim was tossed forward when we hit the beach, she scurried back to him, lying in a tight ball, her hands over her ears and eyes closed tight. I stayed low on the deck, watching Kahuna and waited for the cracking sound of the pistol. He scanned the waters, his pistol at the ready.

"Captain," a man's voice said. Kahuna quickly turned, the pistol still in his hand. I came to my knees and looked over the side. A man resembling a biker but in a flack vest with D.E.A. written in yellow across the chest was approaching us. "I'm agent Parkhurst, I need you to put the gun away, Captain. It's over. They got 'em out there."

"Thank God," he said, dropping the magazine and ejecting the chambered round, then tossed the pistol into his bag.

"Is everyone OK?" Agent Parkhurst asked, waving over two medics who were standing by.

"I took one in the shoulder, but other than that, I think we're OK," Kahuna said, kneeling next to Kim who was still curled on the floor at his feet. I sat down next to her and put my hand on her back.

"Are you ok?" Kahuna asked her, touching her shoulder.

She opened her tear-filled eyes and slowly lifted her head. "Is it over?"

"It's over," Kahuna said.

She sat up and looked around, dazed from the experience. Kahuna offered her his left hand and helped her to her feet. Seeing his bloody shoulder she gasped.

"Oh my God… are you OK?"

"They got a lucky shot," he said, flipping open the tuna door and stepping onto the beach. "I'll be alright though, I've had worse," he said.

"Thanks, old girl," Kahuna said, tapping the gunwale as the medics approached and moved him to a chair for examination.

Offshore we could see the police boat tied off to the Coast Guard response vessel and surrounded by two other unmarked RIBs with blue lights.

"Good shooting," Agent Parkhurst said to Kahuna.

"I did hit something then?" Kahuna replied, leaning to see the boat. The medics pulled him back and implored to him to sit still. He grunted disapprovingly, but did as asked.

"Oh yeah. They tried to turn and run when they saw the Coasties out there but had smoke pouring from a motor."

"That's all great," I said, "but what about Preston, Larry, or Winters? Where are they? Those guys were just the muscle."

"Sir, I was only told to meet you at the ferry dock and get you into protective custody. An Agent Ramirez from the FBI is coming in tomorrow. He'll be taking over from there," Agent Parkhurst said.

"All of us?" Kahuna asked.

"Yes sir. For now, the three of you have to come with me. For your safety."

"What about my boat?"

"We'll worry about that later. Just make sure everything is turned off. I'll have someone secure the gear. Right now, we have to move. The chopper is on the way and should be landing soon at the helipad."

"Where are we going?" Kim asked.

"For now, Puerto Rico. We have a safe house there. We'll get the captain here to the hospital first though."

Kim let out a disapproving sigh.

"Don't worry, ma'am. This is definitely the nicest place you'll ever hide."

"Well let's hope it's the last place I ever have to," she said.

***

Kim was asleep, her head on my shoulder as we flew over open water. Kahuna sat in the right seat, next to the pilot. I thought about how lucky I was to have met him. I felt bad he got dragged into it, but if he hadn't, things would've gone much differently.

He must have felt my stare because he turned and looked back, meeting my eyes. I just nodded to him. He grinned, chuckled to himself and reached back and patted my knee, then turned back around with a nod.

For the first time in days, I felt safe, but I couldn't fully relax yet. I knew the journey wasn't over. John was flying down as legal counsel and until Agent Ramirez had a handle on what happened, he said we'd have to stay put.

I put my head back and looked out of the window to the horizon, lightly stroking Kim's hair. I felt the tension in my chest release and my eyes grew heavy.

Quickly I drifted to sleep and dreamed of my little boat, on her mooring, floating peacefully on still waters.

CHAPTER 37

OUR TWO WEEKS STAY AT THE SAFE HOUSE PASSED SLOWLY. The first few days felt more like we were prisoners, with a constant line of interrogation and repeatedly asking the same questions. Thankfully John had brought Carl down and they both mediated the meetings, representing all three of us. Finally, the FBI felt satisfied and, aside from someone being posted there to protect and keep an eye on us, mostly left us alone.

After that, it wasn't so bad. The house was nice. It had a pool, was secluded on a large property, and faced a beach with a decent surf break. After some cajoling, the FBI even rented us a couple boards so I could teach Kim to surf. But as nice as it was, we still couldn't leave. So, when the phone call came from John that he was arriving in two days and we should be able to go home, I was relieved.

A few days later John gathered us in the living room with Agent Ramirez and another agent from the Miami office, to debrief us. We all listened with wide eyes and disbelief as the FBI laid out the details.

"Well, folks," Agent Ramirez began, "I'm happy to say that tomorrow you can all go home."

"So, you have everyone?" I asked.

"Almost. Jones, Larry, and the two detectives are all in custody. Larry actually turned himself in. Sarah is wanted for questioning, but no charges have been filed on her yet. Winters is a ghost, but we don't feel he's a threat."

"How can you be so sure?" Kim asked.

"He vanished. Which means he knows we're looking for him. So, he'll lay low. His only real threats, that aren't already in custody, would be Sarah and his wife."

"His wife?" I asked.

"Cindy's been working with us for some time," the other agent said. "She knew about his infidelity and had overheard enough to bury him. She even went as far as wearing a wire once. We've been looking into his and Larry's business practices and building a case against them. It's actually not so strange a coincidence, Mr. Bennett, that you're here."

I sat up. "Why's that?" I asked.

"The Waterford project," he said.

I stood and leaned over the agent. "I was cleared of any wrongdoing in that. Preston even said he had evidence that it was Larry who manipulated that entire thing. Or was he never really an agent?"

John grabbed my arm. "Sit down, Mike. You're not in trouble here. Just listen," he said.

"OK, well — what does this have to do with me?" I asked, returning to my seat.

"Look, he likely used that information to coerce you. But he is, or rather, was, an agent. He was suspended a while ago for unethical behavior. But he's been on Winters' payroll for a long time. But, he is correct. It was all Larry. What you didn't know was, Winters was a silent investor in that project and stayed in the shadows. He's very good at making sure his hands stay clean. So, when it all went down, Preston found substantial evidence of crimes Larry committed. But Winters chose to keep Larry out of jail and the evidence to himself, allowing you to take the fall."

I sat back deep into the couch and stared at the ceiling. "So, Larry threw me to the wolves to save his own ass."

"Yes and no. Larry was the cause of everything that happened. That's true. But he didn't know about Preston. Never has. Winters told him about the evidence he had, and it was enough to send Larry to prison. So, he held it over him to control him."

"And you've known about all of this? For how long?" I asked.

"We've known about some of it. Preston is facing a long prison sentence, so he's been very helpful in filling in the blanks. Larry is being cooperative as well. I think as a way to get back at Winters."

"Winters is the one that wanted you on the project," Agent Ramirez said. "He forced Larry to call you and directed him to offer you everything he did."

"Why?" I asked.

"Honestly — because you'd be the perfect patsy. It'd look like you were up to your old tricks and trying to get back on top. The position, the money, all of it was leverage to incriminate you if the plan failed."

"The good news is," John said, "now that they have the full picture, not only will Larry be held responsible for what he did, but it's enough to vindicate you completely."

"Good. Fuck him. He had Dave Killed. I hope he rots in prison."

"We don't think it was Larry," Agent Ramirez said.

"What? I heard his voice on the recording!"

"We've heard it too. Sarah also dropped a copy to Winters' wife, Cindy, and they had a little chat. Seems the governor called Winters because he was anxious about the leverage Sarah could have over him, given how much she knows, and how their 'work relationship' looks. Winters told the governor not to worry because he has enough on Sarah to discredit anything she says and send her away for a long time if she stepped out of line.

Well, Sarah overheard the discussion and decided not to give him the chance. She told Cindy that she heard them discussing plans to meet on *Bottom Line* where it was safe to talk. So, Sarah planted the recorder. When we arrested the governor, he broke quickly in interrogation. He said it was Sarah's idea, that she is the one who pushed him to even suggest it and even came up with the plan. He went along, trying to look confident to Winters."

"Wow, greedy Gary, our illustrious Governor, is a killer. Never would've guessed that," Kahuna said.

"Yeah. And when we started wrapping people up, we grabbed him. We actually caught him at the airport about to skip town."

"So, when I brought up the recording, Larry thought he was being set up. – That's why he attacked the detectives."

Agent Ramirez laughed. "Yea, he shot one of them in the arm then him and his bodyguard cuffed them to a tree and ran. It took a while, but someone found some bolt cutters and freed them."

"I know politicians are greedy bastards, but to kill someone?" Kahuna said.

"Unfortunately, if Governor Edwards is telling the truth, Dave was a sacrificial pawn for Sarah's plan to get some leverage on him and Winters."

"I still don't see how they planned to pull this off," I said.

"It's quite the plan they had. From what we can tell, this thing was dead in the water, and they were getting desperate. But a change of personnel at the Army Corps gave them an in. The original person handling the application was moved to a new project. We still don't know how, but Winters found out that the guy they put in his place was about to hit retirement. He came down for a site visit and Winters bribed him with a nice position and pay if everything went through smoothly."

"Even with someone on the inside, there's no way in hell that original plan wouldn't have raised a flag somewhere," I said.

"Right. According to Larry, they knew you'd suggest an alternative. Their plan was to go along with it. Their guy would then greenlight it and the follow-up assessment would be done by a hand-picked biologist. Two permits would be issued. The one you did would be sent to you via official channels. Another, approving the original plan, would be sent to Larry via other methods. The Corps of course will have no record of the latter, and the permit you'd submit to Larry would disappear.

"The plan was to ensure that by the time anybody caught on to anything, the project would be too far along to stop and if anything blew up, it would look like you worked with the Corps guy and forged the permit. You were both lined up to take a fall. We also have him in custody as of this morning."

I got up without saying anything, walked out to the beach and stood in the water. I watched the waves curl and break as they crossed the reef. A pelican flew just ahead of the curl, pushed forward by the air as it closed. The water rose to my knees then fell to my ankles with each wave and my feet sank a little more into the sand as it was pulled out with the falling water.

I walked deeper then swam towards the breakers just before the reef. I watched as a larger wave built and moved closer, growing taller. It pulled me towards it. I closed my eyes. The powerful wave lifted me, and I felt the sensation of falling as I plummeted with the crest back towards the sand. The weight and energy of the rushing water slammed me into the sandy bottom. But I didn't try to swim or fight against it. Wave after wave rolled over me until my lungs begged for air.

Finally, I found the bottom with my feet and thrust myself upwards, gasping a breath of air just as the next wave broke over me. I ducked and came up behind it, pulling backwards then paddled quickly as the next one approached. I caught it and body surfed towards the shore, allowing the waves to push me into the foamy white water near the beach. Once in shallow water, I crawled away from the surf and laid in the sand on my back. My chest heaved as I caught my breath.

"Mike, what the hell are you doing?" Kahuna asked, standing over me.

Kim kneeled in the sand next to me. Her hand on my chest. "Are you OK, hun?"

Still breathing heavily, I sat up then leaned back on my arms, letting my head fall back. Panting as I spoke.

"From day one… as soon as I got on that plane… it was all stacked against me."

"Maybe. But you came out on top. And it's over now, cuz. You can go home," Kahuna said.

I looked back towards the house. The two agents were standing on the deck watching all of this. John was walking towards us.

"Decided you needed a swim, buddy?"

I took a deep breath and stood up. "Yeah, I just… I needed to get away from all of that," I said.

"I figured. That was a lot to take in. I told them we're done for the day. They'll have more questions down the road, but for now, relax. We'll get you back to St. Thomas tomorrow then you and I are flying out in style on the FBI's private plane. One way back to Key West."

DURING MY STAY AT THE FBI VACATION HOME, the Coast Guard had to move *Second Wind* from British waters or it'd impounded there. Thankfully agent Ramirez called his contact in the Coast Guard and they put her back on her mooring in Coral Bay as a favor. I had to delay my trip home a couple days so I could clean her up, but John and the two agents had to return home. So, my private plane turned into commercial first class. A gift from John.

Kim though had decided to take them up on their offer. She said she needed some time away from the islands to regroup and wanted to be around her family. I gave her my address and personal cell phone number and she said she'd see me soon.

While on St. Thomas I got a new phone to replace the one I lost in the water at the start of my trip. I was back at the resort, packing up my things, when it rang.

"Hello," I said, placing the phone on speaker and tossing it on the bed as I continued to pack.

"Damn man, finally. I've tried to call you a bunch of times. Thought maybe you met some island girl and sailed off on my boat." It was Chris.

I laughed. "*Second Wind* is safe and sound my friend. I lost my phone and just got a new one today. Sorry to worry you."

"No worries, man. I figure you were just having fun. Plus, I know how the service there can be. But, how's the trip?"

"Long story for another time my friend. Suffice to say, it was memorable."

"You still down island?"

"Yeah. I fly out tomorrow."

"Well, how would you feel about sailing to Key West?"

"On *Second Wind?*" I asked.

"Yup. I just landed a new job that is going to have me based in London for a while. Maybe a couple years. So, I was thinking, I know you have a small charter business on your boat, so just add her to the fleet. We'll be business partners. I'll fly out next month sometime and we can work out the details."

I didn't hesitate. "It's a deal," I said.

"Great. I was hoping you'd say that. Look, I am still a few weeks over here before I can get home so we'll catch up later. Enjoy her, Mike. Cheers."

I'm not sure of the expression that was on my face, but Kahuna walked in just as I hung up.

"Oh boy, now what?" he said as he walked into the room.

"Want to sail to Key West with me?" I asked.

"Hmm — well my boat is going to be in the shop for a while with a cracked hull and bullet holes. But, tell ya what, let me sleep on it."

I grabbed the last two beers from the fridge and opened them, handing one to him.

"Works for me, brother."

Epilogue

Months later

I WALKED OUT OF THE POST OFFICE ON WHITEHEAD STREET into the thick Key West air sorting through my mail. On the bottom of the stack was a large manila envelope post marked Augusta, Georgia. It was from Kim. I sat down on a bench under a shade tree and opened it.

Inside was a newspaper article from the Virgin Islands Daily News. It detailed how the Corps and FBI had shut down the project and an investigation into Bowling Green Holdings had revealed years of false reports, payoffs, and bribery. Winters was finally arrested, and Sarah was charged with several crimes but was still at large and the police had lost her trail. At the end of the article was a quote from the Bowling Green President and CEO, Audrey Stein.

"All of us here at Bowling Green are shocked and saddened at these revelations. First and foremost, we offer our deepest condolences to the family and loved ones of Dr. David Blankenship. I am working personally with his family to see how we can assist them during this difficult time.

Mr. Vincent and Mr. Winters have been trusted employees for many years. Needless to say, this comes as a surprise to us all. And as this happened on my watch, I am deeply embarrassed. We will be launching a full-scale internal investigation into the matter and are cooperating fully with authorities at the FBI as well in Miami and the Virgin Islands.

At the bottom of the clipping, in red ink, Kim had written,

October 1ˢᵗ: ATL —> EYW —> ?

See you soon!

Kim, XOXO

I put the clipping back into the envelope, stood and placed it in my pocket, then pulled my bicycle onto Whitehead St. and peddled towards Mallory Square. A warm breeze blew, gently shaking the limbs of the huge Banyan Tree.

***

The trip across the busy harbor was quick and the waters were smooth. The small dinghy skipped cleanly as I passed under the Fleming Key Bridge with the tide. I waved to the tenants now staying on my old boat as I passed.

A hundred yards ahead of me, *Second Wind* sat on her mooring. Tied to her stern was a brand-new Yellowfin center console. She had Mahalo II written down her side and had three Mahi-Mahi pennants flying from her outriggers.

Kahuna and Chris were sitting on the aft deck and raised a beer to me as I approached.

The End

Mike has returned to Key West, and the horizon looks bright.

But Coral Bay was just the beginning.

The next story in The Michael Bennett Chronicles is coming in Summer 2026.

Stay updated at ShawnMDean.com and be the first to know when the story continues.